Published by Lark
This edition published in the UK in 2022

ISBN: 978-1-8383744-3-3

Cover design by enough (www.enoughdesign.co.uk)

Also available
As an ebook edition: ISBN: 978-1-8383744-2-6
As a hardcover edition: 978-1-8383744-4-0

Praise for *The Twenty-Seven Club*

"Perfectly evoking small-town 90s culture, this is a moving exploration of mental health, enduring music myths and why love can help us through."

Stylist

"Dazzlingly funny, dark and insightful. A brilliantly nostalgic blast from an era where shoe choice was everything, 'townies' were a thing, and the bands you followed told the world who you were about to become. Lucy Nichol is a stunning new voice in fiction."

Dr Guy Mankowski, author of Dead Rock Stars

"An honest and raw depiction of someone battling anxiety and deep-rooted fear. It also screams delicious 90s porn with a real working-class heroes vibe."

Claire Eastham, author of FK I think I'm dying**

"Warm, joyous and thought-provoking. Music lovers will adore it!"

Stephie Chapman, author of Swipe Right

"Full of warmth, wit and humour."

Yorkshire Post

"A heart-warming flashback to the mid 90s."

Ben Harding, Senseless Things

"A funny, perceptive and often moving debut."

Louder Than War

PARKLIFE

LUCY
NICHOL

LARK BOOKS

To the recovery community - who I continue to be in awe of every day.

PROLOGUE
1996

I prodded open the CD player, grabbed a disc, placed it inside, let the lid slowly close...and pressed play on Pulp. *Disco 2000.*

Der da der da da da da der der

Der da der da da da da der der

I gripped my wooden spoon, holding it in front of my face, and belted out the chorus. Then I slammed the block of butter into the bowl, spoon beating down hard, mushing and squidging the fat and the sugar to the beat of the song...

Dur da der da da da da dur dur

...my trainers turning and squeaking on the lino. If only I could hear them above my kitchen Top of The Pops.

I was in Brit Pop disco heaven.

Trevor appeared in the doorway, a whippet on a mission. For cake mix. I picked the spoon back up to serve as my microphone…

Oh Trevor, do you recall?
Your nose is very small.
You pissed up Barbara's wall
When I let out a call!
You didn't follow me at aaaaaaaalll!
And I said….

Trevor simply cocked his head. Meanwhile, I swung back round with my spoon to continue in my baking mission. What next...? Hmm…

I leant across to read the recipe book, noticing my hair fall into the white flour, dusting it up from the kitchen top. I didn't care. My knees were bending in turn, back and forth to the beat.

Der da der   da da da   da der der

Eggs!

I grabbed a couple, whacked them on the side of the bowl and let their insides flop out casually on top of the mush.

More flour puffed into the air, falling like snow on the worktop, the contents of the bowl still shiny with sugar and gooey with egg.

Whisk!

I grabbed the bowl, dancing with it in my arms, clutching it tightly, stirring the big wooden spoon around, the music happy and high, until I paused, struck an awkward pose, embodied Jarvis and, spoon to my lips, whispered his words...quietly...quietly.... before

...AND I SAID…

Shit! I forgot to preheat the oven.

CHAPTER 1

I could feel Trevor licking my fingers as they dangled lazily off the edge of the sofa. It took a moment to realise what day it was - let alone the approximate time.

I went to wipe my dog-spitty hands on my jeans when I noticed…ah, cake mixture, no wonder he was keen to give them a clean.

As the memories of my kitchen disco started to break through my sleepy haze, I realised that the whiff of pop music and birthday cake that had previously hung happily in the air had long gone. And, unfortunately, it had been replaced with banging cupboards and crashing crockery. My heart sank and my fingers felt even scuzzier.

'John?' I called out, sitting up on the sofa where I had obviously dozed off. Trev jumped up next to me ready to take my spot and curl up on the warm fabric.

'In here!' He yelled from the kitchen, his voice flat and tired. I peeled myself off the cushions, feeling as far from refreshed as you always feel when you've had an accidental afternoon nap, and headed into the kitchen.

'Happy birthday gorgeous!' I said, flinging my arms around him.

He hugged me but kept me at a distance. My mouth felt dry. Maybe I had bed breath?

I'd had high hopes that today was going to be fun. I thought that we'd forget all the shit that we were arguing about last week. It was all over something or nothing. It's living together, isn't it? You become kind of…impatient with each other, over all the little things that you used to ignore because you were truly, madly, deeply in love. Him forgetting to put the bin out one too many times. Me playing music too loud when he was trying to sleep. We'd talked it through. We'd agreed we needed to be more patient with each other. We'd even joked about it, laughing that we must've made some good progress to get beyond the honeymoon period and into the daily bickering.

But today he seemed.... really fucking flat.

'You, OK?' I asked.

'Emma, man, seriously.' He sighed, his eyes on everything in the kitchen except me.

'Seriously what?' I could feel my hackles rising. Stay calm Emma. It's his birthday. Maybe he's just had a really shitty day. After all, he did say that one of the residents was in major relapse. I don't know how he did that job. I certainly couldn't. It made sales admin at Shaw's Static Caravans a walk in the flamin' park.

He just looked at me, intimating that I should know, eyebrows slightly raised.

I said nothing.

'State of the place.' He finally filled in the silence, his eyes now darting around the room. 'Honest to God, it looks like Mr Blobby's hoyed up in here.' His description made me smile, but *he* was definitely *not* smiling. He was...furious.

'I was just baking you a cake. Chocolate and butter cream. You know it's not my forte, but I thought I'd have a go for the man I...'

'Don't.' His voice was quiet and empty. He moved away from me, continuing to pile the used baking stuff in the sink. Every clank of crockery made me wince. He turned the tap on and squeezed Fairy liquid into it, steam rising above the bubbles. He simply looked ahead out of the window into the garden. It was as though there wasn't any tension. It was as though there was…nothing.

My chest felt tight. 'John, I thought we'd got past all this.'

'It was one last chance, Emma. I said I couldn't do it anymore.' He didn't even look round as he spoke, just continued washing up the bowls and the cake tins in the bubbly sink, plonking them on the side, covered in suds.

I couldn't believe it took this. One little, tiny thing. Making a mess in the kitchen. I was making him a cake. Surely this wasn't it.

'But what? Seriously? You're really fucking angry because I messed up the kitchen baking you a birthday cake. Are you serious, John?'

He just looked at me and I knew. I knew there and then. It really *was* over this time.

CHAPTER 2

'Come on, it'll take your mind off it.'

'I guess.'

'It'll be a laugh.'

'Maybe.'

'And you'll…'

'I said OK! Jesus Christ Dave.' I was furiously flicking through the pages of Ally's magazine while Dave, Sega controller in hand and eyes fixed firmly on the telly, tried to talk me into watching the Euro semi-finals at the Angel. I'd left John's in a hurry only hours ago, gathering a few bags of essentials and random crap, pulling Trev on his lead while he hung his head low, occasionally stopping to look back. Dave's was, of course, the first port of call. But I knew it wouldn't be long-term. Not now Ally had all but moved in.

I'd known Dave forever. We'd grown up living down the same street, going to the same school and even, somehow, managing to land most of the same classes. He was always there for me. And given how his family life was so pants most of the time, my mum and dad always invited him on our family holidays to Tenby or Torquay or wherever was on the cards that year. We'd been through everything together.

I guess nothing had changed. Other than his dad moving on and my mum, well, leaving us and everything.

I continued snatching at the corner of every page of the glossy magazine, trying with all my might not to stop for a single second and think about what had just happened with John.

'Fuck's sake, Dave, what does she read this shite for?'

He turned and raised his eyebrows briefly before focusing

back on the telly, where he was expertly navigating Lara Croft through some dangerous tombs or something.

'*Get body beautiful for summer.* Fuck off. *How to snare your man.* Fuck the fuck off. *Boss your break-up.* Fuck the fuckity fu…'

'Hi Emma.'

'Oh, hi Ally. Hope you don't mind me having a read…'

'Sounds like it's right up your street.'

I felt my cheeks flush and continued flicking through the pages a little more quietly.

She walked over to Dave and stooped forward to kiss him on the cheek. He didn't look away from the screen, but his face said everything she needed it to. She smiled a contented smile as she walked past me, roughed Trevor's head and went into the kitchen to unpack the shopping like some kind of domestic goddess.

Trevor put his chin back on the carpet and harrumphed.

I made a mental note. I absolutely was *not* jealous of *I've-got-my-shit-together* Ally. And I was *not* going to cry in front of her, either. Although, on my next intake of breath, I felt my stomach muscles flutter involuntarily reminding me that staying happy and calm was going to be tough.

'You coming to watch the match then Em?'

'Yeah. If you don't mind.' I said, following her into the kitchen and knowing full well she did mind.

'Course not,' she replied, forcing a smile.

They'd got together not long after me and John had. They'd met at the Angel. I think Ally and her mates must've taken a wrong turn or something. They were dressed to the nines: high heels, jeans with statement belts and cropped vest tops. Ally was pristine. A strawberry blonde bob, a perfectly sculpted pair of barely-there eyebrows and a big beaming smile. He was always going to fall for her. It must've taken all of two minutes for him to make his approach while me and John looked on. Oh, and she's a big Oasis fan. I guess that was always going to be a pre-requisite for our Dave.

'Fancy some tea?' She asked, setting a jar of sauce and some chicken onto the work surface.'

'Oh, I couldn't…'

'Don't be daft. You need to eat. I'm doing chicken cacciatore.'

'Thanks,' I said, clueless as to what I was about to eat. 'Want a hand?'

'No, it's fine. Grab a drink, go help him find whatever he's trying to find in that bloody computer game.' She laughed. 'Might take your mind off things…'

I smiled back, wondering what exactly Dave had told her, and opened the fridge door to find a few bottles of Bud, a pack of Diet Cokes and a few cans of Stella. I grabbed a Stella.

'So, how long are you staying?' She blurted out before I left the room.

I knew she'd be keen to know. As much as it irked me that she had the ultimate say in who got to kip in the spare room at my best mate's flat, I had already tried to think about it the other way around; Dave staying with me and John. It would have been great…*for a bit.*

'I'm gonna head to Doreen's tomorrow. She said I could stay with her a while.'

Ally's eyes lit up. 'Ah, that's great. I mean, you're always welcome here, but you know, great you've got somewhere longer term.' She turned back to her chopping board dicing slimy chunks of chicken breast.

'Yeah.' I said, sipping the froth that had escaped from the top of the can. It was my hair of the dog. I'd already had a few baking that bloody cake before I nodded off. It was *meant* to be a day of celebration.

I walked back into the lounge where Dave had his tongue sticking out over his top lip while staring hard at the TV screen. He was completely lost in the violent stunts of a pointy-titted cartoon girl in a vest top, hot pants, and walking boots. I stood behind him to watch for a bit and see what was so mesmerising about Tomb Raider.

Trev hadn't moved from his spot, chin still flat on the floor, sad eyes flicking towards me every so often.

I tried to ignore my guilt by focusing on the upcoming game. 'Are we gonna win then?'

'Eh? Oh, um. Fuck. I don't wanna say. Don't wanna jinx it.'

I nodded.

'And whatever you do…' Dave continued, pausing the game to look me square in the eye. 'Make sure you don't go to the bog in the second half.'

It was some ridiculous obsession he had. Once, when we were teens, we were playing Argentina, and I nipped to the loo twice. Both times Maradona scored. Dave always thought it was a bad omen if I nipped to the loo during the footy. He practically banned me from watching if I was having one of my attacks of cystitis.

England being through to the Euro semi-finals though —I don't know why Dave thought this could possibly cheer me up, because, frankly, deep down, I knew we wouldn't win. Not on a day like today. My breakup was inevitably going to jinx things. Loo break or no loo break.

After picking at our tea, the three of us wandered along to the Angel, two pairs of trainers and one pair of heels tottering up the street. I decided to leave Trev home alone tonight, because, well, a) he was used to Dave's house and felt comfortable there and b), the football could always get a bit lairy and I didn't want him to get stuck in the middle of all the angst and noise.

He whimpered at the door as we left, and I was sure he was just as aware as me what John's final words meant for both of us.

As we walked into the pub, my dad and Barbara were seated at a table positioned perfectly in line with the big screen, their coats around two empty chairs, keeping them back for us.

The Angel was like our home from home. Honestly, I'd

eaten my Christmas dinner there with Bob and Bren more times than I can remember. Dave too for that matter. And Dor. I think they all took pity on me and my dad after Mum left. And Dave, well, his dad used to be present, just not in a good way. So, escaping to the Angel had been a bit of a routine for him, too. It was like a compulsion. Not for the drink, necessarily, you could get that anywhere. But for the comfort. For the familiarity.

'Hi Dad,' I said, kissing him on the cheek.

'Emma,' he said, just as his half empty pint glass connected with his mouth.

'Hi love.' Barbara leapt up full of beans, her mousey layered hair barely moving under the heavy-duty lacquer. 'Saved you a seat.' She moved her big fake fur coat from one of the seats and motioned for me to sit. Dave nobly offered the other seat to Ally and headed to the bar.

'So then ladies!' Barbara said. 'We gonna have it large tonight or what?!'

I was beginning to warm to Barbara. I was dubious when I first found out she was shagging my dad. Ugh, that thought...But he'd been on his own for so long, and she was definitely making him happier. And, God, she tried *hard* to make friends with me. I had to appreciate her efforts.

'Don't go leading our Emma astray Babs,' Dad said, straight-faced.

I smiled. 'I can look after myself.'

'Knew I could count on you doll,' Barbara beamed.

'Yeah, it's just…' Ally glanced at Barbara before turning to me. 'Just…take it easy tonight, Em. You know, what with everything that's happened. And you didn't eat much…'

'What's happened?' Barbara instinctively put her hand on top of mine…

'John finished things,' Ally mouthed quietly.

My dad's head spun round, and he looked like he'd seen a ghost. 'You what love? Johns dumped you?'

'Dad! Shh!' I said, conscious that I didn't want the whole

pub looking on with pity. If anything was going to set me off, sympathy would be the very thing to summon my tears. 'Anyway, I was *not* dumped.' I said, just as a full pint appeared in front of my nose. 'Ah, cheers Dave…'

'Emma's trying to take her mind off things,' Dave said. 'Let's guess the score instead, eh?'

I mouthed a silent *thank you* as Dave shuffled a stool across from the next table and took a seat. He winked back at me.

'I'm going 2:1, and extra time,' Barbara said with an air of confidence.

'To who?' Dad asked.

'The Germans.'

'Fuck's sake Babs.' He placed his pint down firmly on the table in the centre of his beer mat and shook his head. 'That's no way to start one of the most anticipated games of the decade.'

'He's right there Barbara. Bad luck that,' Dave said in support of him.

'How can it possibly be bad luck?' Ally asked, looking bemused.

'Because…well, because it's a bad omen. And I'll tell you something else, Emma better not be nipping to the loo in the second half again.'

'Why ever not?' Barbara asked, looking towards me and Ally and letting out an audible tut.

'Bad omen!' My dad and Dave said in unison.

I caught Ally's eye and she smiled at me. It felt comforting. Maybe I *did* need some female companionship right now. I was inevitably going to blub at some point during the evening.

'Well. Whatever the score, and whatever happened with me and John,' I said, directing the words towards my dad. 'I'm going to get pissed tonight. Because, well, why the hell not?' I held my glass up and it was immediately met by four clinking glasses reminding me that I was the odd number now.

CHAPTER 3

'Go on son!'

'Get the fuck in!'

'Sheeeeeeearer!'

By now, the pub was rapturous. But I couldn't get excited. Besides, anything that gets off to an unbelievably brilliant start always has the potential to knock you back down to earth with a nasty bang.

Yes, I was comparing my breakup to the impending heartbreak that every single England fan in the country was destined to endure.

'Fuck's sake.'

'Shit the bed!'

'For fuck's sake!'

An equaliser. I knew it wouldn't last…

The blokes on the table behind us were getting lairy and I wasn't in the mood.

'Anyone want a bevvy?' I offered.

'Cheers Em.' Dave held out his pint glass. Ally was still sipping her wine, and Dad and Bren were seemingly lost in the moment.

I grabbed mine and Dave's empties and headed to the bar, carefully squeezing past the lairy table overflowing with pint glasses, crisp packets, and cigarette ash swimming in pools of now-stale beer. They weren't regulars. They stuck out like a sore thumb.

'Two pints please Bren.'

'Coming up love.' She turned and picked out a clean glass….

'And a vodka too. Thanks.'

She eyeballed me, before placing the two fresh pint

glasses back down and turning to the optics to measure me a single.

She never offered me the option of a double.

I downed the vodka as she went on to fill our two pint glasses, then I paid, shoved the leftover shrapnel back in my jeans' pocket and headed back to the table.

'Flamin' extra time,' Dave said.

I rolled my eyes.

But at least it meant more time in the pub, taking my mind off things. At least here I had the overwhelming sounds, sights and anticipation all battling for my attention. Ashtrays were overflowing, beers were being poured down throats and onto carpets and tables, chants growing louder, especially from the table behind. But here, at least, I had booze to numb the pain. It was certainly helping, despite me feeling relatively sick - even before kick-off.

Maybe I should have forced more of that posh chicken dinner down my neck after all…

After a tense but ultimately fruitless thirty minutes of extra time, everything quietened in a collective hush. We were going to penalties. Fuck! This was going to be a killer. The moment of jeopardy where someone loses out in an instant.

The moment I heard those words, I knew it was over.

Everyone was on tenterhooks. Knees jutting out over seats, bums perched precariously on the edge. Pints held by tensed arms, veins bulging, and brows being wiped with backs of hands.

With every goal scored there was a palpable, albeit nervous, relief. Anxiety was coursing its way through everyone's veins as one by one, the brave players made their way to the penalty area.

Then Gareth Southgate went to take his shot…

'Fuck.'

'Jesus Christ. No way!'

'Fuck's sake.'

'You are fucking kidding me!'

The energy drained from the pub like a deflated balloon… but on the table behind us, anger was rising like bile.

'Fucking daft cunt.'

'Useless fucking cunt.'

My stomach jolted in disgust at these pathetic drunken fans, beer bellies dictating how closely they could sit at the table, a crappy plastic bag by their feet full of bargain booze from the offie. They were daring to judge a world-class footballer who, up until the last moment, had incited cheers and roars bursting with compliments. I couldn't help but feel the almighty sting in Gareth Southgate's chest.

'You what?' I said, my head snapping round. I felt Dave's trainer on my foot and my dad whispered something in my ear.

The table of three now all had eyes on me.

'Fuck off love.'

'What did you call me?' I could feel myself rising to their jibes. I knew I shouldn't, I knew it, but I couldn't stop.

The three stared, smirking, laughing…

'I said, what the *fuck* did you just call me?'

'Emma, come on, we're off,' Dave said, standing up, tugging at my sleeve.

'The fuck we are until these cunts apologise.'

'What you gonna do about it sweetheart?' They were all laughing, but at the same time, there was menace in their eyes. My rage was overflowing like a pint poured far too quickly.

Barbara and Ally had already left the table and were making their way to the exit. My dad was now standing trying to get Bob's attention from behind the bar.

'Fucking birds.' One of them piped up. 'Shouldn't let fucking fanny watch the footie. Too fucking hormonal.'

And with that my ears rushed with blood, and I grabbed my pint glass, hurling its contents towards the three of them, lurching forward with all my weight and hate behind me.

I felt my elbow being grabbed from behind me. My dad was pulling me backwards, away from the group and towards the bar. Meanwhile, Bob had made his way to the table and he and Dave were fronting up to the three pissed up pricks.

Dad pulled me into the back of the bar, knocking over boxes of crisps as I stumbled towards the stairs.

'Sit!' He said, his voice slightly elevated above his usual monotone repertoire. 'And don't move.' He stood in front of me blocking my exit while within the bar the volume had snuck back up to pre-penalty levels. But the tone was different.

Then I heard smashed glass.

Fuck. What have I done?

CHAPTER 4

'Honestly, I wasn't expecting you to…'

'What the fuck *were* you expecting, Em? That those pricks would pass up the chance of a scrap?'

'But it was my…'

'Emma! It's like fucking Brid all over again.'

I pulled my knees towards my body and tried to disappear into Dave's armchair.

'What happened in Bridlington?' Ally asked, handing Dave a bag of frozen peas.

I looked at Dave.

'Nothing,' he said, placing the ice-cold plastic bag on his eye and wincing. 'Doesn't matter.'

It wasn't nothing. I'd had too much to drink on a night out. And I'd given as good as I got when some wankers started grabbing my arse and calling me love. And perhaps I *did* overdo it a bit…

Perhaps I did tonight, too.

Dave lost a tooth that night.

'I'm really sorry.'

'It's alright, Em. They *were* total fucking pricks,' Ally said, trying to reassure me.

'Yeah, they were total fucking pricks,' Dave said, wincing again. 'Which is precisely why we fucking ignore them.'

'But I can understand why she…'

'Look, it's always the fucking same with blokes like that. Whatever you say to them, however much you think it's about you, you're a woman. They're not gonna fight *you*, are they?'

'Sexist pigs,' Ally said.

Dave shook his head and sighed while kicking his

trainers off on the carpet in front of him near to where Trevor was sitting. Trev didn't flinch but looked around at me with his sad doggy stare. Dave tapped his chair to invite him up. 'Let's just…forget about it, eh?' He said, stroking Trev's head. 'It's been a rough day for everyone. Especially…'

'Ah let's not go there, shall we?' I said, shifting around in Dave's armchair. 'Not sure I can keep myself from blubbing.'

'I'm just saying,' he continued. 'That maybe that's why you over did it. You know…at the bar.'

'Over did what?' I asked. 'I matched you pint for pint.'

He raised his eyebrows. 'Anyway,' he said. 'Thank fuck Bob was there with his lucky pool cue or I might have been making another trip to the dentist tomorrow.'

CHAPTER 5

'Oh lovey. Get yersel inside.' Doreen gave me a squeeze as I trundled through her front door, whippet in tow and my bags of random belongings falling haphazardly off my shoulders onto the floor of my second temporary home in as many days.

'Where shall I put my stuff?' I asked, my voice quivering and my lip so close to wobbling that I decided to bite it hard to stop it showing me up any further.

'You just leave yer stuff on the floor and come through for a brew.'

'Got anything stronger?'

She sighed. 'I heard about last night,' she said.

'Hair of the dog that bit me and broke my heart,' I said, my whining reminiscent of Trevor's when I dragged him from what was supposed to be his forever home.

'Why aren't you at work anyway?'

'Couldn't face it.' My eyes were welling up.

'I'll get you a whiskey,' she said. 'I guess if there's ever a time for it...' Dor walked away, her slipper boots shuffling along the hard wooden floor.

I left my bags in her hallway, the sun shining through the frosted glass of the front door, making me feel sick to my stomach because feeling crap feels twice as crap when the sun's out and the rest of the worlds in a great fucking mood. And now the drama of the Euros was officially over, my new reality was starting to sink in. I was single.

And hungover.

I kicked off my Converse and wandered through to Dor's living room, falling carelessly backwards onto the sofa. Trev immediately jumped onto my knee for a cuddle and looked up at me with his big, sad puppy-doggy eyes. Poor little lad. He loved John as much as I did. And Dixie. And that house with its mini back garden that our two canine bezzies took ownership of, always on guard for patrolling neighbourhood cats who loved to wind them up.

A whole little way of life, gone.

I felt completely empty except for the palpitations in my chest that were gearing up for a familiar mammoth panic. Great. My heart certainly wasn't dancing to a happy tune. Death metal simultaneously mixed with bangin' hardcore trance. Out of sync, out of time…

It made me nervous my heart going off like that. I thought I'd gotten over all that panic months ago, but the anxiety had been creeping back in - especially in the mornings. Mornings were the worst.

I could hear the return of shuffling slippers and the comforting jingle of ice in a glass as Dor wandered through with two whiskeys in her hands in mismatched glasses. 'Here you go lovey,' she said, handing me a heavy glass.

There was always something I found incredibly beautiful about Doreen's home. Sure, she was in her early 70s and there wasn't exactly an abundance of contemporary influences, but she had a real knack of drawing out the design highlights of every decade and combining them to create a beautiful sort of...chaos. Tiffany lamps really shouldn't work anywhere, but in Dor's place, mixed with 70's wicker furniture, knackered leather sofas, huge cheese plants, Victoriana, and imposing rugs it just, somehow, worked. Even her silver trainers in the hallway effortlessly complemented the old rickety coat stand.

I took a swig of my drink and exhaled a tiny proportion of my stress.

'Do you want to talk about it then?' She never asked me much on the phone when I called her. Just said that, yes, of course I could move in for a while. She knew she was my first choice because, after all, Dave's got Ally and Dad's got Barbara and I wasn't about to gate-crash those romantic parties. All of them blissfully drowning in the romantic haze of early-stage love affairs. Bastards.

'I don't know,' I said, taking another sip of whiskey, the smoky fumes dancing around my nostrils, hitting the back of my throat like a warm blanket of fibreglass. She might get her furniture from the car boots and her clothes from the charity shops, but she never scrimped on the whiskey.

'I think it was for the best, darling,' she said.

'What? Why would you say that?'

'The truth sometimes hurts, but, you know, once it's faced, it's faced.'

'Cheers for that,' I said, knocking back the rest of the drink and holding out my empty glass like a spoilt brat.

Dor rolled her eyes and took it off me, stopping in the doorway briefly. 'This is the thing though, Emma, love. John's, well, he's been through a lot and...'

'I guess…but we all have, haven't we?'

'Well, yes, you certainly have.' She paused, giving me the kind of look you might give a nervous kitten. 'But with his family stresses and the stress of his job too…. you know…'

Dor had been in my life since day dot. She'd seen me through everything - my mum leaving us, my dad being unemployed and melancholier than a Shakespearean tragedy. And she'd picked me up off the floor more than once when I was attacked by panic or trying to strangle the panic with copious amounts of booze.

My fingers pulled at a loose thread on the arm of the sofa. 'I get that his job is tough…I know he sees a lot of bad stuff…'

'But it's how we respond to these things isn't it.' She pressed on. 'It's given John a taste for...calm, for responsibility. You've responded completely differently.'

'How do you mean?'

'He wants to just chill with you Emma. He wants a quiet life. And who can blame him?'

'Cheers for that.'

Dor finally headed into the kitchen to grab the refills while I sat sulking. I *wanted* John to chill with me. To chill and have fun. To not get so wound up with the mundane. I don't know. Part of me could see why he got so irritable with me. Our lives were always clashing one way or another. His night shifts at work. My night shifts by the record player with a bottle of cheap wine and Nirvana or Tori Amos blaring out through the stereo depending on what kind of mood I was in. I always tried to wait up for him if he was due home in the middle of the night. To greet him. But that involved keeping my spirits up with booze to keep me awake. I was usually half cut when he got home.

He was usually half asleep having been pushed to the limit by one of his clients trying to hurt themselves or over-dosing or something equally awful.

I guess Dor had a point. But also, we weren't exactly middle-aged. You could just as easily chill out from the stresses of adult life by getting merry and having a laugh. We all needed some of that in our lives, surely?

I looked to Trev for some kind of affirmation, but he just cocked his head to one side and lifted an ear as if to challenge me.

As the slipper shuffles and ice cube jangles got louder, Dor reappeared, handing me my second cold drink.

'Thanks,' I said, realising how grumpy I'd been. I mean, the woman was putting me up. For free. For as long as I needed. 'Sorry for being an arse.'

'No bother darling,' she said, settling into her armchair, smiling. 'I'm used to it.'

Dor made anyone and everyone feel at home. She was often perched on her favourite stool at The Angel bar, her hair perched neatly on her head in a kind of Judi Dench style pixie cut. She'd be sipping her milk stout, telling stories, observing the world in a completely different way to everyone around her. She was The Angel's angel. My mum and dad had known her since they were young, so she'd been an eccentric and homely presence my entire life. The less-than-cuddly grandma I never had.

'But, Dor, I mean, even you don't have a quiet life. That can't be it. I have to wonder…'

'If he's having an affair? Don't be bloody ridiculous.'

'How is it ridiculous?'

'I don't think you can blame John for this one, love. I think maybe you need to take some responsibility for it.'

'Dor!'

'Well come on love, John deals with some shitty stuff at work all day, he's spent years looking after his sister and all her dramatics. I think he could do without your night-time antics on top of that.'

'What night-time antics?'

'You know what I mean.' She said, her eyes making contact with my glass.

I drank it down in defiance.

'I'm 28 Dor, going on 29. I'm bound to be cramming in the fun before things get serious and I hit my 30s. Your twenties are meant to be for living life to the full.'

'Well, that depends on what living life to the full means, and whether you've interpreted it correctly.'

'You're talking nonsense now. Besides, you're at the pub every day.'

'Sitting at the bar, not falling asleep under it.'

'Once Dor. Once!'

She shook her head. 'I hope you left on good terms. Lovely fella is John.' She sipped her drink, her eyes downcast as she focused on her whiskey rather than the pitiful state squatting in her house.

'Thanks for making me feel worse and yes, for your information, we did. Well, fairly good terms, anyway.'

'Good.'

'It was a mutual decision,' I lied.

'Right.' She looked unconvinced. 'Anyway, make yourself at home, I'm off out tonight.'

'Ooh where we going?'

'Sorry lovey. I'm seeing to some business.'

I didn't want to know what that meant. She was always up to something. Selling knock-off ciggies to the punters in The Angel or brewing Hull's own version of moonshine. I mean, bit rich telling me to be more responsible. She was an old-aged-criminal. Dor was like Supergran's nemesis.

She left the room, and I heard her footsteps on the stairs as I picked up the remote and stuck the telly on. *Watchdog* or *MasterChef*. Great. I switched the telly back off, rummaged through my bag in the hallway and grabbed the first CD I could find then chucked it into Dor's hi-fi. *Linger* by The Cranberries came on, Dolores' haunting voice whispering through the speakers like the ghost of romance past. I went to top up my glass then returned to the sofa, snuggling up to Trev and feeling as though I might never move from here again.

I took a big gulp of my whiskey. How did I so royally mess it all up?

We'd only been together two years - not even that. I really, truly believed that John was 'The One.' That I could finally stop all the nights out where I was so desperate to find that someone special that I'd end up snogging some onion-breathing curtain-haired townie with shit aftershave at the taxi rank. They probably felt the same as me, to be fair. I'm sure they didn't *really* set out to pull a lank haired, Dr Marten-clad tomboy, either. But come 2.30am you take what you can get. The fumes and the looks get a bit faded and blurry in the midst of it all, but the next day it always hits you like a big fat belly of regret, sharpened by daylight and heightened by nausea. I was too old for all that shite. I was delighted to find someone to go to Pier Luigi for a spag bol with and relax back into the sofa to finish the night with a bit of Euro Trash on the telly.

The restlessness never actually vanished, though. It just shape-shifted into a hopeless energy. A nagging anxiety, knowing that I should've been far more relaxed and happier than I was. But it wasn't John that was the problem. No way was it, John.

I love John.

'See you later sweetheart,' Dor shouted from the hallway. Before I had chance to reply the door had shut, and I could hear her heels outside. Curious, I got up and walked to the window, pulling the net curtain to one side to see her tottering down the path in '40s style shoes and a big fake fur coat. Lord knows what she was up to tonight. No doubt getting some of what I *won't* be getting for the foreseeable.

Dumped. No matter how I dressed it up I was well and truly dumped. The man I dreamt of marrying. The man whose eyes made me swoon. The man who took me on a mini break with our little family of pooches. The man I loved so bloody much I could just squeeze him to death.

And now I'd split everyone up. Now, I was living back down the road from my dad, with nowt to my name other than a crappy job, a whippet with dodgy bowels and a... nope...I'd already drained my third glass dry.

CHAPTER 6

Dave

Ally was doing that thing women do with mascara – she was talking away while layering her lashes with the stuff, mouth gaping open in concentration. 'You're gonna have to keep an eye on her. These next few days, they'll be tough' she said, popping the little brush back in the pot and digging around in her make-up bag for whatever was next.

Lipstick, apparently.

She was standing in front of the hallway mirror getting ready to go out with her mum. Some play about a night on the town at that little theatre on Spring Street. I couldn't really understand why you'd go to *watch* a night out – why not just have one?

But then I suppose there's no chance of your best mate dragging you all into a scrap with a bunch of fuckwits if you're just *watching* a night out.

'What's the show called again?' I asked, hovering behind her, chatting to our reflections in the mirror.

'Don't go changing the subject. Emma's gonna need to talk to you about stuff. You need to be prepared.'

'We've been talking for over twenty years.'

'Yeah,' she said, smoothing her hair down, 'but this isn't talking about top ten movies or critiquing Liam Gallagher's lyrics.'

'Noel's,' I said.

Her reflection shot me a death stare. 'She'll need to *really* talk.' She said, giving her hair a wild shake - having only just this second smoothed it down neatly. Honestly, I didn't understand women.

But I *really* didn't understand Emma. Not anymore. I couldn't just sit there and tell her that John must be out of his mind for finishing things. I couldn't lie to her. She knew me too well for that. Although it felt like, these days anyway, telling Emma what she *wanted* to hear would suffice. In fact, if anyone was cutting off the conversation when it got too close to the bone it was her.

I leaned in to kiss Ally's head just as she picked up the hairspray. 'Jesus fucking Christ, Al.'

'Bouncers,' she said, stopping the spraying momentarily while I choked on the fumes.

'Eh?'

'The show. It's a John Godber.'

'Right,' I said, none the wiser.

'Maybe you and Emma should try the theatre one night?'

'Not sure that'd be a good idea.'

'It's pretty laid back at Spring Street.'

'It might be, but Emma's bloody not.'

Ally shrugged, gave herself a final check in the mirror, then kissed me goodbye.

The door slammed shut behind her, shaking the wall so that the framed pic of me and Ally now hung at a wonky angle. I straightened it back up – a familiar routine.

I walked into the kitchen and grabbed a coke and a packet of ham from the fridge, before diving onto the sofa in the lounge.

No drama. No chatter. Just me, a pile of cooked meat, and a documentary on reptiles. Bliss.

CHAPTER 7

'Come on, Dave. What the fuck am I going to do, sit home alone all dumped and pathetic?'

'But it's a Monday night, Emma. And besides, I'm still recovering from last night.'

'You soft shite.'

'I wouldn't go there if I were you.'

'OK, OK. It's just that Dor's gone out, and it's all kind of hit me, you know. And I'm here all alone and it's really doing my head in if I'm honest.'

'Nah. Sorry. Putting my foot down.'

'Dave please. It's not like I wanna go clubbing. We'll be back early doors. It's just a gig at the Adelphi.'

'You've already started, haven't you?'

'I've just been dumped, Dave. D.U.M…'

'All right, Jesus.…'

'Ah you'll come then?'

'Fuck's sake. All right. Meet you out the front in half an hour.'

'You fucking beauty.'

I immediately felt chirpier. Like, really fucking chirpier. If there was one thing that was going to kick my misery into touch it was live music. And beer. And yeah, I was already on the up in that respect. But. For. Fuck's. Sake. I'd just been dumped. If there's one time you can be excused for getting completely and utterly off your face, it's now. At least, that was the plan.

I changed my jeans and pulled on a fresh vest top, shoved my feet in my Converse, chucked Trev a chew stick and headed out the door, my quick steps taking me there hurriedly. Everything would be all right tonight. Tonight,

I'd have Dave, oblivion, and King Rupert.

That was the great thing about Hull. No matter what day of the week it was, there was always some band playing. And these guys, King Rupert, they were just a bunch of kids, like 17 or 18 or something. But I'd heard they were good. And they could draw a crowd. So maybe.... maybe I'd find some face to snog in said crowd and forget all about John and my hopelessness.

Yes. That's *exactly* what would happen.

Dave was smoking a ciggie, kicking his feet when I arrived. He had that look on his face...

I elbowed him. 'Cheer up. I'll pay us in.'

'Nice one Emma.' He chucked his cigarette butt on the floor and immediately took another out from his battered packet of Embassy No. 1.

It was still light outside, and I was desperate to get lost in some dark and moody noise. Smoky, dark, loud, *really fucking loud*, oblivion.

We paid and made our way into the venue, the walls beautifully decorated in overlapping flyers and posters. As we headed into the main venue area, the band had already taken to the stage. Amps were being set up, cables uncoiled and leads plugged in.

'Christ, Emma, how old are these lot?'

'18 or 19, I think.'

'Shit. I feel really fucking old. I'm like...like a dad or something.'

'Ah get away! What you drinking?'

We ordered a couple of pints and stood towards the back of the room.

'Ciggie?'

'Cheers, Dave.'

It was just like old times. Who needed boyfriends when you have a best mate and live music? I lit my cigarette and inhaled deeply. Ahhhhh.

The guitarist and bass player built up the sound, low and

heavy, there was an almost eerie Doors vibe to it. The singer, bright ginger curly hair, took stock of the room, the audience numbers. It wasn't bad for a Monday. He was happy. He started singing, almost a whisper, then the drums kicked in and his voice screamed a nice healthy scream.

'Nice vocals,' Dave said.

'What?'

'Nice vocals.'

'Sorry?'

'NICE VOCALS!'

'Yeah. Read some good reviews. They're like fresh out of college or something. You never know, we might be watching the next Oasis here.'

'Yeah.' Dave somehow managed to make taking a sip of his pint symbolise cynicism.

'Are you taking the piss?'

'What?'

'Are you taking the piss?'

'What?'

I sighed. 'Don't you like them?'

'Yeah. Course. I just mean. Nobody ever fucking makes it do they? Like, these bands, slogging their guts out, we've seen, how many?'

'What, bands?'

'Eh?'

'BANDS?'

'Yeah.' He picked his drink back up to mark the end of the discussion. There was no point trying to have a real conversation. Nobody could hear a thing other than the dirty, heavy melody. And it was exactly the medicine I needed.

'Same again?'

'Cheers Dave.'

He headed to the bar, returning with another couple of pints and a weary look on his face. 'Here you go.'

'Thanks.' I took the cold pint glass from him, a dribble of beery froth making its way over my fingers. 'You all right?' I asked.

'Yeah, why?' He immediately looked away towards the stage. I decided to end it there. Maybe we could chat more once the band had finished, and it was quieter. I'd get it out of him eventually, I always did.

The gig was fun, but things weren't like they used to be. He was only here because I'd nagged him to come.

I guess I had a part to play in it, whatever this weird drifting feeling was. I mean, I'd met John. Dave met Ally. Life kind of took a turn, got serious. We were still seeing my dad for a drink every so often, but our less sensible nights had come to a pretty strong full stop. Time to hop off the fun bus. Time to grow the fuck up.

We'd always been a bit behind in the maturity stakes. When growing up is far from stable or happy, you feel like you've earned the right to take some extra time to fuck around. Both me and Dave spent far too much of our childhood having to consider adults. With my mum leaving us and Dave's dad being…well…being the absolute cunt that he is…we kind of tried to create as much fun and laughter outside of our stressful little houses as we could. In our teenage years that meant overdoing the Diamond White. As we moved into our early twenties the only thing that changed was the choice of beverage.

Goodbye strong cider and hello tequila.

Music, pubs, quiz nights, The Word on the telly just before we passed out. Waking up to Going Live! and that weird puppet thing on TV as we opened our eyes. Hmm… I guess we had to grow up at some point.

But now wasn't the time. Now I needed Dave all to myself. I was glad his other half didn't come with us tonight. As selfish as that sounded. Ally was far too bloody sensible for him, really.

After the band finished their first set, the crowd showed

their enthusiasm as loudly and proudly as they could. Cheers, claps, whoops, and whistles rang out. That was what I loved about small venues like The Adelphi. The small crowd always made up for the limited capacity by hollering as loudly as possible. You felt closer to the band in spaces like this. You had an obligation to make them feel appreciated.

'Not bad, not bad at all,' Dave said seriously, as if he was a Guardian music critic or something. 'Wasn't expecting anything of any quality to be honest. Not at their age.'

'Yeah, I read good things.'

He looked at his feet stretched out in front of him. 'You said.'

'Dave, have I done something to upset you?'

'No.'

'You just seem. I don't know...'

'I'm fine.'

'Fine. Right.'

'You trying to start a row?'

'No. Fuck's sake. I am worried about you is all. Especially after last night. I thought you might be angry with me.'

'I was.'

'I'm sorry. Really am.'

I felt like a wounded puppy, what with Dave being so off with me…I needed him so much right now and I felt like a burden. And that was new.

I hit myself in the chest with a boatload of self-pity that was threatening me with tears. Catastrophising, the therapist used to call it. But it didn't matter what she said it was, it felt real. It felt horrible.

Dave shifted himself to a more upright position. In his chair. 'Look, I'm grand. I'm just knackered. It's a Monday night. I've got an early shift tomorrow.'

'Just one more though? I could really do not to be alone tonight.'

'You're never alone these days.'

'What's that supposed to mean?'

'Nothing.'

I looked down towards the table and realised I had been peeling the top layer from the beer mat with one hand the whole time.

Dave noticed it too. 'Sorry,' he said. 'I'm being a boring bastard. Get 'em in.'

I smiled and hopped over to the bar, ordering a cheeky vodka to enjoy before my pint. Some of the band started to gather in the bar area so I did my bit.

'You guys were great! We loved it. Great set.'

'Thanks,' the singer said, looking pleased with himself. I thought this could be an opportunity to liven things up. It might be a Monday night, but if there's one group of people who are always up for a laugh it's musicians.

'Yeah, well impressive, what with you guys still being in college and everything.'

'Ha. I think I can take that as a compliment?'

'Ha-ha yes. It was absolutely meant as one. Sorry, didn't mean to sound like your mum.' There was a slight awkward silence as he got his drink from the barman, so I filled it. 'I'm Emma by the way.'

'Martin. And this is Phil and that's Chris. And er… where's Rich?'

Phil looked around. 'Think he's sorting things out with the manager.'

'Ah.' Martin turned back round. 'It's a good job someone makes sure we get paid. So, you enjoyed it then?'

'Yeah, 100%. My mate did too.'

'Ah that's good to hear! You always worry, especially on a school night.'

'School? I thought…'

'Turn of phrase. Fewer syllables than college. Or something.' He took a sip of his pint.

Martin was dressed in jeans and a dark T-shirt. He probably didn't need to do much to stand out given the mass of ginger curls adorning his head. Chris was tall, skinny, and wearing a fitted '70's floral short. Phil was in jeans and a relaxed shirt. I was yet to meet Rich.

'That's my mate, Dave.' I nodded over and Dave raised his almost empty glass up in response. 'Come join us if you want? I mean if we're not too middle aged for you.'

Martin laughed and gave Phil and Chris a 'shall we?' kind of look. They shrugged. I took that as great enthusiasm, coming from teenagers.

'Dave. Meet the band! This is Martin. Chris. And…hang on…Phil?'

'Well done!' Phil laughed. We began chatting about being music fans, who we'd seen live, best tracks on our favourite albums, the usual cheesy stuff that fans geek out over.

Luckily, Dave was starting to perk up. 'Get this for a lark,' he said excitedly. 'You know Senseless Things? We only ended up getting backstage passes and partying on their tour bus.'

'No way.'

'Really?'

'Yeah,' Dave continued. 'It was great, 'til we passed out and woke up in fucking Portsmouth. I was due to have surgery the next day in bloody Hull.'

'Surgery?'

'Ball cancer.'

'Shit, man.'

'Ancient history.'

'So, did you make it to the hospital?'

'Yeah. Just.'

'How did you end up backstage anyway?'

'Emma?' Dave smirked at me while rolling his cigarette ash in the overflowing ashtray. 'Want to tell them?'

'Ha. The drummer caught me pissing in a bush and being ambushed by the security guard. Think he felt sorry for me.'

'Ha-ha nice one.'

'Hilarious.'

'He gave us backstage passes and we spent the rest of the night, after the gig, partying on their tour bus. It was ace. Until, well, like Dave said…'

We carried on drinking and gabbing away, feeling like the experienced gig-goers that we probably really weren't in comparison, even with our decade head start. We never played in a band, for starters. Karaoke at The Angel was the closest we ever got to performing. And that was usually Especially for You by Kylie and Jason. Trying to be ironic but actually really enjoying ourselves.

I realised, regardless of what major catastrophe had *happened* earlier in the day, I was having fun. This was just what I needed.

'Who are your musical influences then?' Dave asked.

I rolled my eyes, looked at the band apologetically then back at Dave. 'Jeez. Could you be any more cringe?'

'Valid question. My question, I mean. Not your sarky comment.'

'Whatever.'

As the band reeled off a list of musicians they loved, including some of the covers they played, we rejoiced in forgetting about shit and wallowing in the sounds of now.

'Sultans of Ping's always a favourite,' Martin said.

'Could I hear a touch of some bittersweet melancholy Lemonheads there too?' Dave asked, trying to impress them.

'A touch of some Lemonheads? Piss off Dave, they played an *actual* Lemonheads cover…it wasn't hard to work that influence out.'

'Fuck off Emma.'

'Fuck off Dave.'

I gave him a playful, yet forceful punch on the arm and he returned the gesture by nipping me.

'You twat,' I laughed, rubbing the smarting skin on my arm that was no doubt blazing bright red already.

The music was no longer live, but it was buzzing and crashing through all of us thanks to the Adelphi's stereo system. *Black Holed Sun* by Soundgarden had us all singing at the top of our voices complete with dramatic '80s style action accompaniments, *Come out and Play* by The Offspring had us up out of our chairs doing some serious moves, twisting our feet around on the old, carpeted floor to the lively Arabian riff. And when *Today* by Smashing Pumpkins came on, I was genuinely feeling it. It *was* the greatest day. Right now, was all that mattered. It was bittersweet. Tomorrow didn't bear thinking about.

I leapt up animatedly. 'I'll get another round in.

CHAPTER 8

'Emma what the fuck...Mate, look, I'm dead sorry.'

'Give over it's only a pint.'

'Anyone'd think you were the fucking teenager.'

'Stop it Dave, you're embarrassing the band.'

'*You* just chucked a fucking pint over them.'

'Lighten up. I was having a laugh.'

'Lighten up? How fucking old are you.... Yeah, no worries, sorry again mate. Dunno what else to say.... nice to meet you. See ya. Bye. Bye.... You're a fucking liability Emma.'

'You're a fucking bore. 'Ere do you want one an' all, might chill you out?'

'I'm serious, Em. Put that fucking glass down or we're done.'

'We were anyway.'

'What's that supposed to mean?'

'You've hardly been a mate in months. You never bother anymore.'

'Any fucking wonder?'

'I've been dumped.'

'Yeah, and don't we all know it.'

'Well, you could be a bit more...'

'What? You drag me out on a Monday, I do my bit, turn up, say nowt when you start to get lairy...'

'Fuck off Dave.'

'Yeah, d'you know what. That's a fucking grand idea that.'

'No Dave. Sorry. I didn't mean it. Don't go. Dave, please...'

'Fuck's sake, Emma come on...there's no need to... Right, I'll walk you home, OK? But you need to chill the fuck out. Honestly. You're getting right on everyone's tits.'

'What because I've been dumped? Because I had a drink?'

'Yeah. Yeah OK. That *is* the problem. This isn't you. It's not you.'

'What's not?'

'This. This…God Emma. There's having a laugh and then there's….'

'We *have* had a laugh.'

'You always take it too far. It *used* to be a laugh.'

'You try waking up and being me.'

'We've all got shit going on, Emma.'

'So, what now? I lose John, and now you.'

'Get off your pity pot. Fuck's sake. Nobody said that. Christ, take it on the chin. You've been fucking out of order. If I wasn't a mate, I wouldn't be standing here telling you that.'

'What making me feel like shit?'

'I've had enough of this. Come on.'

'But you're like my brother. You've always been…'

'Jeez, Emma. Stop crying. Just…get your jacket. I'll walk you back.'

CHAPTER 9

'You look rough as arseholes'

I pulled my rickety swivel chair out from behind my desk and plonked myself down. 'Cheers Claire.'

'Mike's on your case by the way.'

I checked my watch and rolled my eyes.

'For twenty-bleedin' minutes?'

Claire was clicking her mouse and frowning at her monitor. 'Something about pulling a sickie, too.'

'But I never pulled a sickie. He's just a grumpy bastard. Anyway,' I said. 'Brew?'

'Yeah, why not, fill her up.' Claire handed me her manky mug without allowing her eyes to leave her computer screen. Ugh. Those brown tea stains made my stomach churn. If I had the energy, I'd be bleaching it with a scrubber and a bit of elbow grease. Funny how she's pristine in looks but...

I wandered through to the kitchen, manky mug in hand and went to find mine.

My mug didn't appear to be in any of the cupboards. 'Fuck's sake.'

'What's up with you?' I didn't have to turn around. I knew from the waft of cheap aftershave and the smarmy tone that it was Shane from sales. The last person I wanted to see today.

'Someone's stolen my fucking mug. Again.' I continued opening and slamming doors, ignoring all the other empty clean mugs that were left standing on the shelves.

'Woah, it's not the end of the world. Chill yer boots.'

'Fuck off Shane.'

He responded to my words by walking backwards, hands in front of him, shaking his head and tutting.

'Twat,' I mumbled.

'I heard that.'

'Well, I'm clearly in a bad mood. You winding me up doesn't help.'

'Just trying to be friendly.'

He finally walked out of the kitchen, and I gave up on my mug search. I grabbed someone's beloved Hull City mug, also full of brown stains, and dropped a tea bag in it, and one in Claire's, and made a strong brew. With two sugars. And the teabag left in.

God, I felt rough as arseholes.

'Here' I said, clumsily putting Claire's mug on her desk, spilling tea down the side and onto her already tea-spattered promotional desk pad.

'What's eating you?' She asked, her multiple gold earrings jangling as she flung her long, curly, heavily moussed hair behind her shoulder.

'Nothing,' I snapped.

'Well, I'd try to come up with something if I were you. Mike will need a good excuse this time.'

'I guess.'

I slumped backwards in my swivel chair saying nowt.

'Trouble in para....'

'Don't! Please, don't go there.' I could feel my lip wobbling and an involuntary intake of breath force its way to my lungs. 'I'm just. God it really fucking hurts, Claire.'

'Ah no, Em. Come on, tell me all about it.' She stood up to wander over and I could feel a wetness on my cheek and a bubble growing from my nostril.

'It's over, Claire. It's well and truly fucking over.'

'No. With John?'

'No, with Timmy Mallett.' I sneered, rolling my eyes. 'Yes, with John!'

'OK well it's just…'

'Just what? There's not been anyone else in years.'

'I know that. I just mean, well, I don't know. I guess I'm just shocked is all babes.'

'You and me both.'

'You got on so well.'

'I know.'

'It doesn't make sense.'

'I *know*.'

'Why would he?'

'I don't know Claire, but he has. He well and truly has.' I started blubbing, more tears, more snot, and more jangles from Claire's ears as she gave me a rigorous hug.

'Don't you worry darlin'. I'll help you through it. I've got a packet of bourbons and an Anne Summers catalogue in my drawer.'

'Dirty cow.'

'You know you love it'

'Jesus. Have you been possessed by the spirit of Sid James?' I laughed, sniffing the escaping snot back up my nose.

'Carry on caravanning.'

'Ha, it might as well be. But it's Shane who's Sid James. You're Barbara Windsor. And Mike's like that Kenneth…'

'Emma. A word!' Mike's voice boomed behind us.

Fuck. I turned my head slowly hoping that by some stroke of luck I was hearing things. I wasn't.

'Now, Emma!'

'Sorry Mike. Coming.'

He turned and walked towards his office, beckoning me with his arm in the air. I picked up my tea and reluctantly followed him in, wiping my nose with my arm because, what was better, a snot covered arm, or my boss seeing my snotty nose? I had to pull myself together. I was *not* about to have a breakdown in Mike's office.

'Take a seat. Close the door behind you first.'

Fuck. My heart was racing like a trained greyhound and my mouth was drier than my dad's Yorkshire puddings.

'What is it?' I asked nervously, positioning my bum on the knackered swivel chair in front of his desk, orange sponge erupting out of the greying fabric. My feet were fidgeting wildly on the coffee-stained carpet tiles beneath in anticipation of a serious bollocking.

Mike finally sat down. 'I think you know what it is.' He was twirling a biro pen in his fingers while looking at me. Was he waiting for me to say something? Then he sighed, put the biro down and leaned forward over his desk. 'Emma, seriously. The state of you. You reek of it.'

I pointed my nose towards my armpit as discreetly as I possibly could.

'Booze!' He clarified.

I felt myself flush. 'Oh. I um. Well. I've had...'

'You can't even remember your own made-up excuse this time, can you?'

'It's not an excuse. It's…' I tried to collect myself, but my tears were threatening. I wished, I *really* wished, that I was here getting in trouble for being late for no good reason. I wished I *was* making up some daft excuse. I couldn't say what my actual genuine reason was because I didn't want to say it out loud. I didn't want to share it with Mike. It was personal. It was gnawing away inside me, but I didn't want to let it grow by screaming it to the whole wide world.

'I had a really rough couple of days,' I said. 'I know I've had a bit too much to drink. I know I've been late but…. it's just…' I couldn't hold it back. It burst out. I *was* having a breakdown in Mike's office. The tears fell harder than a Shaw's Static Caravan's Deluxe turbo power shower. Mike went white.

'OK. Um. OK.' He stood awkwardly, fumbling around in his pocket, before handing me a tissue. I took it. 'Thank you,' I said.

'Your um. Fella, is it? Boyfriend?' He said, playing with his tie and clearing his throat.

I sobbed harder, louder. Gigantic blobby tears rolling at speed down my cheeks, my nose quickly filling with emotional snot. I didn't care - he might as well see me like this. My life was a fucking shit show right now.

John - you broke my bloody heart you gorgeous bloody bastard!

'Emma?'

I tried to catch my breath, but nothing useful was about to come out.

'OK. Emma. Um...'

I looked up at him. He had no idea what to say or do. He was kind of hovering around me, bouncing from one foot to the next, arms in the air as if I was a delicate butterfly that he was scared of accidentally murdering by being an awkward clod. But he needed to calm me down, he needed to stop my fluttering. Because, well, this was a *hugely* uncomfortable situation for no-nonsense Mike.

At least maybe now he wouldn't sack me.

Oh God - was I actually using John to manipulate the situation? With that thought flashing through my mind I felt even worse. I was a shameful excuse for a human being.

'Look,' he said. 'I'll give you one last chance. But this is your final warning.

I nodded. 'Thanks, Mike.' Then I went to leave, my head hanging low.

'Emma. Erm...'

'Sorry?' I said, turning around.

'Emma you've. Um.' He flapped his fingers around his face, indicating, I could only assume, a make-up malfunction on mine. I wiped my fingertips under my eyes and noticed they were covered in black streaks of Rimmel mascara. 'Thanks,' I said, holding the now disgusting snotty tissue underneath my sore and streaming eyes. Why did I never fork out the extra for waterproof?

I walked back to my desk, my fingers tightly gripping the rogue Hull City mug that was now full of cold tea., I sat down feeling beaten, only to be immediately met with my *actual* mug that was now full of a hot steaming drink.

'Here you go. Take five minutes. Tell me about it.' Claire handed me a biscuit, too, but I waved it away. I needed Caffeine. Food I couldn't much stomach right now. Which reminded me that I hadn't eaten and that thought somehow triggered hunger pains. But in a weird kind of way, they comforted me.

I cradled the hot, Dalmatian-patterned mug in my hand, the heat stinging my palms. I held on to it tightly regardless, as if I deserved to feel the pain.

'It's over, Claire,' I managed, lip quivering but less at risk of a flood of tears after my accidental outburst in Mike's office. I wasn't even sure I had any tears left now.

'I know, honey. Tell me what happened?'

'I'm not sure I'm ready to go there yet. I've just had some kind of freaky breakdown in Mike's office.'

'OK. You take a moment to collect yourself. Pub after work?'

A pang of excitement jolted through me, immediately perking me up. 'Deal,' I said, slurping my tea with renewed energy, delighted I didn't have to wander into the pub on my own again.

'But you must take it easy today, OK? I'll look after your calls. You just keep your head down, crack on with filing or something, yeah?'

'Thanks. Can't really face people today.'

'Aw sweetie,' she said, giving me her sweetest smile as she went back to her desk.

5.30 couldn't come round fast enough. The day was slow. Monotonous. Dull. Everything I worked on demanded so little brain power that I seemingly had all the time in the world to think about John. Since it happened, I'd managed to bury it all by getting drunk and hanging out with some band. Oh, fuck and chucking beer over the singer.

Dave was so angry with me.

With John's seeming indifference and Dave's blatant rage on my mind, perhaps confrontations with the sales team would have been better than sitting here shuffling papers with too much head space? Instead, I was going over and over those last words John had said to me before I left.

Take care of yourself.

I couldn't understand it. He definitely cared. That much was clear. He was the most caring person I knew. But why did it have to end? Perhaps he could change his mind? Perhaps he was just giving me a definite *final* ultimatum?

But then I realised that was just what I *wanted* to believe, and every time I went over and over what happened, what had led to him breaking up with me, it was like it hit me all over again.

It wasn't just a sadness—it was the worst kind of sadness—a restless sadness. I was making cup after cup of tea just to get up from my desk and do something different. Appreciating the constant caffeinated need for a wee just for something else to do. I was pissing like a racehorse. It was all diversion tactics.

But I knew what would really take the edge off. I knew what would stop the relentless loop in my brain. I looked at the clock. It was only 2.17pm. Damn.

Working at Shaw's Static Caravans was something I never really thought I'd spend long doing. It was a stop gap after uni. I was always planning to move onto bigger and brighter things. But now I'd been here almost five years. Five years! The thought of turning 30 in less than two years' time was frankly terrifying. What the fuck had I been doing with my life so far? Getting pissed, getting dumped and getting bored of relentless filing and data inputting on the computer. Why couldn't I just grow up gracefully like everyone else. Not that Claire's especially graceful, certainly not if you hear what she gets up to at LA's on a Friday night. But she was happy, content. She didn't need to do anything different or be anyone else. I envied that in her. No matter where I was in the world, no matter what was happening in my life, I needed to feel different, to do it differently. Even with John, I was never satisfied, never truly content. But I so wanted to be. With him.

If I couldn't be content with him, would I ever be?

I shut my computer down at 5.27pm. I couldn't wait any longer. I couldn't just keep sitting at my desk with my head in its melancholy state of darkness and my body all fidgeting and jittery. If I could go back and tell my 15-year-old self some words of wisdom it would be to not get so smug about getting over break up number one. I always thought the first would be the hardest. How naive. The teenage crush was a walk in the park compared to falling in love and losing it.

I needed a drink, and I was up out of my chair before the clock hit 5.30 with my bag over my shoulder.

'You're keen,' Claire said.

'I know. Today has dragged. Come on. I'll get the first round in.'

'Nice one darlin.'

We headed into the pub around the corner from work. It was a bit of a dive, one of those pubs that looked more like a shop front among terraced houses. It was mainly quiet locals who spent the day there from doors open, to a few of the factory lads on a lunchtime pint-break or a straight-from-work bevvy. A good old Axminster on the floor that had seen better days, and a smell of stale ale hanging in the air. Still, I'd got to know some of the locals and the bar staff over time when I'd popped in on a lunchtime or for a swift one after work. It'd do for me.

'You grab a seat,' I said to Claire, motioning towards a table in the corner. She headed off and I went to order.

'Two pints of Stella please, Col.'

'Coming up.'

As he filled the glasses, the amber liquid rose to the top of each before he straightened the angle and allowed a frothy white head to peek out over the rim. God I was thirsty. I could feel my mouth watering at the sight of it.

'Actually, I'll have a voddy too.'

'Single?'

'Make it a double.'

He presented me with a neat little glass. 'That'll be £6.26 please love.'

I dug around in my purse for the correct change, handed it to him, and downed the vodka as he opened the till, exhaling with an immense rush of relief as I placed the empty glass back on the bar before he'd had chance to pass me my change. As my muscles instantly relaxed, I felt that perhaps, at least for a little while, I could dare to feel OK again.

'Here you go.' I plonked two pints on the table, careful to position them on the beer mats some former punters had kindly left in a soggy state for us, and took a seat opposite Claire, lighting up a cigarette and taking a big gulp of beer. 'God I was thirsty.'

'So, spill, then. Let's get it out there. Did you cheat? Did he cheat? What's been happening?'

'God no. Nothing like that.'

'Is it cos of Dave?'

'Eh?'

'You two are very close.'

I nearly spat my drink out. 'Eueww, he's like my brother.'

'Ah, but he isn't though.'

'He might as well be. Jesus, you're not helping. That's sick that.'

'What then? You two seemed the perfect match. Everyone thought so. Even Shane commented on how sickly sweet the two of you were after the Christmas party.'

'I know. But it's not always enough, is it?'

I went on to fill her in on the bickering. How John didn't like me coming in late. How he always nagged at me for getting too excitable and drunk when we went out.

'I'm 28 Claire. I'm *supposed* to be having fun.'

'So, you broke it off with him then?'

I took another gulp of beer. 'No.'

'OK...?'

'I don't know. I think he just wanted to settle down more

than me.'

'Well, that doesn't make sense. Jesus, we've spent hours discussing the wedding.'

'Yeah, well. Maybe we both have different ideas about what settling down and married life really means?'

She eyed me suspiciously while sipping her drink and all inside my chest felt heavy and low. I knew, really, that John was right. I couldn't blame him. I knew that I'd fucked it up good and proper. I knew I'd behaved like a bloody teenager.

The sadness coursed through my body as I waited for Claire to finish her pint, tapping my feet impatiently as she continued with the pep talk.

'Maybe you could call him?'

I shot her a look.

'No,' she said, suddenly over-animated. 'Pop round unannounced, with some kind of...gesture. Yeah, that's it, a seriously romantic gesture. I know, get him some record tokens. Men like vinyl don't they. Or, ooh, a mix tape.'

My head rolled back with my eyes. 'Christ, I'm not 16.'

'OK then. A ring. A proposal. That's real fucking modern-world-woman stuff that. Let him know you're serious about him, let him know...'

'Need the loo. Back in a sec.'

I hot footed it to the loos, peed, washed up, dried my hands to an almost acceptable point of dryness and walked back into the bar at speed. Claire had her head in the soggy paper that someone had left on our table - what a waste of beer. No doubt she was about to tell me what my horoscope says I should do next to salvage the situation. Either way, she wouldn't notice me gone for another couple of minutes.

'Vodka please.'

'Double?'

'Please.'

I didn't need to explain myself. He knew. It was an

unspoken truth. An understanding between landlord and loyal customer. And I was feeling warmer, calmer by the second. The restlessness was fizzling away. Claire needn't know I was way ahead of her.

As I approached the bar table she looked up from the paper. 'Right then. Capricorn, right?'

'Yeah but…'

'OK. Ses 'ere you're going to be involved in a repair, Em. That must mean repairing the relationship, right?'

'Right,' I said.

'So, there must be some glimmer of hope. There must be some way to salvage things?'

'Maybe.'

'What about that proposal?'

'I don't think that's what he's looking for, to be honest. He'll probably think I was just being impulsive. Again.'

'Again?'

'Yeah like…like that time I gate-crashed his work's do.'

'Ah.'

'Or that time I serenaded him outside his window. At 1am.'

'Ah but that's romantic that, surely?'

'I sang Deeply Dippy by Right Said Fred.'

'Oh.'

'I don't think I need to do anything drastic. I think he just wants normality. I think...' I started to sob again. 'I think I just don't fit the mould.'

Claire rubbed my arm, and her eyes must've scanned the empty glasses on the table. 'Ah shit, look at me. You're sitting here dry while I'm reading the paper with me feet up. I'll get the next round in.'

She went over to the bar to order the pints. I decided all we needed now to make the world a better place was music. After all, the beer alone clearly wasn't working today.

I fumbled around in my purse, found a few silver coins,

and made my way towards the jukebox to line a few good tracks up. I raced past Mariah Carey, Elton John, and Michael Jackson. God, there wasn't much to choose from. Ok, Blur, *Country House*, that'd do. Um...Weezer, *Buddy Holly*. Ooh and Offspring, *Self Esteem*. With a trio of decent songs lined up I headed back to the table as *Country House* started blaring out of the sound system.

'Love this song,' Claire said, placing the drinks on the table.

'Me too,' I said, supping up.

'Yeah. There's a great mix by DJ Voo.'

'Who the fuck's DJ Voo?'

'You know. He plays at Room on a Friday.'

'DJ…. you mean De Ja Vu? It's a night Claire, not a DJ.'

'Well, they play it. At The Room. On a Friday. It's bangin'. Great mix.'

I frowned. 'Fucking blasphemous if you ask me.'

'Anyway', she disregarded my blatant dig at her taste in music - if you could even call it that. 'You seem happier than before,' she commented.

'Ahhh that'll be your charm and wit.'

'Aye. Probably.'

We clinked our glasses and, as Damon Albarn launched into the chorus, so did we. I felt myself smile again.

CHAPTER 10

'Dave! Me main man! Col, look! This is me bezzie. It's Dave! Who I was tellin' you 'bout? Daviiiiiid!'

'Come on, Emma.'

'Shh! Listen! Can you hear? It's the Gallaghers Brothers, David. Do what they say, cigarettes. Alcohol....ahhhh me glass is empty...be a love.'

'Sorry, yeah, I'm taking her...'

'Who you talking to?'

'We've got to get you home.'

'Fucking boring bastard.'

'Emma zip it.'

'Your missus making you have an early night, is she? Ruining our fun...boring cunt.'

'No, that's you.'

'Eh?'

'Where's your bag. Sorry mate? Ah good on yer. Emma just...just sit there a sec. Don't move.'

'Fine I'll sit here a sec. Just do as I'm told by Hull's biggest boringest fucking bastard...fucking stupid lighter...'

'Right, I've got your bag, car's outside.'

'Seen what I've done. Lit the wrong flamin' end. Stupid twat.'

'Right. Up you get...jeez, you want to try and carry some of your own weight or what.'

'What you tryin' to say.'

'It's home time.'

'Ahhhh get that. Ahhh that fresh air...'

'In the car! In fact, get in the back. I'll wind the window down.'

'But I want to walk. It's all fresh and nice. You go...'

'Nope.'
'Don't be a dick, Dave. Just....uh. Hang on...shit...ugh...'
'Nice one Emma. All over my fucking Adidas.'

CHAPTER 11

No. No. No. Not again. Not this not again.

'Emma lovey!'

Shit. I automatically put on my best voice. My voice of health, of calm, my voice of *no I am absolutely not trying to claw my way out of my own body*. 'Yeah, Dor, sorry, slept in.' Ouch. Ugh God, clammy clammy skin. Stale sick. Ugh God.

Not again.

My eyes were open, but everything was grey and fuzzy.

'I've walked Trevor for you. Little mite was crying by the back door.'

'Thanks Dor!'

I don't deserve that dog.

The last thing I could face in the whole world right now was a day of work. The last thing I could face in the whole world right now was losing my job. A last bit of normality. A last bit of routine.

I had no choice. I had to face the day. And I was late. There was no way out of it. I sat upright, momentarily paralysed. My chest felt as though it had pots and pans clattering around in it. Whatever I did, today was going to be absolutely horrific. Again.

I reached under my bed, my hand flailing around blindly on top of skanky tissues and sharp crumbs. Crisps? Pastry? Fuck, where was it? Oh God, did I drink them all? I could feel a polystyrene box. Was that from last night? Did I get chips? I had no idea. I stretched my arm just a bit further...

Thank. Fuck.

I clamped my fingers around the smooth surface of the glass and yanked it towards me, scraping my forearm on the underside of the bedframe. I took an urgent swig. The liquid hit my throat and burned a warm blanket of relief right into me. I can do this.

Now, I can do this.

I stood up, my heart crashing around my chest as heavy as my clumsy feet on the carpet. I don't know how but they managed to get me into the bathroom. I shut the door behind me, clattering the glass panel. I stripped off, turned the shower on cold and stepped into the bath, trying desperately to scrub the dirt from me. But it wasn't *on* me, it was *inside* me. It was coursing through my veins - and no doubt through the memories of every poor fucker who had the misfortune to run into me last night. I washed my hair and left it wet - at least it was clean.

I headed back to my room. Trev was now sat on my bed.

'Please, *please* don't look at me like that.' He turned his head and put his chin down on the bare mattress - the sheet having unclung itself from the corners. My own dog couldn't even look at me. I grabbed a pair of knickers, chucked on a pair of trousers, my shoes, a plain tee and left my boy sitting there. Sad eyes.

'Sorry Trev,' I whispered. He harumphed.

I ran down the stairs and straight out the door. I couldn't bear to make small talk with Dor.

The harsh reality of daylight and fresh air knocked me for six.

Why did mornings always have to come around like this? Why couldn't I just remain in a state of safety? A state of pissed-up, oblivious, wrapped up safety.

Shit what was Mike going to say? He'd already given me my last warning. Literally yesterday! Oh fuck.

No, come on Emma, you can blag this. You can totally do this.

I jumped on the bus, took a seat, and felt like some kind of monster on a stage. Were they all looking at me? The whirring reality of sobriety, of a world that I was no longer part of - just something on the outside. Something I could no longer understand. A world where people got up and drank a cup of tea to get them going in a morning.

I felt sick with every bump in the road, and my stomach was growling, but I couldn't bear to eat anything. I knew how that would go down - it would go down temporarily.

As the bus approached my stop I walked towards the front, carefully grabbing hold of each handrail, my fingers accidentally clamping on top of the grubby fingers of some grubby kid. He flinched. I could feel a sea of faces scowling at me, burning their frowns into my back, as I walked as carefully as I could towards the driver. The bus was slowly edging its way to my stop behind the cramped morning traffic.

Don't be sick, don't be sick, don't be sick.

I jumped off the bus thoroughly relieved and opened my bag, grabbing my water bottle.

I took a glug. Put it back. Took it out again. Shit. Would it see me through the day? I decided to make a de-tour to the dodgy offie near work. It was gone 9. And they didn't care anyway.

I walked into the office after a deep breath, vodka keeping me buoyed - along with the knowledge that I now had extra supplies, double-wrapped in a plastic bag and placed carefully into my work bag to soften the clang.

He was standing at my desk, talking to Claire. The look on her face. I knew. I knew she'd try to cover for me. I made my way over, my brain trying to come up with an excuse but barely able to string words together in any order.

Hang on, we were out together - me and Claire. Where was she? How come she seemed OK?

'Emma - you've got five minutes, then I want to see you in my office.' I could just tell what was coming. No smile. No hello. I didn't deserve any more, I guess.

I sat down at my desk, trying to work out how to blag this. How could I get through it? I needed a strategy.

'You all right Emma?' Claire's tone was flat. It hit me like a bolt. What had I done? Claire was always OK with me no matter what.

'Yeah.'

'You need to get a fucking grip, babe.'

'What?'

She shook her head and looked away. I felt sick.

Had I been sick last night? I had some vague memory of Dave.

'Did, erm, did Dave come out last night?' I had a feeling he was with us, at the pub, but I couldn't remember and couldn't work out why he would have been.

'Shit, Emma, you can't even remember, can you?'

I wracked my brain, desperate to remember. Why was Dave there? Why would my best mate turn up randomly at the end of the night? In Gypsyville? He never came to this end of town. I don't even remember him walking in. I just remember his…presence…somewhere amid it all.

Oh God…I was sick on Dave's shoes last night, wasn't I?

'Emma!'

Mike's voice boomed loudly across the office. Every single person in here would know I was about to get sacked.

I stood up and headed over to his office, my head down. As I walked in, I decided that maybe I didn't need to take a seat for this. Maybe I just needed to apologise. Profusely. It was all I had left.

'Mike. Look, I'm so, *so*, sorr...'

'You need to clear your desk.

'Mike. Look. I promise I'll...'

'No Emma.'

He put his head back down, looking through his diary. A clear sign that this was the end of the conversation. I might have argued, tried to talk him around, put on a smile and a brave face. But what was the point? Plus, I didn't want to be in there a second longer than I had to be.

'I'm sorry Mike.'

In the main office, I could feel those looks again, drilling into the back of my head. Not frowns this time, but whispers - eager minds hungry for the gossip. They knew. They *all* knew. That's how it felt. *I* wasn't even clear on what I'd done last night - it felt like a secret I had let everyone else in on but was keeping from myself. But I knew one thing - I was late again. And this time it was one late mark too many.

'All, OK?' Claire asked, still maintaining a tone that was erring on the angry.

I couldn't speak. I felt so, so ashamed.

She leant forward in her chair. 'Has he…?'

I nodded as I was picking up my bag, chucking in a couple of pens, but I was unable to think clearly about what was mine, what I wanted to keep. I just wanted to get the hell out of there. Pins and needles were racing through my fingers and my head felt fuzzy in a dead weight kind of way. Nothing felt real and yet everything was terrifyingly true. I felt as though I was watching some strange, dead version of me, just alive enough to fuck everything up while inside I was screaming - no! Please! Stop! But that voice was getting quieter and quieter. I knew how to quieten it. I just always went too far. I always strangled it.

I was about to walk out without saying a word, but something stopped me. I needed to know.

'Claire. What happened last night?'

She sighed. 'Where do I start?'

'Why was Dave there?'

'Because I couldn't deal with you, Emma. I called Dean from production. Got Dave's number, asked him to come in and get you home.'

'But what was I…?'

'The fact you can't remember says it all.'

A tear burned my cheek.

'Emma. You need to sort yourself out. It's not fun.'

I shuddered, dreading to think. She continued. 'You were on the seats, hollering along to some song or other, letting that awful old guy from the table next to us letch all over you. It was tragic, Em. Fucking tragic.'

What song? What old guy? Story of my life. I'd no idea. All I knew was that life really hurt and I was a disgusting human being.

'I'm sorry Claire. I really am.' How many more apologies did I need to make today?

'Just. Take care of yourself, Emma. And don't be a stranger.'

I smiled a weak smile to let her know I appreciated everything she'd done for me last night. Well, everything she'd done for me over the last few years, really. It was nice to know she was there. But what now?

Jobless, boyfriendless, homeless...I didn't feel lost, like I was out at sea. I felt lost like…like I was stranded on my own shrinking island. I felt as though I was getting further and further away from civilisation. From hope. But that I was somewhere, trapped in something. Just me in this shitty, shady booze town that I'd built up around me.

I was so scared.

Flashbacks from the night before whizzed through my brain like an old-fashioned silent movie on fast forward. All these snippets that taunted me, like a bonus catchphrase round. Each revealing something potentially sinister that I'd said or done, but not quite revealing enough. I was left guessing. And the problem was, from experience, I knew it was more than likely far worse than I feared. It was all too much to bear.

I opened my bag, and took out my water bottle…

CHAPTER 12

'A fucking ice cream van?'

'No, Em, it's an ice cream *hut*. It's different.'

'How exactly?'

'Well, you know. You can live in a van, or you can live in a house...and...'

'It's a hut, Dave.'

He sighed. 'Look, you need a job. So, stop being a pain in the arse about it.'

Dave had brought the jobs pages round to Dor's. I was amazed he was still talking to me to be honest - I'd pushed him too far recently. Even *I* hated how I was when I was drunk so God knows what it was like for him. Three nights in a row he'd endured my states recently. There were memories flashing through my mind continuously since the other night, always intermittent, broken, and blurry stories. And he still had a faintly marbled ring of purple, yellow and blue around his eye.

I'd been awful. *Really* fucking awful.

Luckily, when I called, it was Dave that picked up the phone. Not Ally. That would have been excruciating. He'd no doubt told her about what a tit I'd been. Saying that, it was awkward just facing him anyway, and when things got excruciatingly awful with Dave, which happened incredibly rarely, it meant shit was getting serious. And that was never a good thing.

The last time things between me and Dave got *that* unsettling was when he told me he had testicular cancer a couple of years ago. Before that, well, I think it was when I ripped the pages out of his completed Panini football sticker album because he told Gareth Laybourne that I was going to let him finger me for a fiver. Dave was never very good at jokes.

He never told any of the lads at school they could finger me after that.

Even when I asked him to.

We lasted about five minutes of being awkward before he asked if I wanted to try out for The Hopefuls on the Word by 'just being me and getting drunk and being a dick' and we both burst out laughing. It broke the ice. He said the baseline for doing 'anything' to get on TV would be easily crossed by me and a bottle of vodka. It felt like we were laughing at our old tricks again. It lowered the seriousness of it all. And because of that, he was happy to come round to Dor's today. Ally was at work on Saturdays anyway, so I knew it was a good day to get some quality 'Dave time' in the bank.

We were sitting in the sunshine in the back garden on Dor's green plastic chairs. My bare feet were resting on the warmed stone patio and, every so often when I dropped my arm on it, the heat of the plastic smarted against my pale white skin. I missed how good these things felt. These *real* things. The things that remind you that you're alive. I had been careful the last few days - barely swallowed a drop. Not really, anyway. I knew I had to prove to myself that I had some degree of control over my life. And in doing so, I paused on the oblivion, managed my intake carefully and started to sense some of the good stuff in life…the sunshine…the friendship…but it all felt too temporary. And in some ways, it made me feel even more unsettled, because I desperately wanted those feelings and times to last forever - hearing Dave's awful jokes, drinking Dor's tea, just being, well, alive really. And being able to feel the lovely warm stone on my feet. But I knew it wouldn't last long.

The stone patio might have been a consistent feature of this house since 1910 or something, but the sunshine isn't especially reliable. Not in Hull, anyway.

But more than anything, I couldn't digest the fact that I was still having to poison my body just to feel normal. Just to get out of bed. There was a fine line between completely losing the plot and appearing to function. And every day, it took so, *so* much energy and logistical preparation just trying to strike the right balance.

I pretended I was completely off the booze. Well, the spirits, anyway. Not a single sip, I said. Who wants to admit they're totally screwed to the people they love the most? Especially when it's those people you turn to when you need some solid company in your drinking.

I looked over at Dave, my great big lump Dave, sitting in his bright yellow Blur T-shirt and cut off shorts, suede Adidas three-stripes covering his feet (no doubt hastily machine washed from the puke incident - but I wasn't going to bring that up to confirm either way). He was carefully studying the paper to help get his best mate out of this cruel, unemployed hole she'd landed herself in. And behind us, in the house busying herself by the kitchen window was Dor - sunglasses on, steam rising from the kettle she'd just boiled, singing along to some Queen song on Radio 2. My heart skipped at how lucky I was to have such lovely people in my life as I flicked through an old copy of Select Magazine mindlessly…

'I don't mean to be, like, snobby about it or anything. I just feel like I'm going backwards. A degree. A sales admin job, now a flamin' ice cream woman?'

'Cheers, Em.'

'No, I don't mean…'

Dave never went to uni. But he was happy in his job. It was manual work at a plastics company, but he enjoyed it. Made a decent wage too.

By now, I'd already turned my nose up at Night Shift Operative and Packer. And there was no way I was going into a fish factory. But I knew he was right - I *was* being a pain in the arse. It was wrong to think these jobs were beneath me. My dad had just got back into work, and I praised him emphatically. Fishy smells and scales or no fishy smells and scales. I think the new romance in his life had put a spring back in his step and turned up his energy levels and drive.

Meanwhile, I just felt so disappointed in myself. So angry. Fucking things up catastrophically. At least that was one reliable part of my life.

Dave tried to buoy me up. 'There's worse than serving smiles and sprinkles.'

'Fair point,' I conceded.

'Anything of interest in the music world anyway?' He nodded towards my knackered old copy of Select magazine.

'Something about rock 'n' roll suburbs.'

'Rock n roll suburbs?'

'British nowheres with pop importance, apparently.'

'Is Hull in?'

'Nah. Colchester. Braintree…'

'They haven't got the fucking, Beautiful South. They haven't got the Adelphi.'

'They've got the Prodigy.'

'Colchester?'

'No, Braintree. Besides, as much as we think Adelphi's the ultimate music haven, maybe there are other versions? Maybe there are little terraced houses converted into music venues dotted all around the country.'

'Doubt it. Can't see Colchester having one.'

'Maybe they converted an ice-cream hut instead,' I said.

'Ha, nope. That's the KLF did that.'

'Ice cream *van*, Dave. The KLF converted an ice cream *van*.'

'What?'

'Nothing.'

'Who's on the cover?'

'Prodigy.'

'What they up to? Apart from coming from Braintree?'

'Hmm…. touring Australia…mind, think this is a few weeks old this…' I said, checking the cover.

'Love their latest one.'

'Firestarter? Yeah. It's gonna be a classic that one. Got the CD single from Woollies in there.' I nodded backwards towards the house just as Dor appeared with a finely balanced tray containing three mugs of tea and a packet of Malted Milks. 'How's the job hunt going?' she asked.

I shrugged.

'Emma thinks she's too good for serving ice-cream.' Dave unhelpfully piped up. I shot him a look. And if looks had volume, that one would have made his ears bleed.

'Emma, dear. Let's be honest now. There's no point you having an uppity attitude given your recent...'

'I know, I know.' I sighed, feeling desperately defeated. I had tried to build myself up. I was full of hope and aspiration as a kid. I wanted to get to uni—to be the first in our family, to make my dad proud. After losing mum all those years ago it was, well, just a way of proving that being brought up in a small terrace in Hull by a wonderfully loving but seriously melancholic and unemployed father, wasn't about to stop me in my tracks.

Well, *it* didn't. *I* did that. I leapt off the train. A wave of nausea swept over me. 'Just nipping to the loo.'

'Bloody hell, Emma. You not got it again, have you?'

'No, Dave. I haven't. I just need the bloody loo, OK?'

'I've got some baking soda in the cupboard...' Dor added.

'I haven't got bloody cystitis you two. I just need the loo.'

I didn't need the loo. But I was going to try and pee at least a drop out to make flushing the toilet less of a charade. I took a detour to my bedroom, well, Dor's spare room. She had it piled full of books and magazines and photo albums. It was like an Aladdin's cave of memories and passages and poetry stacked high on the carpet and overwhelming the mahogany bookshelf too imposing for a room this small, but then that's Doreen all over. At least if I ever felt like staying shut up in my room, I'd have plenty to keep me occupied.

I sat down on the patterned throw. Dor didn't do duvets. Just layers and layers of patterned sheets and throws. I rarely had the wits about me to get in them. More often than not I woke up shivering not long before the sun was due up.

I leant forward, my hand padding around on the carpet. What was that? Felt like a stale crisp. Ugh, I really needed to clean under there. But the chaos of discarded crisps and crumbs and plastic bags and old cups of tea somehow disguised the most valuable of items.

I found the plastic water bottle and took a sip, immediately feeling better, a warmth rising up in my chest and a newfound positivity immediately glowing through my veins. I nipped to the loo, managed to let out a dribble, flushed with conviction, then wandered back downstairs.

'I'll do it. I'll apply. You're right Dave, serving ice creams and sprinkles - it'd do for me.'

They both looked at me inquisitively. I grabbed the paper from Dave's hands.

'Hey! I was just reading about City.'

'I'm going to do it Dave. I'm going to take control of my life. I'm putting an application in today.'

Dave slurped his tea, eyeing me. He couldn't know. Could he?

I stood up, newspaper in hand. 'Right. Off to walk Trev.' I flew upstairs to my room and popped the paper on the bedside table as a reminder. Then I grabbed my things and went back downstairs to pick Trev's lead up from the back of the kitchen door. When I got back outside Dave was stood up, ready to come with me. My heart sank. 'I was just gonna whizz round the block, no need to bother. I'll be five minutes.'

I didn't give him time to consider it before I was gone.

CHAPTER 13

Dave

'What the fuck else can I do, Al? She won't listen.'

'Then you've got to make her.'

'Fuck's sake. It's Emma we're talking about. Even without the fucking booze… you can't bastard tell her.'

Al shook her head, grabbed her bag, and kissed me goodbye. She smelt bloody fantastic. Off on a work's night out. But I didn't need to worry about her, not like Emma - and that made me feel guilty sometimes.

It's not that I don't care as much about Al - I love the bloody bones of her. And it's different with a mate isn't it. Christ, Emma's more like me sister. But aside from the occasional tuneless yelling of some All Saints song in the street at 1am, Al was sorted. Emma, on the other hand…

I chucked myself back on the sofa and grabbed the controller, trying to take my mind off it all with Lara Croft and a bit of tomb raiding. But it didn't take long until I'd gone and got Lara killed by a boulder and had to start the level over again. Fuck's sake. I couldn't cope with all these independent women in my life. What was my role? Was I meant to step in? To be the protector? Al would no doubt call me sexist for even suggesting that. I mean, I wasn't exactly doing a great job. I'd killed Lara at least four times that night already. And Ally was usually the one dishing out the sage advice to me rather than it being the other way round. But Emma…sure she was strong, always had been, but it was like, recently, she'd lost all control. Mind and bodily functions included.

I threw the controller back on the floor. I couldn't shake

the feeling of needing to be alert to something else. I reminded myself that I'd left Emma safely under the watchful eye of Dor and that I should just switch off for the night. But it felt selfish.

It's bad enough watching your best mate fuck her life up big time without wondering what else you could - or should - be doing about it. What the fuck *could* I do? I felt like a swing ball being batted back and forth between 'wasted Emma' and 'not so wasted Emma'. But Tel thinks of me like the big brother - it's a big responsibility, that. And we'd always looked out for each other, me, and Emma. So, with this happening right in front of me, *with* me…

Fuck, how many tequilas have I bought her lately anyway?

I'd never pass a big brother performance review. Although staying calm when she puked on my new trainers was pretty fucking impressive.

She'd made light of it. The pub. I guess I did too - I made jokes about it, I didn't want to start another row. She'd only push me away again.

But I didn't want to push her over the edge, either. I mean, no spirits my arse. She was clearly on the vodka. I made some joke about her not having cystitis again, wondering if it might break the ice, get her talking. I mean, what's more embarrassing, sneaking off and pissing razor blades or sneaking off and necking vodka from an old placky bottle hidden under your bed. Second thoughts…

She was sitting there, in Dor's Garden, pretending everything was normal. Trying to read Select with one eye shut, desperate to focus, pretending she was just squinting in the sun. I said nowt. Dor neither. At least she was there, in front of us.

Well, until she disappeared on her own with Trev for twenty minutes. And she was definitely perkier when she got back.

I couldn't believe it when Claire rang the other night. It's not fucking Emma! The guy was in his 50s or something.

Steaming. Both of them. Claire found her with him pushed up against the wall, on her knees, yanking on his belt. I'm just glad Claire pulled her off him before...

It makes me sick to think about it. He was like some old piss-soaked drunk on some bench on Freetown Way. And John, he was sorted was John. Made her so bloody happy. But I guess Emma was becoming less like us and more like those desperately sad souls huddled together around those benches in town. You don't need to be sitting on a bench in town to suffer. But some things are the same. The chatter's loud and proud, but it's not real. Not when the effect of the booze subsides. I guess that's why she's desperate to stay under, in her liquid oblivion. But it's just getting worse every day.

Hell, Emma. This isn't you. This isn't fucking you.

CHAPTER 14

'Hi'

'Emma?'

'I just wanted...to see how you were?'

'It's almost midnight.'

'I know. I know. Sorry.'

'Have you been drinking?'

'Just a couple.'

'Emma. You can't do this. It's the second time this w...'

'I miss you, John. I really fucking miss you.'

'But it's…this is ridiculous.'

'I'm sorry.'

'I miss you too.'

'Really? Then maybe...'

'No, Emma. I'm just. I'm just saying, I care about you. I miss the good times. But we can't go back there.'

'But I promise, it'll be different.'

'We've been here before.'

'I know. But honest, I'll do anything to make you believe me.'

'Try making yourself believe it first.'

'What do you mean?'

'Look after yourself Emma.'

There's nothing more heart wrenching than the line going dead when you know it's saying the same thing over and over again. That's it. The end. It's done. Over. Please don't call me anymore. This isn't me hanging up the phone in a huff because he's refused to pick me up from the pub after closing. This is because…because it's really fucking over.

Why did I keep doing this to myself? It was masochistic. Nothing had changed, so why was I expecting him to have changed his mind? Why would he want to take me back? I've only got worse since we broke up. That much was true and blatantly bleedin' obvious.

My chest felt heavy again and I wanted to cry it all out or drink it all away. I wandered into the kitchen. The digital clock on the oven was all blurred. I stood still, straining my eyes, desperately trying to work it out, to see what the time was, to prove I wasn't really all that drunk. It was just the dark. It was just the tears.

'Lovey?'

'Ach! Dor! You startled me!'

'What are you doing in the dark down here?' She was stood there, paisley scarf wrapped around her head, dressing gown on, slipper boots sticking out from underneath.

I looked down at my glass, then quickly back at the clock to distract her. But she'd seen.

'Right, Emma. I'm not happy about this. All these tears. I'm worried about you.'

I was mentally preparing myself for the lecture. Going over the well-rehearsed lines I had in my head. *But I'm in pain. I hurt. It's night-time. Everyone enjoys a drink. I'm still in my twenties give me a fucking break.*

Then she said... 'I'll join you.'

She took my glass from my hand, and I sat at the kitchen table. I didn't really want her here. I didn't want to *sip* a whiskey. I wanted to collect two gallons. Do not pass Go. Head straight to oblivion. I desperately wanted oblivion. And the longer I was there the better. But I loved Dor. I guessed I'd sip for Dor tonight. I didn't want to be alone, anyway.

'Ice?'

I shrugged. She handed me a glass. No ice. And beckoned me outside, while finding her ciggies and lighter from the windowsill.

We sat back at the little plastic table where we spent the day earlier with Dave. Dor offered me one of her long

Berkeley menthols. I took it appreciatively and we lit up with her gold engraved zippo, both exhaling clouds of minty smoke into the dark night.

'Have you called him?'

'Who?'

She gave me one of her looks.

'Yes.'

'Didn't go well?'

'No.'

'Oh lovey. I think, now these few days have passed, you've got to end it in here.' She prodded her temple with her finger. 'You've got to say goodbye to him. I don't think he's going to change his mind, is he?'

'I know,' I said, my stomach in spasm. I could no longer complete a cartwheel, but my stomach certainly had the ability. 'I think it's truly over.'

My eyes were now so raw, that the tears were fossilised into my face with dirty make-up.

'Oh, love.' She rubbed my arm. It made me feel worse. I didn't deserve her care. Snot began to build up in my nostrils.

'Here,' she passed me a tissue from her dressing gown pocket. She was always well prepared. I wiped my damp face.

'Thanks,' I said.

'Ooh! I know!' suddenly Dor's eyes were shining bright and white in the dark as she looked out of the window. 'Let's have a boyfriend bonfire.'

'You what Dor? I love the man I don't hate him. Why do you think I'm crying? I'm not making a Guy Fawkes with his image.'

'No! No! Not like that. Remember that episode of Friends?'

'*You* watch Friends?'

'How *you* doin'?'

'Ah, bit of a Joey fan, are we?'

'Who isn't. Anyway, it's not about Joey Tribiani. The girls throw a boyfriend bonfire. I watched it the other week.'

'But I don't want to burn John?' I couldn't quite understand what she was suggesting.

'No! No! We're not burning John. Don't be silly. I thought I'd have a crack at him after you.'

I was about to retort angrily when her cheeky wink made me burst out laughing. There was something about Doreen that made me feel stronger. Invincible. She never, *never* indulged my self pity. She cared - harshly and honestly. And sometimes that was exactly what I needed to jolt me out of the dark.

We clinked glasses giggling.

'Is that going to be your line with my ex-fella then?'

'Sure. Why not. How *you* doin' Johnny boy.' She pursed her lips and winked into the darkness.

'Oh, sweet Jesus. I've *never* called him that.'

We both chuckled, ending in a happy sigh.

'Ah dear. You'll get back into the swing of things, Emma. There're plenty of fellas up for grabs. You just need to get yourself straightened out.'

'Plenty up for grabs? In Hull? Give me just one example! Just one example of someone you'd be happy to take on the role of Maid of Honour for at the wedding?'

'OK.'

I tapped my fingers on the table dramatically. 'I'm waiting…'

'No hang on, there's definitely….'

'See.'

She slapped her palms on her lap. 'Yes! That Shane you're always banging on about at work.'

'Yeah, I might be banging on about him but I'm definitely not up for banging him.'

'Why ever not dear?'

'You can smell his aftershave from East Hull.'

'Obviously takes care of himself then.'

'No. He's a wanker. Absolutely not. Next?'

'OK I'm stumped. You've got me. Ooh. What about one of those Senseless Boys you love?'

'Senseless *Things*, Dor. Very cute. But a bit young and, well, kind of out of reach being Londoners and in a successful band and that.'

'OK. Well…erm…' She was making a point of thinking long and hard about this, but all she was managing to do was prove me right. 'Well look, you've got all the time in the world to come up with your new crush. Not sure why it's proving so challenging.'

'Because I lov…'

'I know! Wait there.' She ran back into the house cutting me off mid-sentence. There was no way she was going to let me dwell.

I sat at the table in the dark, lit only by the rose-orange light shining through the kitchen window, providing that warm cosy glow that houses always give off at night. That tempting glimpse of peace always seemed just out of reach. That I was always trapped outside of. I shuddered in the night air and grabbed another cigarette from Dor's packet.

'Ta-da!' Dor reappeared suddenly.

'What in the hell…?' I said, newly lit ciggie in mouth.

'Do you like him? He's joining us for drinks.'

'I think *he* is a *she*.'

'Codswallop. That Kirk Cobain had long hair.'

'Kurt!' I laughed. 'And yeah, but he didn't have tits and an arse like that!'

'Oh, I thought the jumper had covered them.'

'I think they make blow up dolls' tits big on purpose Dor! Those two would be tricky to hide! Why have you got it anyway?'

She was busy sitting her demonic looking inflatable next to us at the plastic table. The once female-inspired plastic now had a tatty old jumper over its torso and a baseball hat. 'Which do you prefer Emma - forwards or backwards?'

'What?'

'The hat?'

'Oh, backwards.'

'Nice.' She continued preening her masterpiece.

'Anyway, you never answered my question.'

'Oh. Yep. No, I don't remember if I'm honest. It's been in the back of my wardrobe for years.'

'Kinky ex?'

'Most likely,' she laughed.

I'd never known anyone as out there as Dor. Although to be fair, given the huge collections of bric-à-brac in her house she could probably open up a stall at Portobello Market. You could think of any old random item, and she'd have one somewhere in this Aladdin's cave she calls a house.

I just loved how she cheered me up. There was no nonsense. No indulgence. She was all, 'get back on that horse and ride girl!' But I know how much she liked John. *Everyone* liked John. I shook his kind eyes from my mind and looked back over at the monstrosity sitting at the table with us. It was the most ridiculous picture.

'So, why's he joining us then.' I could barely stop giggling. 'What's he called, anyway?'

'Brian.'

'Yuk, Dor!'

'Don't take the mickey, poor fella. He's had to put up with that all his life. Besides, it doesn't mean he's no good in bed.'

I was roaring with laughter as she struggled to keep him upright, and placed his plastic, rather well-manicured hand, around a glass.

'I think he's had a few too many don't you Dor?'

'I'd say. As the Dead Kennedy's song goes, he's…'

'Too drunk to fuck!'

'…Too drunk to fuck!'

We roared with laughter, a more positive deluge of emotion now pouring from my eyes.

'Ha! Dor, I didn't know you knew punk.'

'There's a lot you don't know sweetie. I was pretty punk back in the day.'

'But you must've been…' I was trying to calculate her age when Dead Kennedy's were at their peak. 'What, like…at least in your 50s.'

'They might have coined the term in the '70s…'60s even. But when you think about it…just because they came up with the name then, well, it didn't mean the attitude didn't exist beforehand.'

'Like with the 'Twenty-Seven Club' when Kurt Cobain died,' I said, reminiscing about the tragic death of one of our greatest rock stars aged, you guessed it, twenty-seven. 'They came up with the term in the '90s, but then described Janis Joplin and Jim Morrison as members from back in the '70s.

'Exactly.'

'So, what does punk mean to you then, Dor?' I tapped my ash into the ashtray.

'Well, to me, it's less the music, more the attitude, I guess. It was your mum, you know, introduced me to the term. She used to come into the Angel raving about The Stooges and the New York Dolls. You know, she had that heavy fringe, can you remember? All that dark kohl smudged around her eyes. You were just a nipper then. She'd play all this music on the juke box and try to rouse the whole pub. Bren hated it - poor cow. She was much more a gentle Beatles sort of fan. Ha-ha, you and your mum were so alike you know.' She carefully rolled the ash from her cigarette onto the side of the ashtray.

'Did my mum introduce you to Dead Kennedy's then?'

'No. That was after…well, you know.'

'Oh,' I said, feeling a little tug at my chest. 'I wish I'd had the chance to get to know her better.'

'Yeah, I know lovey. I know she didn't mean to hurt you. She was so young though, Emma. Younger than you are now. She worshipped the ground you… crawled on - ha-

ha.' Dor was giggling at her own joke and went to light another ciggie. 'But she was so young.' She inhaled the menthol smoke and continued to speak as she held it deep inside her lungs. 'Your dad too.'

'I guess.'

I tried to cheer myself back up. 'How in the hell *do* you know that song anyway?'

'Dead Kennedy's? Had mesel' a nice young toy boy at one stage, didn't I?'

'You dirty cow.'

'Ah yes. David,' she said, straightening her dressing gown out in front of her with a wicked grin on her face. 'About fifteen years younger than me I think he was. Big punk fan. I'll be honest though; it all got a bit much after a while. All that hair gel.'

I laughed. 'I can imagine. Spiky too.'

'Ha-ha quite. Yes.'

I took another sip of my drink, trying hard to imagine Dor back in the late '70s, getting it on with a leather-clad Mohican-donning young punk.

'Anyway,' Dor said, nodding towards 'Brian', 'it's your first date since John. And now you've got it out of the way. Phew!' She started pushing the doll's face into mine and making smoochy noises. 'Go on then, give Brian a little kiss.' I was beside myself.

'Dor! I'm going to wet myself.'

'Good. I'd rather you pissed your pants laughing than sat there sobbing. Anyway, come on. We're burning your relationship. It's gone Emma. You need...what do the Americans say? Closure.'

'Right...?'

'Go on then. Gather your things.'

'You chucking me out? I've only had a couple?'

'No, lovey.' She said, standing up out of her chair and wandering towards the firewood that lay in a pile beneath the crab apple tree. 'Gather your relationship mementos.'

'What relationship mementos?'

'For the bonfire!'

'But why do I have to burn things to end it in my head?'

She was gathering an impressive armful of logs and twigs. 'I don't know. Symbolism and stuff.'

'But what should I get?'

'Mementos. Whatever you young 'uns do and keep these days. Letters, photos, tickets from concerts, that shirt of his you kept.'

'No way!'

'It's the *only* way, Emma. You go, I'll get this going and top up the drinks.'

That was enough to fire some energy in me. I walked upstairs, feeling both charged and surreal and, thankfully, refreshingly, chuckling to myself as I went. Dumped women need Dor on prescription!

I checked the clock in my room. It was ten past midnight. Who has a bonfire after midnight? Ah fuck it. It's Dor. If she says it's OK, it's OK.

I pulled my bag out from the bottom of the wardrobe. I still hadn't properly unpacked. I felt so rudderless it didn't make sense. I didn't feel at home anywhere right now. I didn't want to stand still and admit that this is how things were.

I knew there would be things in there. When I gathered my stuff up to leave the other day, I tipped my little box of 'special memories' into the bag. As if leaving them behind would mean saying goodbye to the memory itself.

I found our Oasis gig ticket from when we first got together and invited John on a night out with me and Dave. That was a pivotal moment. Dave getting to know my new boyfriend. What a great night. The ticket, however, was all screwed up at the bottom of my bag. Maybe it was time to get rid of it? Alongside it were some of those stupid tokens you get from the amusements from our trips to Brid. I sat, staring at them, remembering the fun. The stupid talc and Cypriot Delight we won on prize bingo. John pretending to be scared on the little ghost train and me being taken in and comforting him, only for him to suddenly spook me with a crazy demonic voice. And some of those passport photos on a strip, the two of us pulling ridiculous faces and giggling. I cut two of them off to keep and hid them in my knicker drawer by the bed.

But Dor was right. All this, it wasn't going to happen again. I needed some American style closure.

Trevor's nose appeared beside me, sniffing around and snorting all over my things. Little mite. I pulled him in for a cuddle before releasing him and continuing in my mission, heading downstairs with my arms full of relationship memorabilia.

'You got everything?'

'Yep. A photo, gig ticket, amusements tokens.'

'His shirt?'

'Oh, Dor, no.'

'You've got to commit to this Emma. It's a cleansing ritual. It will be good for your soul.'

I reluctantly trudged back upstairs to get his T-shirt. I knew exactly where it was. I pulled it off the shelf in the wardrobe and breathed him in. I felt tears pricking my eyes and knew she was right. It had to be done. I didn't want to feel like this.

I could hear her in the garden. She was only in bed an hour ago and now she was as lively as anything. By the time I got outside she had a little bonfire going in the lawn.

'Think the neighbours'll mind?' I asked.

She prodded at the centre of the smoking heap with a stick, orange sparks flying, wood snapping and cracking. 'No. They'll be grand. I'll bung him next door a couple of extra packets of baccy.' Dor handed me one of the glasses that she'd filled and placed on the plastic green table... 'You ready?'

'I am, but is the bonfire?'

'You're not exactly burning much. Come on, lovey. Let's get you cleansed of your lingering love sickness.'

We huddled around the miniature bonfire, Trevor sitting in seeming awe of the dancing flames. The whippet was apparently hypnotised.

'So, what, I just chuck stuff in? Are you going to say anything? Chant something?'

'Sure. OK.' She cleared her throat, then immediately walked off.

'Dor?'

'Back in a sec, darling.'

My brain was too cloudy to comprehend pretty much anything. So, I decided to take the moment's silence while Dor was doing whatever it was, she was doing, to indulge in some self-directed anger. I knew it was self-pity. I knew that. But surely, I'd earnt it?

I could feel the heat of the fire on my face as I sat on the grass, a slight cold dampness soaking through my jeans around my arse and Brian the blow-up doll looming over me in the background. I didn't even notice it had rained earlier. And I certainly didn't care if my skin got too hot. I was like a dog happily napping in front of the fire and emerging with scorch marks. I was almost daring the fire to scold me. For a moment, I felt hypnotised like Trevor, taken away from the hurt by the dancing flames. Taken away from the fact that I would wake up tomorrow and do all this over and over again. A drink to get out of bed. A drink to get me out of the house and to the job centre. A drink to pass the spare time. A drink to make the pain stop. A drink to get to sleep. A drink to function.

Having to make sure that I had the correct bottles filled with the correct amounts to fit in the right sized bags, was a daily chore. A logistical nightmare. But for now, for right now, in this moment, I could feel the warmth of the alcohol coursing through me, numbing me, and I was enjoying it. I'd earnt that, surely?

My vision was becoming obscured as orange flickers overwhelmed my eyes and my skin felt too warm. The fire was reminding me that there are things much bigger and more powerful than me in the world. A strangely comforting notion. And then...

All hell broke loose!

That newly famous guitar riff screeching its way into my ears, assaulting my hypnotic state, and bringing me right back down to earth with the crash of the drums. I jumped up. 'What the…?'

'Don't you love a bit of Prodigy,' Dor shouted, returning with renewed vigour as the house shook with the song, Firestarter.

'I certainly do, but I didn't know *you* did?'

'I don't. But I remembered you and Dave were raving about it earlier. You left your CD out.'

'The big Prodigy comeback.' I smiled, remembering how me and Dave were dancing around the bar to it like divvies at the Angel a couple of months ago. 'Ha, me, and Dave dancing to this Dor, good times.'

'Yes, Emma, good times. Good times you didn't need John for. And there'll be plenty more I promise you.'

'Not sure the neighbours would see this as a good time.'

'Ah fuck 'em. I've had to endure dogs barking and babies crying for long enough.'

I rolled my eyes. She was nothing if she wasn't bold.

'You and Dave got any gigs coming up then?'

'He's always with Ally these days.'

'Well, it's good he's happy isn't it?'

'Oh, I know. I just. Do you think she's right for him?'

'If she makes *him* happy that's all that matters.'

'What do you mean?'

'I think you should try to make an effort. You might get to like her more if you stop assuming she's bad for him. He's not exactly wet behind the ears our Dave.'

'Er, when it comes to relationships, he's not exactly experienced.'

'Maybe that's because he only gets involved when he

knows he's onto a good thing.'

I shrugged. 'Anyway, who says I don't like her?'

'Your face does. Every time the poor bloke mentions her name.'

'Oh.'

'As much as you're hurting right now, Dave deserves some happiness too. You both had it tough as kids.'

'I guess. But Dor, they don't have to practically get married, do they? I mean, there's two toothbrushes in the bathroom at his now, and I swear Dave didn't buy that jar of Chicken Tonight. Not his style.'

'Right little detective you. Never mind serving ice-cream, get yersel a mac and a cigar and we could have Hull's very own Colombo on our hands. Might help put that criminology degree to use.'

'True.' I smiled at her. She was doing everything she possibly could to cheer me up. Including topping up my drink. The Prodigy finished and I nipped inside to stick a mix-tape on. I chucked one into the deck of the little red stereo with paint flecks on it and pressed play. Girls and Boys by Blur came on as I headed back outside.

'Shut that flamin' racket off.' It was Dor's neighbour, hanging out his bedroom window. 'I'm tryin' to bastard sleep, here.'

'Half an hour max,' Dor hollered back. 'You can cope with that can't you. For me?'

He sighed and shut the window.

'Right then. Go for it girl. Let's burn that pain away.'

With Damon Albarn's vocals and Dor's whiskey keeping me fired up, I stepped forward.

I threw in the tokens first. Followed by the gig ticket. Flames suffocating the little pieces of paper that took me back to happier days. Oasis playing the Adelphi. Parker jackets and beer and this romantic idea that we were all going to live forever…that night I felt like I'd finally found peace, finally content. There were people I had lost in life…but I had *exactly* who I needed by my side. But that was then…

'Good girl,' Dor said.

I turned around. John's shirt was now sitting proudly on Brian the doll.

'Oi, why have you given Brian John's shirt?'

'Suits him don't you think? I wasn't going to make you burn this, Emma. Smells bleedin' gorgeous.'

'Pervert!'

I picked up the photos. I would never get that time in the photo booth back. Our day trip to Scarborough. Chips and seagulls and sandy socks. Those pics were all I had. Well, aside from the two I'd squirrelled away in my knicker drawer. I hesitated, necked the rest of my whiskey, and chucked the photos in immediately turning away. I couldn't bear to watch our happy faces contort and wither. It was like watching our relationship on fast-forward.

'Right. You've done it. You've got closure. You're ready to roll. You're going to kill it baby!'

'Kill what Dor?'

'I don't know. It's what they say isn't it?'

'Who?'

'I don't know.'

As the poppy beats of The You and Me song came on, she grabbed my hands and waltzed me around the bonfire, singing all the wrong words to the song, her burgundy dressing gown flowing out around her as if she were in some kind of elaborate ballgown. I couldn't help it. I couldn't keep it in. I released myself from her grip and bent double laughing at the sight of 70-something Doreen, half cut on whiskey, dancing around to the Wannadies in her robe.

Perhaps she was right? Perhaps there was something in a cleansing ritual after all?

CHAPTER 15

It felt wrong that after all those years of my dad signing on, that his only daughter was now standing in the queue of desperation in the job centre, feeling guilty as hell.

What was it that always made you feel like that? It's like when you're in a car and the police are behind you, and you get this overwhelming feeling like you've done something terribly wrong.

I hated it. I stood in that queue, ready to tell them for the second time in as many weeks that, no, I hadn't found work, and yes, I will look at the job boards before I leave and yes - *of course* I'd accept work if it was offered to me.

Luckily, I had a trial coming up at the ice cream hut for the temporary job I applied for a couple of weeks ago. Perhaps I could placate them with that for now?

As I stood in line trying to keep my head down, I heard a familiar voice.

'Now then Emma!'

It was Hula Hoop Paul. Hull's answer to Pablo Escobar. Or at least, a Fisher Price version of Pablo Escobar.

'All right Paul.'

'You signing on?'

'No, I'm here to pick up my dry cleaning.'

'Really?' He looked around and I rolled my eyes discreetly.

'I lost my job.' I explained. 'I've been applying for a few, got an interview coming up so…fingers crossed.'

'Wouldn't bother if I were you. They never check-up. You can get away with murder in 'ere if you know how to blag the system.' He tapped his finger on his temple as he said the words. 'Got them wrapped round my little finger,' he said, taking in a sharp breath and puffing out his chest.

'Right,' I said, wondering why he was even here given how he was probably earning a much bigger sum from Hull's thriving speed-freak community and student potheads.

I noticed him attempt a discreet mirror check using one of the windows behind us, readjusting the dark curtains that his thin, straight hair hung in. He was all aftershave and swagger. I couldn't really understand why he wore his best Burberry polo shirt to sign on, when he was meant to be claiming near-poverty.

'Ere,' he said, leaning in close, his hot breath hitting my ear and his Joop aftershave smarting my nostrils. 'Got a new batch of Mitsubishis. Done a good deal on them, what with me connections an' that.'

'Mitsubishis?'

'Yeah. Doves are out. These are purer. Clean, like. Had some proper bangin' nights down Room on them.'

I figured he was talking about ecstasy pills. They were never really my bag. Too unpredictable for my liking. 'Thanks. I'll probably pass all the same.'

'Ah come on Em. Way better than that shite you and Dave do. Cleaner. Cheaper too.'

'Shh, Jesus, Paul.' I looked around me to see if anyone might have been listening. Who tries to sort a deal in the bloody job centre? I was already feeling bad for being here, I didn't need my former coke habit bringing up. 'Me and Dave don't really bother these days.'

'You fell out?'

'No, I mean, with, you know…' I said, feeling highly embarrassed about discussing our historic coked up Friday nights, while in the context of signing on at the job centre.

'Right.' He moved backwards, finally giving me some of my own air to breathe. 'So, um, you still with that Geordie lad?'

'John? Um. No. Not really…'

A smile spread across his face. Oh God…

'Would you, um…I mean, might you fancy…'

'Next!'

Saved by the bell.

'I'll call you,' he said, then swaggered over to the desk, throwing himself back on the plastic chair, his bum barely touching the seat and his knees jutting out into the aisles between the desks. A stern looking lady with a Margaret Thatcher hairstyle sat opposite him, ready to dismiss his excuses.

I stood idly, looking at everyone around me. The mood in the job centre was generally not like Hula Hoop Paul's. It was sombre. Sad.

I glanced at the job's boards on the wall next to me, wondering what I would end up doing - serving ice cream, mopping floors or processing invoices? Hmm…

As I looked around, I noticed Hula Hoop Paul jolt upright in his seat. Someone else - who looked vaguely familiar, but I couldn't think why, had approached the desk. He was wearing a grey suit and looked about the same age as us.

'Congratulations Paul!' I heard him say.

There was a bit of commotion, Paul shaking his head, leaning back in his seat, fidgeting. I couldn't hear the full conversation but managed to pick up Paul saying, 'there was no way he could get there' and familiar suit guy saying something about his souped-up Vauxhall Calibra.

Eventually Paul stood up and turned, looking like he'd just been informed that he'd caught the clap or something. As soon as he clocked eyes on me, he transformed his face and slapped on a smile and said, 'I'll call you,' before giving me a wink and swaggering outside.

'Next!'

Grey suit guy seemed to have taken over from the lady who was on before. I couldn't place him, but he seemed so familiar…

'Hi there. How can I help?' He said, his voice flat as he flicked through some papers on his desk. Then he looked up at me. 'Emma Barclay. My God!'

'Ha-ha.' I tried my hardest to think. Who the fuck was this guy?

'Keith. Keith Crabtree,' he said.

'Oh God. Yes of course. Sorry. It's been…'

'Years. I know.'

'Yeah,' I said, trying to remember whether we got on back in school or not.

'You still in touch with Hula Hoop Paul then?'

'I err…'

'Saw you chatting.'

'Oh, right. Yeah. Just bumped into him. Getting to be a bit of a reunion this place.' I laughed, still trying to remember if Keith Crabtree from school was likely to be on my side or not.

'Isn't it. Signing on then?'

'Yep. It's only my second.' Why did I constantly feel as though I needed to justify my presence. 'Lost my job just the other week.'

'Ah, sorry to hear that. I've just got Paul a nice cushy job,' he said, a thin smile spreading across his face.

'Oh really?' That must've been the congratulations.

'Yep. Farmhand over near Cottingham.' He started sniggering as he was going through some papers.

'Farmhand?'

'You know how he was with me back in school don't you?'

'Paul?'

'Yip. I'll never forgive him for flushing my new trainers down the loo.'

'Ah, right, I didn't rea…'

'It wasn't the worst of it.'

'What else did he do?' I asked, intrigued.

'The rumour.'

'Rumour?' Then I remembered. We used to call him 'mummy's boy.' 'Oh yeah…'

'Bastard,' he said.

'Well, yeah, but nobody really believed you were…you know…'

'Well…'

'Nobody really believed you shagged…'

'Anyway.' He cleared his throat.

'So, you got him a job?'

'Yeah.' He started chuckling again. 'He'll be a fleece wrapper. Well, more specifically, he'll oversee removing the winnets from sheep's arses before they're sheared.' He looked increasingly pleased with himself. 'My brother-in-law works there but, er, don't tell anyone now, will you.' He tapped his nose twice.

'Course not,' I said, smiling along. Perhaps if I stayed on his good side, I wouldn't run into any trouble with my own giro?

'And he kind of needs to turn up really, given what I know about his, extracurricular activities, shall we say.' He tapped his nose again. Jesus, I forgot how irritating this guy was.

'Extracurricular activities?' I tried to play it cool as if I was oblivious to Paul's main source of income.

'Drug deals,' he said, as if it was the most obvious thing in the world. Well, it was really. The bloke had just tried to sell me an E in the job centre queue.

'Anyway. That's cheered me right up that has. So, now then, we'll get you signed on shall we.'

'Thanks,' I said.

CHAPTER 16

'OK, slowly.... slowly....no, no, slow it down, sloooooow it doooooown....no! don't...!'

'Oh.'

'See this is what happens when you go too fast.' Isabella snatched the cone off me. 'You've created a dog poopy ice-cream, Emma. We do not serve dog poopy ice-cream.'

I sighed. I couldn't quite believe how much skill there was in building a Mr bloody Whippy. After being invited in for a trial at the ice cream hut, the big day was finally here.

'Once more. Ready?'

I grabbed the hollow wafer cone, and carefully positioned it below the ice-cream dispenser as Isabella watched me like a hawk, her hands hovering around me as if they were omitting a magical force that would transform me into the perfect ice-cream maker if she was just still enough and quiet enough.

Isabella was of Italian descent and had a no-nonsense attitude about her. She was probably in her late 60s, early 70s, but she didn't look like a frail old lady needing an op to keep her on her feet. She hobbled a bit, sure, but she carried herself with such assertiveness that you saw right past her age. She was fairly large, in a nice way. She wore her dark hair in a short, curly style, and her clothes were made of flowing patterned fabrics. She was like a fierce hippy, if such a contradiction could exist.

I held the cone as steady as I could, and pulled down the lever as slowly as possible, Isabella's hands still hovering around me like some kind of ice-cream queen aura. I let the first spurt of Mr Whippy make its way towards the bottom of the cone, gradually circling the cone expanding as it filled, moving it back in again for the finishing touch.

'Ta-da!' I said, proud as punch. Isabella's lips remaining narrow and flat. She grabbed a flake, shoved it in the top and said, 'we need to talk about volume, Emma.'

Bollocks.

The day continued much in the same vein. It seems it's incredibly easy to mess up when it comes to ice-cream. Surprisingly, at the end of my painful—and rather messy trial—she offered me the job. I was to look after the hut on a three-month basis while Isabella had her hip replacement operation at Hull Royal. It would take her quite some time to recover, she said, and doctor's orders were *no more standing on your feet in the ice cream hut for hours on end.* She'd lined up me and some friend of hers who was going to cover one day a week, so I could get a day off each week. Perfect.

After finishing my first shift as an ice-cream lady, including being allowed to serve a customer unsupervised while Isabella nipped to the loo, I collared Dave for a pint down the Angel feeling proud of myself for actually achieving something.

'Thanks. I'll get the next round,' I offered, as Dave plonked the glasses on the table, the frothy liquid spilling out over the top and pooling between my pint glass and the paper beer mat.

'No bother. Just the one though tonight, eh?'

I shrugged, imagining Ally had him on a tight leash again. I never really understood how things changed so damn quickly. One minute he was my bezzie Dave. My daily pint-drinking, tea-slurping best mate. The next.... Well, I guess I had neglected him a bit when I met John. So, I could hardly blame him for getting lost in the romance of his relationship. They seemed to get on, and she was nice to me. She just seemed far too sensible for him.

And then there was that matter of trainer puke. And pints over lead singer's heads. I shook away the guilt by picking up the ice-cold glass. 'Ahhh. Needed that,' I said.

'So, how was it then?' Dave asked.

'OK, I think. Although I'm not sure I'm the best Mr Whippy maker. Takes some bloody skill you know.'

'But they offered you the job?'

'Yeah.'

'Nice one, Emma.' He supped his pint.

'Yeah but....'

'But what? You get to hang out in every child's favourite place, surrounded by every child's favourite dessert...'

I shrugged. 'But I'm 28. I mean, where do you progress to, in the world of ice-cream?'

'Aye. But it's fun for now. And you've surely got *some* good fun left in you?'

I shot him a look, but he was right to raise it. Ironically, as much as I had been the one who was always still up for a night out, the one who always accused him of getting boring, it wasn't really the same. *I* wasn't really the same. Just like he said. Nights out were not the light-hearted affair they used to be. Or perhaps they were the same, it's just that we'd grown up? And chucking pints over heads wasn't a laugh anymore. I don't know. Whatever it was, things were different. There was good fun and there was bad fun. Unfortunately, these days, I always ended up having the latter.

'OK,' I said, with a little more joy and enthusiasm. 'You've got a point. I'll embrace the sprinkles and flakes. But first, fancy another? Just one for the road?'

He glanced, unsmiling, at his half empty pint, then up at my empty glass. I was already standing ready to head to the bar.

'Just get us a half, I'll pour it in.'

'Sure.'

I came back with two pints, plonked the drinks down. He shook his head when he realised I'd doubled his order. I filled him in on the workings of an ice-cream hut as he finished his pint and picked up another. I told him about how I had learnt to handle the Whippy machine as though I was using clutch control in a car. About the signature flavours. About the ice-cream tempering...

'What the fuck is tempering?' He asked.

'Don't you know? I thought everyone knew what tempering was,' I joked, putting on my version of Isabella's voice.

Dave laughed.

'It's when you have to bring the ice-cream temperature up. But very carefully.' I explained. 'I swear, you'd think she'd given birth to the Mr Whippy given how protective she is over it. Get this - I'm not to fill the entire cone if it's busy - spread it thinly by just filling the top bit.'

'Good bit of business sense, I'd say.'

'Maybe,' I said. 'But oh my God, Dave. She's giving me a crash-course in up-selling the number of scoops tomorrow. For every adult sale we make, we offer the special as an extra scoop for half the price.'

'The special?'

'Pistachio this month apparently.'

He laughed. 'Seriously though, Emma. It's summer, a new start, a happy place. Honestly, I think this will be just what you need to reset and get back on track.'

I felt an involuntary frown flash across my face and immediately tried to turn it around. We'd got past my denials that life was fine and dandy. The anxiety that I thought I'd left behind me, was gearing up again. I couldn't remember the last time I woke up without feeling a horrible, snowballing sense of fear. And I couldn't remember the last time I went to bed sober. But if I didn't calm the fear with the booze well...it didn't bear thinking about.

The panic attacks had been creeping back in since I stopped therapy a few months ago. Talking about my mum's affair and living with a desperately sad, unemployed single father for years was the focus of the conversation when I sat in that beige armchair, glass of water sitting neatly on a coaster on the little round table in front of me. But when we got onto what she called 'coping mechanisms' it all became a bit like a lecture. And they're not supposed to do that are they? Counsellors? They're not meant to advise you; you're meant to work it out for yourself. That's what she said way back when we had our first session. But somehow, she was doing exactly that. Try *cutting back on the alcohol, Emma. Why not speak to your doctor about coming off the Zopiclone, Emma.*

Jesus Christ. Yep, that's it, drag all this historical pain out of me then tell me to go on my merry way and handle it cold turkey. No thank you. Sleeping through the night was bad enough even with the crutch of zopiclone. And the mornings, that's when it always hit me like a sucker punch. The mornings were the worst.

Dave got up to leave, giving me a cheeky punch on the arm before turning to make for the door, lifting the back of his arm up in the air and shouting 'see you later'.

I walked over to the bar.

'Vodka please Bren.'

'No can do love.'

'You ran out?'

'Nope.'

'Then…? Fuck's sake. Dor?'

'She's only looking out for you.'

'I'm a 28-year-old adult, Bren. I can look after myself.'

She raised her eyebrows. 'Pint?' She offered.

'Go on then.' I sighed and took a seat.

I was like a self-proclaimed vegetarian dining out on fish, and I knew it.

CHAPTER 17

I walked through the doors, music pounding in my ears and sending a prickle of excitement through my head. As I headed over the hard steel steps and into the main bar and dance floor area, the familiar whiff of dry ice hit me, and I felt instantly alive.

I surveyed the room, a few people propped up the bar. A guy, standing alone with a pint in no hurry to move, coat still on.

I made my way over.

'Pint of Foster's please.' I rummaged around in my canvas shoulder bag for some coins before handing them over. 'Thanks,' I said, taking a sip and turning to the man on my right. 'Fucking love the Stone Roses.' I said, nodding towards the dancefloor where groups of students were swaying, heads backwards, feeling every pulse of the music.

'Yeah,' he said. He seemed quiet. Maybe he was sad.

'You not staying?' I joked, tugging at his jacket sleeve.

'Just popped in for one.'

'On a Friday?'

'Ha. You got me there.'

He must've been about thirty, thirty-five? There was something sad about him. It felt as though I knew him even though I'd never seen him before.

'I know,' I said, turning back to the bar that was relatively quiet thanks to the Stone Roses' draw on the dance floor. 'Two tequila slammers please?'

His face seemed to light up. 'So, I'm having more than one then?''

'It's not a second drink, it's a chaser, so…'

He laughed.

'I'm Emma.'

'Jake.'

The barman handed each of us the shots, two pieces of lime and some salt.

'Bottoms up.' I said, licking the back of my hand to sprinkle the salt onto, passing the saltshaker onto Jake who followed suit.

'1, 2, 3…'

Salt. Neck it. Lime……aaaaahhhhhhhh!

We laughed.

'I'll get the next ones,' he said.

CHAPTER 18

I was kicking around aimlessly in bed, awoken by an almighty churn in my stomach that hit me before any hint of consciousness did.

Oh God, no.

The light summer skies illuminating the gap between my curtains made everything feel much darker. The contrast between how I was *meant* to feel and how I *actually* felt was stark. I craved a truly dark morning sky.

I heard Trev groaning and felt him shifting around by my feet. 'Morning Trev,' I said with barely a whisper. He stood up, circled, and plonked himself back down, but this time a bit closer to me.

'Why'd you put up with me, eh?' I said, stroking his head, trying desperately to distract myself from the fear, my shaking hands.

I leant over and felt around on the carpet for my water bottle. Locating it, I took a sip, quenching my thirst, and immediately felt a little better.

I lay back down, my left forearm resting on my hot forehead, and contemplated the day ahead. How the hell was I going to get through it? My new job, a step backwards from my former Sales Admin role, which was a step backwards from my uni degree and, worse still, I knew there was a high potential to fail at this too.

I dangled my right arm down by the side of my bed and could just about reach the bottle again without leaning over too much. I didn't want to twist around too much. My stomach was already one huge pile of twisted knots. I desperately needed it to unknot itself.

My fingertips hit the plastic and, just as I almost had it in my grasp, I accidentally rolled it further away. Fuck's sake.

I wedged myself up in bed, leaned my torso towards the floor and grabbed the bottle as quickly as I could.

Ah. That's better.

As my stomach began to settle, my mind began to calm too, and the piercing daylight started to feel friendlier. Perhaps there was hope.

'Right then Trev.' I said with a renewed vigour. 'Let's do this!'

I pulled on a pair of jeans and a T-shirt, threw the curtains open and took in a deep breath. 'I'll be OK' I said to nobody in particular - neither hearing it nor really believing it. But then I could feel it. In my throat. My muscles were involuntarily clenching. I ran to the loo. It all came back up in an instant.

Fuck.

I ran back into my bedroom, grabbed the bottle, wrapped a towel around it and legged it back into the bathroom. I needed to get my levels right or I'd be worse than useless today.

I drank a sip and immediately felt my stomach lurch again. More sick came up. For every bit of vodka I lost, diluted in vomit, I knew I needed to replace it. I had the taps running to cover up the sound of retching and stayed until I had got just enough inside of me.

Then I picked up my toothbrush before putting it straight back down. Sticking that in my mouth wouldn't help.

Feeling slightly better, I went downstairs and fed Trev his revolting slop. God why was everything making me retch this morning?

I poured a cold drink of water, sipped it slowly then held the empty glass to my cheek. I could hear Trev's bowl scraping along the floor, which usually meant he'd all but finished and was trying desperately to get every last morsel into his mouth.

His lead was dangling idly from the back of one of the

kitchen chairs. I never left it on the chair. I realised that Dor must've been the last person to take him for his walk. I grabbed it and called him. 'Come on then.'

He bounded towards me, jumping up my legs with glee as I hooked the lead to his collar and grabbed my bag.

We passed the grocery store and walked to the corner shop. The little independent one that didn't play by the licensing rules. I unhooked Trev's lead, looped it around the bottom of the railings, securing him while I popped inside for my supplies.

When we got back to the house, I let Trev off his lead and, noting that Doreen was in the living room watching TV, I walked to the kitchen sink, emptied the full bottle of water I'd just bought and poured the vodka into it.

'Right, I'm off,' I hollered as I walked back past the living room where Dor was now chattering on to Trev, rollers in her hair, seemingly oblivious to the fact he was a dog. Apparently, they were going to watch the Big Breakfast together and discuss Johnny Vaughan's cheeky-chappy looks or something. It was a particularly involved conversation for a whippet.

I wandered through the little green alley to cut into the park, the space opening in front of me like a scene from a chocolate box. I hadn't really visited the park with Trev much this summer. I was often taking him out, don't get me wrong, but it was usually to the corner shop rather than the lush green park he was used to. I was a bad dog parent. He was rarely off his lead with his tongue lolling out his mouth and the wind through his ears these days.

The ducks were lazily floating about on the pond and doing their business on the curvy little path that bordered it, a green poop-spattered walkway that still looked endearing because, well, ducks. The Victorian greenhouse looked eerie peering out from among the trees with its doors still closed, and the little ice cream hut was just opening its eyes - or rather, Isabella was just propping open the shutters.

I took a deep breath and headed over.

'Morning!' I said, in as cheery a tone as I could muster, forcing a big friendly smile. I really hoped the vomiting hadn't left my eyes looking too red. I'd forgotten to do my make up today.

'Morning Emma.' She looked a little flustered, rearranging everything by placing all the items in their daytime spots.

'Can I do anything?'

'Please, love. Could you refill the Chupa Chups and put them out by the ice cream menu on the ledge, please?'

I looked over to a half empty cardboard box pierced with Chupa Chups lolly sticks and spied a few full crates stacked up on the floor behind me. I unwrapped the cellophane from the top and began transferring its contents across to the half empty crate. I couldn't really understand why she didn't just let the first one sell out before opening another, it seemed to me like there was going to be a lot of Chupa Chups lolly transitions on a daily basis doing it this way but, hey, it was my first day. I wasn't about to kick up a fuss. Especially after my stern warning about Whippy wastage!

'So, when do we officially open?' I asked.

'9.30. School holidays bring the crowds early doors, see.'

I nodded and looked out across the park, where I could indeed see a few dots in the distance making their way towards the hut, passing the duck pond - some flapping their arms and quacking at the ducks who quickly scuttled off towards the pond to make their escape.

I tried to make conversation. 'How's your hip today?'

'Well, it's bloody painful hence the op.' She sighed. 'But thanks for asking' she quickly added with a half-smile. I could see we were both putting on a front today.

'So, what's the most popular? Which do I need to keep a close eye on stock-wise?'

'Well, the special, obviously, given how you're going to

up-sell the pistachio today right?'

'I've not forgotten,' I said.

'And, oh the Whippy, of course. Kids' favourite. Red Bull energy drinks for the teens. And keep the sparkling water topped up. The mums seem to like it.'

'Do we have any regulars, then?'

'The day usually begins with the nice middle-class mummies bringing their little ones for an ice lolly. They're pretty calm until one of the kids drops said lolly and mum becomes all animated about it all.'

I giggled. Isabella continued. 'The teens are often down by the park around 1pm-ish. After their lie in. They usually come for cans of pop and chock lick.'

'OK. Any bother?'

'No.'

'Oh good,' I said.

'No that comes later in the day when they've drank all their energy drinks!'

'Right.' I gave a knowing smile with a nod, while trying to discreetly eye the energy drinks because I could really do with one right now.

'Ah, and there's *him*.' Isabella nodded her head in the direction of the park bench where an old guy was just taking a seat. He seemed unsteady on his legs, poor guy.

'Who's he?' I asked.

'He's here most days. I'm not sure if he's after a freebie or if he fancies me.' Isabella said. 'Anyway, he's clearly a drunk. So, keep an eye on him.'

I studied the old man carefully. He was sitting on the bench, a long shabby tweed coat falling away from the seat, and a baggy-ish pair of old grey trousers covering what looked like skinny legs. His hair was kind of shaggy and untamed. He looked like he'd lived a life.

'Is he homeless?' I asked.

'What? Oh, no, I don't know. It's never really crossed my mind. But whatever you do, no freebies, OK? Homeless or not. I'll be homeless if I start giving away my profits.'

'Gotcha,' I said as I looked back across at the old man, who was now expertly rolling a cigarette, a pouch of baccy dangling from under his palm as his fingers crafted a scrawny cigarette. His face was a map of heavily etched lines, but somehow, he looked kind of happy and peaceful. I smiled and gave him a nod. He waved back.

'Don't you go encouraging him,' Isabella warned me. 'Anyway. Can you remember what I said about the till?'

'The number 5 sticks so press it hard?'

'That's it. And the ice cream volume?'

'Never fill the bottom of the cone during the afternoon rush?'

'Excellent.'

'And the sparkling water?'

'Keep an eye on the levels for the mums.'

'Yeah. Although out of everyone, they're the ones I care least about. They're stuck up, some of the pushchair brigade, you know. Look out for the ones who speak about themselves in third person. They think they're Tara-Palmer-bloody-Tomkinson or something.'

I nodded. Perhaps we'd get on after all.

'Right then, here's the keys. I'm off.'

'What?'

'For my op'

'What, today?'

'Yes today.'

'But?'

'You assured me you were more than capable.'

'Did I?'

'It's just a few ice creams, Emma. You'll be grand. Honestly, you'll have a whale of a time working in my little hut. Promise you that.'

I felt panic rising, overwhelming my usual daily panic levels. Why was anybody putting me in charge of anything? I was a disaster. But then my chest deflated when I suddenly realised, I would be alone. When there were no customers to attend to, I would be alone. I could just *be*.

Isabella grabbed her jacket and hobbled out of the hut, stopping in front of the window to remind me where her phone number was kept, along with the supplier directory and the scoop wash.

'Just call if you need anything. I'll be at home with my feet up.'

'I will!' I hollered.

'And careful of those bloody pushchair mummies. They can rile you right up but try and bite your tongue.'

'Ha-ha I will.'

And with that I was alone, Isabella shrinking in the distance, her clothes flowing gracefully while her legs hobbled awkwardly.

I looked around me, taking in the bright colours of the hut. The Chupa Chups, the boxes of crisps in every flavour all stacked on top of one another haphazardly, the green, red, and orange cans of pop, Mr Whippy and the Slush Puppie machine, the syrups and flakes and cornets and wafers. Ice cream was a serious business. You could practically re-create someone's personality with ice cream. I pondered this while looking around.

Dor would be…unconventional. She'd go for the sugar cone over the common wafer. Or perhaps a tub. But like her home, she'd have a mash up of different flavours all competing for the limelight. Pistachio and coffee, maybe, then she'd surprise you once again by going for vanilla.

Dave, he'd go for something safe with a dollop of something childlike. Vanilla and mint choc-chip with some strawberry cheesecake and a flake in a wafer cone.

My dad…bless him…. he'd be straight-up vanilla…or perhaps things might have changed since Barbara Carpenter moved in?

And John…John…he'd try something different every

time. He liked variety. And he always changed his mind. His favourite might be mint choc chip one month, and raspberry the next, then back to mint choc chip but mixing it up with something sophisticated…. like Bailey's ice cream or something.

Maybe he would change his mind about me too. It was possible. Maybe with a few tweaks here and there, I could be good for him again.

As I mulled over the prospect of being reunited with my Geordie man, I realised that I was running this little place. I was in charge. I didn't have time to daydream. It might not be a big turnover caravan company, but it didn't matter, because for the next few months, in Isabella's absence, I was my own boss. I had my own little sugary empire packed full of sprinkles and monkey's blood, Wham! bars and rainbow drops. As the morning sun began to stream through, I felt a strange feeling wash over me. I couldn't quite put my finger on it. But I *could* put my finger on the little radio's 'on' button.

Immediately greeted with Meatloaf, I fiddled with the dial until I found something more pleasing amongst the classical sounds and hissing conversations. There! With a little bit of gentle adjusting, I removed the fuzzy sound to reveal…The Boo Radley's. Wake up Boo!

Perfect.

I grabbed a quick swig from my bag, leaned on the counter ready to serve my first customer, my trainers tapping on the floor of the hut, as I breathed in the fresh air. And God, it *was* a beautiful morning! Then I realised what that strange feeling was. That foreign feeling that weirdly calmed my stomach. It was hope.

This really could be the start of happier times.

CHAPTER 19

'Who's next? Sorry, a what? With a sugar cone? Oh, hang on…'

Cones and Whippy and scoops of pistachio and mint chocolate were flying out and I could barely catch my breath. A little bit of sunshine and the park was swarming with people of every flavour, tiny little dots of colour placed randomly around the grass and surrounding paths. Just as Isabella had predicted.

By the end of the day, I was shattered. It had been non-stop, with the trendy boho mums, the teenagers who came, went away then returned high on taurine, complete with added wings demanding crisps and more Red Bull. I hadn't figured out how to get out for a loo break and had to hang on in there until there was a break in the relentless queueing. I needed a plan for toilet escapes tomorrow, I couldn't hang on like this every day!

The radio kept me company so even in the dips I felt busy - with Newsbeat and traffic alerts occasionally interrupting the pop music of Radio 1. The Humber Bridge was at a standstill. And Chris from Hedon had apparently called in to say there was a sofa on fire on Spring Street. But I was here, safely cocooned. Lifted by the sunshine and the sounds and the happy chatter as kids tried to pick from the colourful array of sweet treats on offer. A bittersweet flashback to times when your choice of chewy sweets was the heaviest thing that played on your mind.

The hut had kept me happy and energised all day. And by the end of it I was completely knackered – which was probably the most welcome feeling I'd felt in a long time. I never felt tired. Not like this, anyway. My brain was too tired to berate myself.

As I was locking up feeling pleased with myself, the old man wandered over, a tin of sweet corn in his hand. I waved as I struggled with the lock and got a gentle wave back. He was alone again, so, once I sussed out the knack of turning the key with a certain amount of pressure at a very particular angle, I decided to go and chat.

'I'm Emma,' I said. 'I've just started working in Isabella's ice cream hut.'

'I noticed. How was your first day?' He seemed surprisingly…normal. Maybe he hadn't been hanging around the park on his own for too long after all? Maybe he'd just lost his wife? Or his house? Or both. Who knows? He was, however, wobbly again. His legs didn't seem to be doing what he wanted them to. Weirdly, though, he didn't sound drunk. But then I didn't really know him so…

…maybe he was good at hiding it, like I was.

'It was good, thanks. Busy.'

'Aye it does get busy in the holidays,' he said. 'I'm Les.'

He held out his hand and I took it emphatically, shaking it with purpose. His skin felt coarse, it was covered in intermittent ground-in dirt and yellow baccy stains. I drew my eyes away quickly.

'What you doing with the sweet corn?' I asked.

'Ducks.' He nodded towards the pond.

'I thought we fed them bread?'

'No! Never,' he said, sharply. 'Never feed ducks bread. It's bad for them.'

'Oh,' I said, thinking how he'd just ruined some happy childhood memories for me. All those times I was excitedly chucking bread in for the ducks, watching it bloat in the green water, strings of tasty weed catching in it, I was just malnourishing said ducks. Oh God, what effect might I have had on the ducklings? It didn't bear thinking about. According to Les, who decided to educate me on duck feed whether I liked it or not, the bread swelled up in their stomachs. It meant they couldn't digest enough of the stuff they actually needed. They got the immediate satisfaction of the bread, which felt like a treat to them, he said, but afterwards, they were so full on rubbish they were missing out on all the good stuff.

I felt that.

By this point, I was unable to shake off the image of me and my dad at the very same pond when I was a kid, bag of Mighty White bread in hand, tearing off chunks and seeing which duck reached the soggy wet prize first as they raced across the water flapping and quacking and splashing. It reminded me that I *did* have some good memories of being a kid. Regardless of duck malnourishment.

He seemed a nice old man, Les. He was stern about the bread, but I think he was just protective of the ducks.

'Do you come and feed them every day?' I asked.

'Oh no, God no. I haven't enough sweet corn for that.' He chuckled, quickly turning it into a hacky cough that overwhelmed him momentarily. He beat his fist on his chest a few times before clearing his throat. 'Need to quit those smokes,' he tutted to himself with a smile.

'I'm always saying the same,' I added.

'You should, you know. Before it gets too late.' It was a no-nonsense delivery of a no-nonsense fact.

'True,' I said. I wasn't about to argue with an old man with a terrible hacky cough. His facial contours demonstrated far more life experience than I had. 'So do you live round here?' I asked.

'Yeah, just on the park,' Les said.

I *knew* it, I thought. I *knew* he was homeless. Poor fella was probably sleeping on a park bench at night. He'd be cold after the sun went down. And what if he got hassle from those artificially energised teenagers on their bikes when nobody else was around? Worse still, I knew there were some right dodgy types hanging out in the park late on. I even got flashed at once when I was walking home from Silhouettes by some weirdo in the bushes.

All of a sudden, I felt overwhelmingly protective of this shaky old gent with a hacky cough.

As we continued to talk the ducks began circling us, lazy quacks echoing around the park. The sun was starting to drop but showed no sign of defeat just yet, its beams divided by tree branches but still stretching out confidently towards us.

'I better feed them; the little blighters are getting impatient,' Les said.

'Well, it was nice to meet you. I'm sure I'll probably see you tomorrow?' I said.

'I'm sure you will. Have a nice evening,' Les said and wandered off, a rabble of mallards quacking impatiently around his feet. He was the Pied Piper of ducks.

I watched him as he strolled along peacefully, taking his time, as though he had all the time in the world. He seemed a pleasant, content man. Maybe when you remove all the crappy modern day stuff we get accustomed to, life becomes somehow, nicer. More peaceful?

I started to walk away from the park to go home and, as I made it out onto the main road, it hit me. The nothingness. A great big fat void of nothing.

First day at work - done. Now what? I wished I could find comfort in feeding the ducks, kicking back on the grass under the diluted sun. But somehow, I knew it would take more than that to occupy my mind. It was starting to race again…leaving me restless, predicting the anxiety that would inevitably follow. And the hopelessness of it seemed to spur it all on.

I wished it was earlier. Wished I could keep serving up scoops of pistachio and bags of chock lick. I wanted the teenagers circling like sharks on their bikes and the children dropping their ice creams and screaming 'til they were redder than Father Christmas. I wanted the crappy music on the radio that I didn't have time to turn over because I needed to refill the Chupa Chups again in between customers.

It was new and shiny and novel. I needed this so much. But once it was over, nothing had really changed, had it? It was Saturday night too. *Now what* had become even bigger.

There was only one answer to '*now what?*'

CHAPTER 20

A whole week of serving ice creams had passed and I was feeling pleased with myself. I hadn't been late once, not really, and I was really getting into my stride.

I was just stacking up the wafer cones, positioning them between the sugar cones and ice-cream cups, when Les made his way to the duck pond. This time he didn't have sweetcorn, he had what looked like…peas. Maybe that's why duck shit is so green?

I waved over…'Morning!'

'Morning Emma. How are you today?'

'Good! Come over for an ice-cream when you're done. I'll treat you.'

He gave me an affirmative nod and I felt good being able to help somebody who was clearly lonely. A little shot of warmth that my brain so desperately needed.

Today, his clothes looked heavy and drab. I couldn't understand how he wasn't melting in the sun in that knackered tweed coat. It must be tough when your home doesn't have walls and you have to carry all your worldly belongings with you. I wondered if he really was sleeping on a bench or maybe he had some kind of tent set up in the bushes somewhere?

I continued getting the hut set up and ready for the customers who were likely to descend sharpish, building up steadily to a busy lunchtime of impatient adults, crying babies, five-year-olds having a paddy because they were only allowed the one flake and teenagers swearing for attention. It made me realise that nothing changes as we age - just the way we express ourselves. Being dissatisfied and cranky seems to be a staple of modern life.

Les stepped back from the pond, having emptied his little sandwich bag of peas, the ducks going crazy for the tiny green balls floating on the surface. I set to making him the perfect ice cream. I grabbed a cone and held it expertly underneath the Mr Whippy machine, and I made sure that Les' cone was filled solidly with ice cream - Isabella's words of warning ringing through my ears…

We need to talk about volume, Emma.

Ah well, she wasn't here. And while life might have been far from a party, at least I had a home and a warm, dry little hut filled with every sugar-laden treat imaginable. I wasn't sure if feeling better about myself because of someone else's misfortune was a good or a bad thing?

When Les arrived at the hut, I handed him the huge, rather professional looking even if I did say so myself, Mr Whippy, with a big smile on my face and a rainbow of sprinkles lodging themselves in the soft ripples of the ice cream.

Les began patting his pockets.

'No - this is on the house.'

'Oh, I couldn't.'

'Of course, you could. You're feeding the ducks, so I'll feed you. What goes around and all that.'

'Ah well thank you very much Emma that's very kind of you.'

He took the ice cream, holding it in his trembling hand, and I was amazed at how he savoured every taste. Up close, you could see how skinny he was under those heavy clothes. I was surprised he wasn't devouring it in three seconds flat.

He looked up at me and I felt immediately embarrassed for staring at him. 'You not having one?' He asked.

'I already have,' I lied, wiping the sprinkles off the side as we chatted, collecting them like brightly coloured iron filings on a magnetic wet cloth. In truth, I couldn't stomach any food right now. 'So, what are your plans for the day?' I asked him, taking advantage of the quiet hour I had before the usual rush.

'Oh, it's just a quiet day for me. As ever.' He was so chilled about life he almost made me feel ashamed for making such a drama out of everything - and for moping so much. But I realised when I chatted to him that I didn't feel quite so angsty. There was something really calming about the old man.

'So, what is it you're feeding the ducks today? Peas, is it?'

'Oh yes, they love the peas. Greedy little blighters,' he said, looking over towards the pond affectionately. 'Some cute little ducklings have arrived recently. Can you see them?'

I leant forward, squashing the wet cloth in my hands to keep tight hold of the sprinkles, and stretched my neck to peer out of the hut. 'Oh yeah, I never noticed them before!' A fluffy arrow of yellow and brown babies trailed behind Mumma duck, bobbing like contentedness itself.

I quickly tried to squash the unwelcome mental image of them being ripped apart by a prowling cat.

'Teeny little creatures aren't they.' He chuckled, his hacky cough making another unwelcome appearance. He beat his fist on his chest again. 'Anyway,' he said. 'Enough about me and the ducks, how's life treating Emma?'

It was such a direct question and one that I had no idea how to answer. My life was the pits. But surely, I had it better than he did? So why did it feel so damn dark all the time?

'Fine, I guess.'

'Fine. Now that's a word with a double meaning.'

'Well, I'm hardly going to stand in the sunshine whingeing, ruining everyone's day. I'm an ice cream lady now,' I laughed. 'I have a responsibility to make people smile.'

'Well, you're doing a grand job'. He tapped his hand three times on the countertop reassuringly as he spoke. 'But…' he took a pause to study my face. 'You'll make me smile more if you answer the question honestly. It's funny how nobody does. We all say we're fine when we're not. If you were fine, you'd probably say you were good, or great.'.

'Ha, yeah, it's weird how we do that. Well, in that case if you must know, the last few weeks have been hard. I was dumped by the most wonderful man I've ever met and sacked by the most patient boss.' I smiled to show I wasn't after sympathy. 'So that's why I'm here, I guess.'

'Oh Emma,' he said, his voice gravelly but soft. 'Sounds like you've had a right old time of it.'

'Yeah, well, let's be honest, it's the last thing you want on a sunny day, me banging on about how unfair life is. I should be serving up smiles and sprinkles, not tales of woe.'

He nodded in response while making his first crispy dent in the wafer cone.

'But I can tell you one thing,' I continued. 'There's always a silver lining isn't there? I've learnt how to master the art of the Whippy, and I get to go to the pub as late as I want without getting grief when I get home. So, you know, could be worse,' I laughed.

'He didn't like you going out, this boyfriend?' He enquired.

I suddenly felt guilty for how I had inadvertently portrayed John. 'Ah no it wasn't so much that. Not really. No, he just, well, I guess I can get carried away sometimes. So, I was always a bit loud and late.'

'Too much of the old plonk, is it?'

'Thing is, I'm 28. I let my hair down. And why not?' I argued my case directly to him, wondering why on earth I was telling him all this. He was practically a stranger after all. Why did I need him to agree?

I *did* need him to agree though. I needed everyone to know that it was OK. It was all in hand. Because really, I wasn't letting my hair down. I was just keeping up appearances.

Les narrowed his eyes slightly. 'Well, there's nowt wrong with letting your hair down. As long as it's fun.'

'It is,' I lied.

'So, how are you finding the world of ice-cream?'

'You know what? I was dubious. But it sure beats faxing off orders for caravan parts.'

'You worked in caravans?'

'Yeah, Shaws.'

'On Gypsyville?'

'That's the one. I was in sales admin. It wasn't exactly making best use of my degree. Well, neither is this considering I studied criminology,' I joked, gesturing at my sugar-laden surroundings.

'Maybe not,' he chuckled, before erupting into another cough. I stopped what I was doing until I was happy he'd recovered. 'But my word,' he said. 'To get to work, to get paid, and be in such beautiful surroundings.' He glanced around, his eyes taking in the greenery and wildlife with wonder. I was amazed that he still saw the place like that. I didn't.

He turned back to me. 'It's something special isn't it. Right on our doorstep. And people think Hull is dull.'

'*Exactly*,' I said. 'And yeah, I'm lucky in that respect. Nice fresh air every day instead of being stuck in an office with crappy old windows that refuse to open.'

'I couldn't bear that,' he said. 'I've always loved the outdoors. I was a bit of a twitcher in my younger days.'

'Twitcher?' I asked, wondering if it had something to do with his shaky problem.

'Birdwatcher.'

'Oh. I've never really…'

'Can you name any of them?' He asked, focussing carefully on the last little bite of wafer cone before popping it into his mouth.

I took a moment… 'Robin. Pigeon…ooh, sparrow.'

'You've not been looking hard enough Emma. There's so many that you'll find in here.' He cocked his head and listened to the sound of the skies. 'Hear that?'

I listened hard. But I couldn't distinguish between the distant chatter, the traffic off the main road and the birdsong. 'I think so….' I said.

'That's a chiff chaff,' he said. 'Listen. Can you hear it….?'

We both stood there, listening for a sound.

'Ah I hear it,' I said. 'Like a cackle?'

'No... That's a magpie - completely different. Little scoundrels those magpies sometimes. Here, listen…' He stood stock still, eyes pointing towards the top of his own head, his yellowing finger in the air. 'Hear that. Chiff chaff chaff chiff chaff chaff chiff.'

I smiled. 'Oh yeah…I can hear it.'

'It's onomatopoeic.'

'Onomata-what?'

'It's named after the sound it makes.'

A vague memory of our English teacher entered my head. 'Oh yes…cool. What does it look like then? This…'

'Chiff Chaff.'

'Yes, Chiff Chaff. What a funny name.'

'It's a cute little warbler.'

'Bit like Kylie Minogue?'

'Eh?'

'Nothing.' I said quickly. I was ashamed of my poor, blatantly-not-feminist excuse for a joke. I must've got it from the pub or something. 'So, a twitcher. A Chiff Chaff. Never feed bread to ducks…I'll be a bird specialist in no time. David Bellamy eat your heart out.'

'You mean Bill Oddie, don't you?'

'Yes.'

He winked at me then took in a lungful of air. 'So, you don't need booze to enjoy what's on your doorstep.'

Where the fuck did that come from?

'God, Les. You sound like my dad.'

'He's a clever fella.'

'I like that. Clever fella.' I sighed, my face still gently smiling.

'I'll bring you a book of birds, so you can spot them.'

'You trying to turn me into a birdwatching geek.'

'Nowt geeky about birdwatching. There's this whole soap opera happening right in front of you, and you don't even know it. The pubs at closing are nowt compared to the drama in the skies.'

I raised an eyebrow. 'Really? What are they getting all dramatic about then? Worms?'

'Oh, there's so much goes on up there.' He said, looking towards the trees. 'They tell each other to fuck off, 'scuze my French, it's very territorial. Like West Side Story…but with gangs within gangs. Then there's the flirting. You'll often see two Mr's going after one Mrs. That can be entertaining. Then there's the real jeopardy, the real drama…'

'What's that?'

'When the babies fledge.'

'Fledge?'

'Oh yes' he said getting suddenly serious, 'it's when the parents kick them out of their nests, encourage them to fly, gain some independence.'

'Because they can fall, or break a wing?'

'It gets much, much worse than that. That cackle you heard.'

'The magpie?'

'Yep. Well, you don't want them around when you've baby blue tits fledging, I'll tell you that for nowt.'

I shuddered to think. Surrounded by beauty and all I could see was predatory cats and cackling magpies with feathers and blood and guts flying in every direction. 'Crikey. It all goes on up there then,' I said, trying to remain upbeat. 'I'll try keep my eyes open. See what I can spot.'

'Good on you. You'll get hooked, I'm telling you.' Then he wagged his finger at me 'Besides, it's better for the soul than getting pissed up down the pub.'

'Dad chat again Les,' I said, copying his finger wagging.

'Your dad a twitcher?'

'Ha-ha no. He loves the pub. I'm talking rubbish. But he'd love to say something like that if it didn't make him a huge hypocrite. I used to worry about how much he drank,' I said. 'I think he might have been depressed. For a long time, I think he was. But now he's got a woman…'

'He's woken up.'

'God yeah, tell me about it. Still manages to keep his monotone voice though. I think it stuck.'

'It's what habits do.'

'True.'

And as we carried on chatting, I realised that I'd gotten into the habit of lots of things. Just like my dad had become accustomed to being sad over the years, I had become accustomed to feeling angsty. And, in my never-ending mission to *not* feel angsty, I'd got trapped in a vicious cycle.

None of it was fun anymore. Having that first sip from the water bottle each morning *never* felt fun. It felt…like taking my daily meds. It was the only thing that made me feel normal enough to brave the world. It was the only thing that kept the tears and the racing heart and the anxiety at bay.

For a little bit, anyway.

CHAPTER 21

'So, what, you're singing? Like karaoke?'

'No Emma. Not like karaoke. Like a pro.'

'I didn't even know you could sing.'

'Of course, I can sing.'

'Well, I guess that's why they gave you a slot.'

Dor was filling me in on her news. The other week, when I first moved in, turned out she'd gone to audition for a support slot with some band at The Angel. Apparently, Bob had pulled some strings with someone he knew to get this band on as a warm-up prior to some big gig they were doing in town. And Dor, being Dor, had managed somehow to create a support act slot. Which she was more than happy to step into. I'd honestly never, in all the time I'd known her, heard Dor sing. Well, not properly anyway. But she never fails to surprise me.

'So what numbers are you going to do?'

'Well, I've got a little repertoire lined up. I'm going to do a bit of your sort of music too. I think the young 'uns'll like that. Thinking of a bit of Blur. Boys and Girls.'

'Girls and Boys.'

'Yeah, that one. And maybe some Tracey Chapman. I like her. But I might throw an Eartha Kitt number in too. Keep it real, you know.'

I couldn't tell if she was being serious or taking the piss. 'Sounds great,' I said. 'How did I not know you could sing though? I mean, are you going to be pulling rabbits out of hats or indulging us in a bit of stand up while you're at it?'

'You never know…I've been known to fire the odd ping pong ball.'

'Ugh, Dor, Please. Who's the band anyway? Anyone I'd have heard of…'

'Yeah, I think so. They're some band from down south. Can't remember their name, but they're from down south. Quite big I believe. They're playing at the ice arena tomorrow, see. Anyway, better get down there and set things up. You coming?'

It almost felt like a gift from the heavens. A huge distraction from an otherwise long, monotonous night ahead. It was only a Monday, but I had a bloody good reason to go out for the night. And I could hang out with family and friends, rather than propping up the bar with Hull's lonely souls.

'Why not,' I said full of cheer. 'I'll follow you down though. I'll bring Trev, give him a quick whizz round the park too. And I'll give Dave and me dad a call. See if they're up for it. None of us can miss this.'

'Good on you girl!' She slipped on her sparkly sandals and suddenly appeared to transform into a cross between Dorothy from the Wizard of Oz and Vivienne Westwood. She pursed her lips, reapplied her pink lippy then grabbed the door. 'OK, see you down there Emma love.'

I rang my dad.

'247398 hello.'

'Dad.'

'Oh, hi love.'

'Dor's singing. Down the Angel. We have to go watch.'

'Dor? Singing?'

'Yes Dad. Down the Angel. I know it's short notice, she's not given me any either. But shall I knock for you in say, half an hour.'

'OK, love.'

'Is um...Barbara coming?' I asked, feeling as though I should show willing but desperately hoping he'd take the hint and say no.

'Babs? No love. It's Monday.' He said it as if I should know why she wouldn't go out on a Monday.

'Monday?'

'Yeah, bingo. She always does bingo on a Monday. Big group of them.'

'You don't go?'

'You kidding? They're all women and, frankly, when those lot get together, they're terrifying.'

I laughed. 'OK well I'll call round in half an hour.'

'No don't worry love, I'll see you in there. I just want to grab a meat paste sandwich to keep me going.'

'OK.' I said, almost balking at the idea.

Of course, Dave wouldn't miss this for the world either. 'You what? Dor, singing? Jesus Christ. It's gonna be like watching Eartha Kitt or something isn't it.'

'Funny you should say that' I laughed. 'See you in there? Half an hour?'

I was relieved to have an excuse to get them both out. And secretly delighted they were coming alone. It would be just like old times.

I walked through the doors of the Angel, Trev in tow, and waved over to Bren and Bob who were both chatting to my dad from behind the bar. He was already perched on a stool, pint of bitter in one hand and a packet of peanuts laid out in front of him. A meat paste sarnie never satisfied anyone.

'Evening all!' I said, feeling chirpy as anything.

'Emma, love.' Bren said. 'What you having? On the house.'

'Aw thanks Bren. Pint of Stella please. And a bowl of water for this one.' I said, putting on a daft voice for my little lad.

'Coming up...'

'Cheers Bren.'

As I heaved my body up onto a bar stool, and Trev got ready to curl up around the foot of it, I noticed my dad's peanut packet was already balancing a puddle of beer in the middle of it. Maybe he wasn't on his first.

'So, who's this band from down South then? Dor said I'd know the…?'

'Eh?' Bren said, as she was placing a huge bowl of water and a chew stick at my feet. Trev went straight for the chew stick.

'The band, tonight?'

'Ohhhh no ha-ha. They're not from down south. Ha Dor must've misheard.'

'Oh.'

'No, they're from Hull.'

'Ah right.'

'It's the Beautiful South.'

'What the…noooo?' My jaw must've dropped all the way to the ale-drenched carpet.

Bren shook her head in mutual disbelief. 'I know. I couldn't believe it myself love. Bob was chatting to his mate, who has a mate, you know, in the music business. Heard they were playing at the Ice Arena and somehow, well, you know my Bob…'

He always did have the gift of the gab did Bob. He and me dad were good mates. In fact, Bob and Bren had been family friends since I was tiny. Since before I was even a concept. I guess that's why they felt entitled to limit my vodka intake. She babysat me a load of times when I was a kid, making me ice cream sodas and stuff. I guess they were bound to be protective.

Plus, it didn't hurt having the legendary Angel landlords on side. You certainly didn't mess with them.

'Go Bob!' I said. 'So, the *actual* Beautiful South are playing the Angel?'

'You what?' Dave had just arrived. 'Pint please Bren.' He nodded towards the beer taps

'Yeah, Dave. It's not a band from down south. it's the *actual* Beautiful South!'

'Yeah, good one Emma.'

'No, it is. Bren, tell him.'

'It's the Beautiful South Dave,' Bren said, filling a glass for him.

'No fucking way. I thought the guy I just walked past looked like…'

'Fuck, is Paul Heaton outside?'

'Well, they're hardly going to perform without him are they,' Bob laughed.

'Shit, Dave. This is big!'

'Oh my God. Is Jacqui Abbott here?' Dave's head was spinning around frantically like that one from the Exorcist. 'Love Jacqui Abbott.'

'Don't you go letching all over her now David,' Bren warned him.

'Oi, I won't. I mean, I respect her music Bren,' Dave retorted. 'How's things Tel?' He turned to my dad who had his mouth full of peanuts.

'Aye grand Dave. Grand, fella.' He continued munching.

'Nice one. I was wondering if you might be getting up and doing a turn too?'

I blurted out a laugh. 'Yeah, he could sing Amadeus. I always catch him singing that when he's in the kitchen,'

'Bloody good song that Emma. Don't take the piss. Very successful record that one.' My dad took things far too seriously. Or perhaps that was just part of his monotone that seemed destined to linger.

Me and Dave smiled at each other. And God it felt good. Me, Dave, me Dad, all together. All in good spirits. What a treat.

'I just can't believe the Beautiful South are playing. I just… can't believe The Beautiful South are playing,' I said, looking up to the ceiling as if the music gods were shining down on us all in the Angel, before being brought back down to earth with Trevor sloshing dog bowl water onto my jeans.

'I know. And in *here* too,' Dave chipped in.

'Watch it, David. There's nowt wrong with our pub,' Bren interjected, wagging a stern finger.

'Nah, I know that Bren. I just mean. Jesus Christ. The Beautiful South are playing.'

'Check check 1-2 1-2'.

'Ha-ha Dave look! Dors on the mic.'

This was fast becoming the most unimaginable, wonderful, and unbelievable night I'd ever had. There she stood, confident as you like, sparkly Mary Janes donning her feet, short hair curled tight with some kind of bohemian scarf styled into it and a velvet 40s style tea dress. She was a fucking delight was our Dor.

And then…. then Paul Heaton and Jacqui Abbott walked in.

We were in a daze. We'd never, *never* seen Beautiful South live. And now, we were going to watch them play in the bloody Angel. Of all places.

'Right then,' Dor said, expertly adjusting the mic to the right height. 'Who fancies a bit of Tracy Chapman.'

The slow, melodic intro to *Fast Cars* came on and I saw the rest of the band pile in and take their seats. Dor didn't have her own band. She was using the karaoke machine.

'I did wonder how she knew the words to Blur songs,' I whispered to Dave.

'She's doing some Blur?'

'Oh yeah. And some Eartha Kitt.'

'Eclectic.'

I looked over at the band. 'Don't they need, like, a backstage room or something?' I asked Bren.

'Nah. Proper down to earth this lot.'

'Does that mean we can go and chat to them, Bren?' Dave asked, not taking his eyes off the band, as starstruck as I'd ever seen him.

'No,' Bren said firmly.

Dave looked like a hurt puppy. But we did what Bren said. Always.

Then Dor got into full swing as the Tracy Chapman song climaxed. Me and Dave looked at each other, jaws still dropped. And that wasn't just in response to The Beautiful South drinking in the Angel…

'Fuck me. She's got some pipes on her,' I said, in awe of Dor's husky deep and smooth vocals. She was a good singer, a great singer. Well, she was in tune, anyway, but she did have an edge of…Eartha Kitt about her. 'Did you know Dave?'

'What, that she could sing? Nope. Had no idea.'

'Bren did you know?' I asked.

'Course,' Bren said, snapping a packet of peanuts off the cardboard crisp hanger behind the bar.

'Dad,' I said. 'Did you know?'

'Course love. Me and yer mum saw her play live back in the 70s.'

'Aw you two, we forget how young you are sometimes.' Bren chuckled.

'I'm just, I'm living with some kind of legend,' I said.

'Ah come on now,' Dad said. 'We've always known she was legendary. We were just never sure if she'd be remembered for something like this or getting nicked for flogging knock-off baccy.'

We all broke out in proud laughter.

After a questionable, jazz-style version of Girls and Boys by Blur, and a straight up cover of Real Gone Kid by Deacon Blue, Dor finished her fourth song - a bit of an about-turn with Eartha Kitt's 'This is My Life'. A strange choice, I thought, but superbly executed.

Then Oasis blasted through the jukebox.

I turned to Dave. 'Was that you lining up the Gallagher brothers for the interlude?'

'Aye,' Dave said, supping his pint looking rather pleased with himself as his favourite guitar riffs were belted out.

The band were getting their stage ready, and the buzz was gearing up.

'We're going to be part of music history. One day, this gig will be reported on all around the world.' I said, in a bewildered stupor. 'Like, this is one for the flamin' archives this.' It was like having them play in my living room.

Once cables had been plugged in, and guitars tinkered with, the full band took to the stage and, as Paul Heaton opened with *Song for Whoever*, the entire pub exploded in excitable, high octane, applause.

'See this, this is Hull at its best,' Dave yelled across to me and me dad.

'Well, technically….' Dad was about to bring the mood down I could tell… 'Technically, only about 50% of the band is from Hull.'

'Eh?'

'Only 50% of the band is from Hull.'

'Ah but Tel, they're Hull through 'n' through,' Dave said.

'If you say so. But I'm pretty sure there's some Manchester in there. They get all the best things do Manchester.'

Dave put on a wobble of his head and a bad Mancunian accent. 'What? Madchester?'

'Manchester.' My dad responded flatly.

'I know. We call it Madchester,' Dave said, showing off his vocabulary like a kid.

'Why?'

'Because… well it's because…oh…doesn't matter, Tel.'

Dad just picked his pint back up, sunk what was left and waved it at Bob who quickly took it off him for a refill. Bob had only just emerged from behind the bar, and we all had a sneaking suspicion he'd been hanging out 'with the band.' Probably making a dick of himself, but still, he bloody got them here so credit where credit's due.

I loved watching my dad and Dave, the pair of daft oafs, trying to connect through music. They never did. If there's one thing they could connect through, however, it was politics. But there was never a good time to bring politics up - most people knew that, but I don't think they ever got the memo, even tonight.

'What's the deal with Manchester anyway Tel?'

'Oh, please,' Bren said. 'Don't bring politics up.'

Dave looked baffled. 'Eh? I didn't.'

'Manchester gets bloody everything,' Bob said wincing and shaking his head.

'Too true,' My dad said.

'What do you mean everything?' Dave asked. I stood on his foot, desperately trying to get him to stop.

My dad's voice strengthened, as though he were giving a lecture 'Hull is forgotten. Even with Mr John Prescott himself in his seat. We are never…'

'Right, that's it. Zip it the two of you.' Bren stopped them in their tracks. 'I'm not having some kind of Question Time dragging on in the background while we've got the Beautiful South in.'

'Here, here,' I said.

Even when you're on the same side, even when you agree, you can't help but argue about politics. Especially when there's beer on draft. You're basically saying the same thing in two different ways and thinking you're arguing with each other.

Dad and Dave were bad enough, but Dad and Bob? I mean, have you ever heard of two almost fifty-year olds getting chucked out of the Question Time studio? Well, they managed it when Question Time came to Hull Uni. The berks.

But I did love how my dad and Dave bonded over stuff. And, more importantly, how they genuinely loved each other. Like father and son. He truly was like my big bro was Dave. Well, bigger in size, anyway. I loved him with all my big fat stupid heart. And for some reason, tonight, and after pissing him off so much recently, I remembered just how important he was to me. All of them. This eccentric little motley crew of mine in a corner of Hull. I loved the bones of them all.

The band played all the greatest hits, everyone in the pub knew them all. Every single one. We hollered along to *36D*, we took it in turns and added 80's style accompanying actions for *A Little Time* (I was particularly impressed with myself for coming up with the pointing-to-my watch action as the word 'time' was sang).

I shifted around uncomfortably at *Old Red Eyes is Back*. Bit close to the bone…

But all in all, the night was simply perfect. A reminder of who I really was and why this place, as inelegant as it was, as rough round the edges as we all were, was the perfect place to call home.

The Beautiful South united us all in the North. It was beautiful. Poetic. A coming together of hearts and minds.

Or maybe I was just drunk.

CHAPTER 22

I opened my eyes, and the dread was strangely absent. I smiled over at Trev who was in his usual spot at the bottom of my bed.

'Morning Trev.'

He lifted his head up, then put it back down. 'Not ready to get up then?' I smiled at the little sweetheart.

I was feeling content. I'd done it. I'd gone out and had a laugh. There was nothing terrible to reflect on. Nothing awful that I'd done. I had been a normal drinker on a normal night out and I bloody loved it. No fallouts, no cringey moments, nothing out of the ordinary anyway, and there were no pints poured on singer's heads.

God, imagine if I'd done that to Paul Heaton? Dave would have disowned me indefinitely.

I grabbed a drink from my water bottle and headed downstairs where I could hear Dor bustling around as I walked into the kitchen. I switched the kettle on.

'Fancy a brew, Dor?'

'Blimey Emma. Made me jump. What you doing up at this time?'

'Having a cuppa. Want one?'

'Go on then.'

I popped tea bags into two mugs and waited for the kettle to boil as I stared out of the kitchen window through to the back garden. The charred remnants of our little boyfriend bonfire had left the lawn scorched and black, but it seemed to do little to dampen the delights of Dor's urban cottage oasis.

'Do you do all this yourself then?'

'All what love?'

'The garden. It's practically Chelsea Flower Show out there.'

'Ah don't be fooled. Yes, I do it myself but it's fairly easy to be on trend when it comes to garden fashions. Chuck a load of seeds down, plant plants on top of one another and you end up with a beautiful chaos. Simple.'

I scanned the edges of the little garden. There were indeed ferns and big showy evergreens towering over cottage-style borders bursting with leaves and petals of every colour, shape, and size imaginable. 'So, you actually plan for it to look untidy then? I mean, untidy in a good way.'

'Yes love. Just like you young 'uns do with your clothes and your hair.'

'Fair point,' I giggled, looking down at my knackered old jeans and well-worn trainers. 'Yeah, it took a long time to get my Vans looking like this.'

'I'm sure it did.'

As the kettle boiled, I filled the two mugs, added sugar for me, none for Dor and allowed a tiny amount of milk to trickle in creating the perfect builder's brew that we both loved.

'Do you get many birds in the garden then?'

'Birds? Well lovey, you should know, given where your bedroom is positioned. Perhaps you should open your curtains more often? You're like a bloody teenager sometimes.'

'Yeah, yeah, yeah,' I said, smirking at her. I was in too good a mood today to overreact to anything.

'But yes, we do get birds. Not sure what birds. But there are a few kinds that flutter about the place. Different colours on them and that.'

'Chiffchaffs?'

'Chiffchaffs?'

'Yeah, you know. Cute little warblers that make the sound like, you know, like, they sing the sound that sounds like their name.'

'Onomatopoeic?'

'That's the one.' I said, pleased with myself, as if I had come out with the word myself.

'I don't know, Emma. I wouldn't know a Chiff Chaff if it pecked me on the backside.'

'I don't think they're renowned for doing that.'

She opened her eyes wide and wrinkled her forehead. 'Then there's no way I'd know what they were then,'

I laughed along with her.

Dor continued scanning her garden from the window. 'There are tonnes of them about. I guess having a couple of apple trees and a hedge out back makes them congregate here,' she said. 'Where's all this come from anyway? Never had you down as a twitcher…'

'I'm not. I know about Chiffchaffs is all. And I can spot a robin or a pigeon. That's the extent of my knowledge really.'

'Oh,' she said. 'Well, I would suggest getting some seeds for the garden, but you know…'

'Know what?'

'Rats.'

'Rats?'

'Yeah. Apparently, they like the bird seed.'

'Oh,' I said looking out across the gardens at the neighbour's bird feeders. 'That's a shame.'

My recent chat with Les still ringing in my ears (along with his impression of the little Chiff Chaff) and Dor's pretty cottage garden sprawling out right in front of my eyes, I was feeling sprightly. Kind of lighter on my toes.

'The problem is when you get damage or disease in the plants,' Dor said, looking back out of the window.

By this point I was in a world of my own. 'Eh?'

'See those two ferns, in the bed, there?' She said.

'The green one and the shrivelled one?' I asked. 'What are those weird things on the green one? They look like plant snails?'

She chuckled sweetly. 'I suppose they do. They're the fronds. New growth, basically. They'll unfurl soon and it will look bright and bushy as anything.'

'Might as well dig that scraggy brown one up don't you reckon?' I asked, nodding towards the second fern.

'No. There's some green still present. It's got life in it yet. I just need to manage the bad bits. Remove them before they take over and destroy the good parts of the plant. You have to do that with lots of evergreens. Sometimes the leaves turn bad and, if you don't remove them, collect all the dodgy leaf litter, it can really damage the core of the plant.'

'Right,' I said, wondering if she was hinting at me to tidy her garden up. 'Want me to do it?'

'Why not? Let's do it together at the weekend. Have a tidy up round the garden?'

'Sure.' I was right. I owed her some domestic help anyway. I wasn't exactly paying my way.

'It's rare anything's inherently bad.' She went on. 'You just need to stop the rot.'

'Dor, are you trying to say something, because it's all sounding a bit metaphorical. And not in a good way.'

'It is good, though. That's the point. You just need to stop the rotten stuff getting inside and eating you alive.'

'What are you on about?'

'You need to look after yourself Emma. You're a diamond. Really, you are.'

'But I don't understand where the lecture is coming from. I wasn't out of order last night? We had a right laugh. I didn't do anything…'

'I know. You were a dream. Back to your old self. And it was seeing that which made me think about you like this. Let yourself shine, love. All the bits of you, the good and the bad.'

'I do, I certainly do. In fact, you lot are always telling me when the bad bits come out.'

'They're not the bad bits of you, Emma. They're not you.'

I couldn't understand what she was getting at. I supped the last of my tea and took Trev for his morning walk, feeling buoyed at the fact I was up and about early, already a cup of tea down and feeling OK about myself.

It just didn't make sense to me. She was obviously talking about the booze, it seemed to be all anyone talked to me about these days. Even the Angel had instructions to monitor my drinks order. It really fucking irritated me If I'm honest. But the point was, I'd had a good night. We all had. I let myself shine last night. Whatever that means. And I'm up early today, ready for work. It just proves things - I can drink like everyone else. I can drink and not end up on the floor. It was fine, I was handling it. And having a laugh in the process. And why the hell not? I maybe just need to wean myself off slowly. To not have so much. Besides, it wasn't like it always made me drunk. It mainly just…. stopped the angst.

I took another swig from my water bottle.

As me and Trev completed our brief whirl around the block before heading back, my mind was trying to make sense of why last night was fine, and yet the other night… Was there something I drank that was different last night? Do I drink differently when my dads there? Maybe when I was at the Angel I was better behaved?

I was trying to find the answer so I could keep on drinking with everyone but do it more responsibly, more normally. Maybe things just all got a bit out of hand when John broke things off. Maybe it was just shock. That's it. Maybe emotional shock has an impact on how I handle alcohol. You know, like if your immune system is down, you can develop allergies and things that you never had before. And now, because I've had time to come to terms with things, I'm better with it? I can handle it again. I will not be breaking out in a rash or a pool of vomit.

I decided that this must indeed be the answer. And I felt satisfied with the conclusion I'd drawn. After I dropped

Trev back at home with a chew stick (which he proceeded to munch on Dor's lovely sofa, getting red bits of dog chew everywhere), I grabbed my bag, re-filled my water bottle, and headed into work. Even that felt good. I was working in the park with ice cream. Things were starting to get better bit by bit. John or no John.

Then I proved myself entirely wrong as I felt a pain radiating across my chest. I still pined for him. He wasn't some stupid teenage-style crush, he was the real deal.

I just didn't *deserve* the real deal.

I took another swig from my bottle, popped it back in my bag and opened up the little hut.

It was a gorgeous day; the birds were out in full force singing - or shouting at their tree neighbours to keep off their territory. But whatever the meaning, it sounded lovely. I paused for a moment to see if I could hear Les' little warblers, but I couldn't be sure, there was too much of a community tree chorus going on.

People were already starting to mill around on the park; a couple of joggers, a couple of mums with their pushchairs, kids that were meant to be in school but were obviously looking for a place to hang out unnoticed while they smoked Lambert & Butler and drank pop.

I took a deep breath and exhaled happily. I was feeling life today. I was noticing it all. I figured Dor was just being overprotective. But maybe I should be thankful for that?

Les appeared in the distance and I waved him over.

'How you doing today, Les? Not feeding the ducks?'

'God no, I can't feed them every day, they'll get too reliant. What if I pop me clogs?'

'Ha I can't see that,' I said. 'Same as usual then?'

'Thanks, and I'll try a bit of that monkey's blood you have on the top of it today.'

'You'll not regret it,' I said, as the ice cream made its way to the bottom of the cone. I wasn't really hungry, so I just filled the top part of mine and didn't really eat it all. I felt too nauseous. But I wanted Les to feel like this was a mutual thing, having an ice cream. I didn't want him to know I felt sorry for him. I didn't want him to think I was patronising him or anything.

He wasn't in his big coat today, but he did have a tatty old cardie on. 'Don't you get hot in this weather?' I asked.

'You wait, Emma. When you get to my age, you'll see that us oldies need the extra layers.'

I nodded, while nibbling the tiniest bit of wafer from the cone, desperate to drop the rest in the bin and be done with it.

'Besides,' He continued. 'Got a bit of a circulation problem.' He held out his hands which still looked ridiculously shaky. Maybe he wasn't drunk, just in need of a drink? That's how mine often look in a morning, so…

'They're very red,' I said.

'Raynaud's disease. My hands and feet sometimes look almost purple. Delightful, eh?'

'Ah,' I said, no idea what Raynaud's disease was.

'Anyway,' he said. 'Enough about me. What's new?'

'Oh God, nothing really. Nice chat about gardening with Dor this morning.'

'Dor?'

'Doreen. An older lady, a family friend. From The Angel. I'm lodging with her.'

'The Angel pub?'

'Yeah. My family have known them all there for years so, well, they're just like my second family. The landlady, landlord, all the regular punters. I can even name everyone one of the pushy sods that comes in flogging jeans or fish or meat or whatever.'

'Do they still do that?'

'They do at The Angel.'

He smiled, a nostalgic look in his eyes.

'Any wild nights out lately then?' He asked.

'I never have wild nights out. Not these days. I don't know what gave you that idea.' I winked at him. 'Although…we had a load of fun out last night. Dor was singing at The Angel; she was supporting this band she said. Anyway, you'll never guess who it actually was…'

I started to fill him in on the events of the night before.

'The Beautiful who?' He asked. He was as clueless as Dor when it came to modern pop music. But they were probably about the same age, he was definitely pushing his late 70s. Maybe they could be a match...?

Maybe not. I don't want everyone around me coupled up and cosy. God, being lonely couldn't half make you selfish.

'I guess the sad thing is that John's not here to share all this funny stuff with me anymore. I was used to getting in and telling him some story or other.'

'You still miss him?'

I nodded.

'Well, you never know.'

'Oh no, he was quite final about everything.'

Les cleared his throat. 'Well, the most important thing is looking after yourself now. You must find your happiness before you can share it with someone else.'

'How do you mean?'

'Just that. You need to find some love in that heart of yours for yourself.'

How could he know whether I had any love for myself or not, I thought. 'That's a tough ask at the minute,' I said.

'Why?'

'I …well, I just keep fucking up basically.'

'Fucking up? Like, as in you don't mean to.'

'Yeah.'

'But you don't *intend* to?'

'No.'

'Then give yourself a break in here.' He pointed to his chest, then pointed to his head. 'But sort it out up here'.

'How do you mean?'

'You'll figure it out. But you just need to stop punishing yourself.'

He was like some kind of philosophical oracle. Dor too, what with all the plant chatter. She was about as subtle as a brick at times. Honestly though, Les seemed sort of…. spiritual. In some of the stuff he said.

'Are you religious?' I asked.

'Me? God no. Why do you ask?'

'I don't know. Just some of the things you say. They're kind of…spiritual.'

'Well, there's a big difference between spirituality and religion. Hell, there's a big difference between faith and religion.'

'You reckon?'

'Sure. Religion is like the set of rules, faith is like the values, the beliefs.'

'That makes sense. I've never really been religious either.' I straightened up the precarious crisp boxes. 'Found myself in church a couple of years back, confessing all to a Catholic priest. My mum's side of the family were Catholic…so….'

'What prompted that then?'

'My best mate, Dave, he was unwell at the time. I was really worried about him. I guess it was like some kind of last-ditch attempt. You know, you practice all these ridiculous magical beliefs trying to control the world around you, and then, because something in you knows, deep down, that they won't work, you think, well, I'll give that God a crack.'

'Hmm. Many of us have been there more than once. How is your friend now?'

'He's good, recovered. It was cancer. But he's had his check-up recently. Went well by all accounts. I just, I felt responsible for some reason.'

'How could you possibly be responsible for your friend's cancer?'

'I know now how daft that was. I didn't then.'

'It's a control issue I think.'

I instantly recognised that. My life was all about controlling and balancing and planning. 'Are you calling me a control freak Les. Is that cos I spend so long perfecting your ice-creams.'

'No Emma, love. I think many of us have control issues. You remind me of me in a way.'

'Well, that's weird because everyone's always telling me I'm *out* of control.'

'You know what, I think it's the opposite. I think you're too pre-occupied with trying to control things, that you're forgetting what you should accept and let be.'

'How so?'

'Your friend's cancer. How did you try to control that?'

'Oh God. I borrowed a tonne of library books about cancer, tried to get him to eat better, tried to encourage us both to cut down on booze and the rest of it.'

'Well, to be fair, those are fairly sensible - depending on how thick you laid it all on.'

'I also decided that because he was 27, he was about to pop his clogs. You know, like all those rock stars? Like Kurt Cobain, Janis Joplin, they all died aged 27.'

'The 27 Club. Yes, my daughter once told me about that. Some media thing, I guess.'

'I became a bit obsessed by it a few years ago. Tried to force him to listen to pop music and stuff. Seems properly crazy now.'

'Well, we all look for reasons when we can't find satisfactory answers. When the world's a bit, you know, random, we try to attach a rationale to it. It's why conspiracy theorists exist. They don't like to believe there are things that are completely beyond their control.'

'I guess. Ha, yes, when I think back, I read up about all those rock stars, tried to find what we had in common with them, then tried to reverse it. Clean living, celibacy, blah blah blah.'

'Right.' He chuckled.

'I know, stupid,' I said, feeling myself blush.

'No, I've been there. You're a bit of a people pleaser too, like me. Like so many of us who struggle.'

'I'm not pleasing many of them at the moment.'

'Probably because you're trying too hard to control the very things you can't. Which is an impossible task. You'll get there. And eventually, you'll realise you don't need to make everyone happy all the time.'

'I hope so,' I said, in awe of his knowledge.

I glanced over and could see two of the mummies and their pushchairs making their way towards the hut.

'Shall we guess the order?' I said, excitedly. 'I reckon you can understand personalities through ice cream choices.

'OK we could try. But I bet sometimes people will surprise you.'

'Not these lot. OK, I'm going for, two bottles of mineral water and mini milks. You?'

'Hmmm…a Diet Coke, a bottle of water and two orange lollies.'

They walked over and placed their orders. I winked over at Les as half my order was correct. He winked back and we waited silently until the mummies had taken their change and were safely out of earshot. 'See Les. I told you I could tell. Maybe you *can* judge a book by its cover.'

'Perhaps that's only when there's no real story to be found in the book,' he laughed. 'Anyway, I'll take my daily stroll now. Catch you later Emma.'

'Catch you later.'

'Oh, nearly forgot.' He stopped in his tracks and was patting his cardigan, before pulling a little book out of his pocket and wobbling back towards me. 'Here you go.'

'The Observer's book of birds,' I said reading its title out loud and flicking through its tiny pages.

'You spot anything in the park, you can look it up, see if you can identify it. Girl, you'll be a twitcher soon.' He sang at me. I laughed.

'You wally,' I said. 'But thanks. I'll use this.'

The day dragged a little after Les had left. I loved having him around. I don't know what it was about him. He wasn't exactly the kind of friend I'd normally look forward to spending time with. He was old. Well, Dor was old, but Dor was Dor. Unique. But there was something both reassuring and fascinating about Les, too. Like, he wasn't judging me and like every line in his face was full of edge and grit. He'd lived a life, I could tell. How else would he have all that wisdom? He made me feel stronger with every word, and I don't even know why.

It was one thing serving ice creams galore in the sunshine, but it could get a bit tedious watching everyone around you laughing and enjoying themselves while you were stuck alone in a hut after the demand had died down. I put the radio on to keep my spirits up and took a swig from my water bottle. Well, I took a few swigs from my water bottle. It was so quiet for some reason today. There must've been something on in town or somewhere. And I just needed something to do. Something to distract me from being stuck in my own head. I didn't like it much in there at the best of times.

As the hours ticked with very little trade, I began to feel woozy. But then, as school bell time hit, the customers started to come in droves.

More mummies with their slightly older children dressed in school uniforms with hats. Seriously! With straw hats! I'd seen a couple of them around before so assumed we must have had a public school somewhere close by. Probably down one of the big avenues. I'd never noticed before, but these little hats were everywhere.

Then there were the other groups of parents, hanging out on the benches as their kids played on the grass, not a care in the world about squashing a straw hat or getting grass stains on starched trousers. Chasing each other around and squealing with delight.

There were the teenagers sharing cigarettes, holding them uncomfortably in their fingers, sharing each one as if it were a precious joint.

And then there were the student couples letting each other taste their respective ice creams, lying on the grass, looking up to the sunshine as if life was one big, beautiful fucking fairy tale.

It made me sick. Sick to my stomach.

All of a sudden, all these thoughts started whirring around my head. What if I had just…. what if I hadn't said…what if he didn't know…

What if things could have been different. Could me and John be lying on the grass, sharing ice-creams, looking up to the sun and clouds in the sky like some romantic movie scene?

I knew, deep down I knew, that this was down to me. And I knew more than anyone why. I knew I was drinking too much. Christ, I was standing in an ice cream hut drinking vodka from a water bottle while the world around me carried on happily, playfully in the sunshine. Why couldn't I carry on like that?

I was tainted now. I couldn't enjoy the innocence of the sunshine and the grass and the laughter. I already had it in me. More would make no difference. I needed more to stay normal, to function.

I grabbed my bag and rummaged around for the bottle. I'd drained it dry. Fuck. Then I noticed, I'd left a strip of zopiclone in there. I'd never taken zopiclone in the day before. At least, not while I was working or anything. But they didn't *really* send me to sleep, did they? They *helped* me sleep when I was desperate to sleep and half the time that didn't even work. They can't have been all that strong.

One thing they definitely *did* do, however, was calm me down. And with the frustration and resentment and anger that was inexplicably rising inside of me just cos two fucking students exchanged ice-creams and tongues, perhaps now was the time to have one. Just the one.

CHAPTER 23

'Sorry. What was it again?'

'Jesus Christ, are you drunk?'

'Excuse me? No, I just couldn't hear you. 99, was it?'

'No, it was a Diet 7 Up, and a Calippo.'

'Ah right, yep. Coming up.'

'Yeah, I think she's drunk…'

'What was that?'

'Well Jesus Christ you're serving children. Drunk.'

'I am *not* drunk.'

'I know. She clearly is….'

'Who are you talking to? Say it to my face.'

'Threatening me now?'

'How was that a threat?'

'Look, she's slurring.'

'You joining in now?'

'No need to get aggressive'

'Me? You're the ones…'

'She's clearly drunk. Shouldn't be serving kids like that.'

'For fuck's sake.'

'Oh right. Because language like that is highly appropriate in an ice cream van.'

'It's a hut. It's a fucking hut.'

'She can't help herself.'

'I'm going to complain.'

'Go on then. Complain to who?'

'Just leave it Susan. We don't want any trouble in front of the kids.'

'Yep, listen to her Susan. You don't want any trouble in front of the kids.'

'Fine, we're going. But we won't be coming back here.'

'Boo-fucking-hoo.'
'Right.'
'Bye then.'

CHAPTER 24

'Coo-ey. Emma! You in there?'

'Yeah.' I said something in response to someone, but I don't know why or who to. Everything felt slowed down. Was I dreaming still? I carefully sat up…my head was banging.

My eyes struggled to focus but soon I could see where I was. Shit. What was I doing in the hut? On the floor of the flamin' ice cream hut. My head felt like it had been invaded, like poison was pulsing through my temples.

I looked up. The shutters were closed. So, I must've known I was going to sleep, surely?

'Emma!'

I sat myself up. 'Who is it?'

'It's Dor.'

Then a second voice yelled. 'And Dave.'

'Oh. Right. Just a sec.'

I slowly stood up feeling confused and bleary. I must've fallen asleep after the lunchtime rush. Was it the lunchtime rush? Did anything happen after that? I had no idea.

I opened the door, the sun streaming in. I can't have been asleep that long - it was still light. But I was confused. And I wasn't expecting these two to turn up unannounced.

Dor walked in through the back door. I pointed towards the little chair, while I slumped back down on the floor, my knees up in front of me. I went to wrap my arms around my legs, mis-judged where they were and jerked forward. Why did everything seem so far away?

Then I watched Dave make his way inside. 'Cosy this for the three of us.' I murmured unimpressed.

'We were worried about you, you daft cow. What's happened here?' Dor asked, gesturing around herself.

'What do you mean? I obviously had a kip for a bit.'

'For a bit? You didn't come home last night.'

'But it's only, what…?' I peeked out of the shutter. 'The sun's still up, it can't be that late.'

'Emma.' Dave looked at me, a seriousness in his tone and his face. 'The sun's *just* come up. It's 7am.'

'What?' I felt a flush of panic wash over me as I tried to take it in. '7am?' A cocktail of panic and confusion jolted through me as I tried to work it all out in my head. 7am?

'Yes, love,' Dor said. 'You've obviously been here all night. Honestly Emma we've been worried sick. We even called John.'

All of a sudden, I felt my consciousness kick into full swing. 'Why the hell would you do that?' I snapped, trying to stand up but finding it too difficult. I wobbled like a weeble and came over faint. I tried to cover it up by sitting back down carefully before I collapsed.

She looked worried. 'Well why wouldn't you come home?'

'I, I don't know. I must've needed a kip, I told you. Besides, I'm a flamin' adult, not some kid with a curfew.'

'This is bullshit Emma.' Dave looked at me in a way he hadn't looked at me since…. well, since he told me he had testicular cancer all that time ago. He was always the joker. Always having a laugh. Not today.

Well. Not for a while, really. What the fuck was up with him.

'Well…well I've hardly done anything wild nodding off in the bloody ice-cream hut. It's hardly the stuff of...'

'Fuck's sake, Emma. You need to get a grip.'

'*You* need to get a grip, Dave. I'm a fully grown adult.'

'Yeah. Well act like one.' Dave stood up and stormed out.

I looked over at Doreen, her eyes fixed on me. No smile. No tenderness. I was still confused. I couldn't understand all the fuss. 'What have I done that's so terrible?'

'What did you have to drink yesterday, Emma?'

'Nothing I…'

She sighed, sounded exhausted. 'Stop the lies, Emma. Please! Just…just stop lying.' Her voice softened by the end of the sentence, but she looked seriously fed up. 'Vodka, was it? I know you've been keeping a water bottle under your bed.'

'Precisely.'

'You think I was born yesterday.'

'You think you can give me grief for drinking water.'

'Emma! This is fucking insulting.'

'OK. OK.' My breathing slowed. I was cornered. There was no way I could explain this other than to admit I had been drinking. Or something.

'OK I was feeling really stressed at work. The women in the queues were giving me grief. I felt a panic attack coming on. So, I took a zopiclone, that's all.'

'You've been on them for two years with no problem. I don't buy it. You were drinking too?'

'Ah Jeez Dor.'

'Admit it.'

'I haven't. You're just worrying. You lot worry too much.' I still felt slightly high. I knew I did because I wasn't feeling like the world was about to end. Not yet.

I knew the worst was yet to come.

Dor lurched forward, swiping the empty water bottle that lay by my feet. I tried to wrestle it off her, but I was too weak. She unscrewed the top and took a sniff.

'OK. OK.' I said, completely trapped. 'I had a small one. Big mistake, I know. I didn't realise that the two would have such a big effect on me.'

'You need help Emma. You'll kill yourself if you carry on like this.'

'Carry on like what. I'm hardly a flamin' drug addict.'

'Really?' Dor stood up and motioned for me to get up off the floor. My head was still banging, and I felt an acute sickness washing over me. But my stomach was empty. I couldn't remember the last time I ate anything. Other than half an ice-cream yesterday morning with Les. Yesterday morning. Jesus. That was yesterday morning? I was still struggling to get my head around it.

I stood up but couldn't steady myself. I grabbed the wall of the hut. 'Must be my blood pressure,' I said. Dor just looked at me.

'I'm just glad Dave was around,' she said. 'Not sure your dad could've handled seeing you like this.'

'You haven't told…'

'No! No, I haven't. He's finally back to some sort of normality. To some sort of, well, happiness might be a stretch but. He's Tel, again. He doesn't need this, Emma. It'll set him right back.'

I walked slowly out of the hut feeling more ashamed than ever. And desperate for a drink. I had no idea how I was going to get out of this situation in order to get my hands on one. Meanwhile, Dave went back into the hut.

'What's he…' I turned around; Dave didn't even look back at me.

'He's stepping in. You should be grateful.'

'Stepping in? For what?'

'For you, you useless twat,' Dave shouted from inside the hut.

Apparently, he was going to look after the ice-cream hut today. Or at least for half the day. Just enough to not raise eyebrows about it being shut, Dor said. He was due in to work his shift at 2pm so that's as long as it would stay open for. Early afternoon.

'I can take over at 1,' I offered.

'You're in no state, Emma.' Dor said. I noticed Dave poke his head outside, shooting me a look. His eyes were dark and his lips tight. I'd been getting these looks from too many of the people I loved recently. Dave, Dor.

John.

'I'll be right,' I said. 'Honestly. I just had a funny turn.'

'Bollocks.' Dave slammed the door behind him, and Dor held her hand out, beckoning me.

'Where we going?' I asked.

'Church.'

'What? I don't need God. Jesus Dor what the fuck.' Had she been talking to Les too? Did she know Les? Didn't I ask him about religion yesterday? Everything felt confusing, like I couldn't remember what was what, who was who, what happened when. It was like a grey tangled mass of pepper-potted wool. I didn't know where anything started or ended, or why I had fallen asleep on the floor.

She snatched my arm. 'No. You don't need God. You need a strong bloody shot of reality. We're off to a meeting.'

'Meeting for what?'

'12-step.'

'What?'

'You need help and, frankly, me and Dave are getting nowhere with you fast.'

'Oh Jesus - you don't mean like those bloody American things on the telly.'

'No. It's in Hull.'

'Same thing though isn't it. Oh, for fuck's sake. What you're expecting me to walk into some room and be all *Hello, my name's Emma, and I'm an alcoholic?*'

'Yes.'

I started laughing. I couldn't take it seriously. I was categorically *not* an alcoholic. I could go a day without a drink if I really wanted. I liked a laugh. Just look at the other night.

And I'm twenty-flamin'-eight!

I couldn't understand the fuss. The drama. The anger. They all seemed so, *so* angry with me. I hadn't hurt anyone; I hadn't embarrassed anyone. Nobody but Dor and Dave knew I had fallen asleep on the job. Christ, it's not as if

Dave's never done it. Cheeky shit used to always fall asleep on our nights out. Everyone laughed when his head was in a pizza or his arse on the floor. Nobody marched him off to flamin' church.

But the whole time I was having this argument with myself I had these solid doubts prodding and tugging at my guts. They kind of have a point. It was like a voice in the distance reminding me…

I'd lost John, my home, my job. And I just fell asleep on the floor of the ice-cream hut. I fell asleep on the job. But still…

'Church though, Dor?'

She continued marching me along out of the park with her. 'Yeah. It's not all God and stuff. Had a friend used to go. You'll be fine.'

Maybe it *was* time to face it. Or, in fact, more than anything, it could be my chance to prove them all wrong. To show them that I wasn't like those people. Like wobbly Les on the park bench. Like the guys that get so wasted they end up getting arrested on a night out. Like the skag addicts that live like zombies. I wasn't like them. Not in the slightest possible sense.

I liked a drink. It had got a bit out of hand. I'd had a hard time. Sure, let's do something about it. But I wasn't one of *them*. And the only thing going to this meeting was going to prove was exactly that.

'I'll only go one condition,' I said. 'We stop at the shop on the way.'

CHAPTER 25

Dave

Me and Emma used to play this daft zombie game when we were kids. Me, Emma, and the little kid that lived three doors down…I can't remember his name. Eric, Eddie, definitely started with an E…

Mikey! That's it!

Me and Emma would pretend we were zombies, eyes dead forward, bumping into things, bumping into Mikey, allowing a little bit of drool to appear from the corner of our mouths for special effect. You know how you can get over involved in your make-believe games as kids that it feels real? Ha-ha poor kid used to freak right out. Me and Emma lapped it up, we used to think we were hilarious.

I wish we could laugh like that again.

When I walked into that ice cream hut, it was like she wasn't inhabiting her own body. Everything was in slow motion. 'Cept for the hammering in my chest. Before she opened the door, I honestly thought…

But then it was like she was trying to prove to us that she was alright by attempting composure - trying to sit up straighter, trying to reach for a drink of water or trying to move a chair. But no matter how hard she tried, it looked as though there was a satellite delay between her brain and her body.

I know it's not just the booze. It doesn't get you like that. But with the booze as well, I mean, it's fucking dangerous, isn't it? Mixing shit like that? We've fucked around with stuff over the years, but I've not seen Em in that state before. I've not seen anyone look as out of body as that -

and I've seen some fucking states out the back of The Angel.

It's like her mind and body are completely disconnected, broken. And she doesn't seem to give a toss about either of them. It's fucking sad. Really fucking sad.

Dor's convinced one of these groups will sort her out, but I'm not sure. She might have lost control of her senses, but she's stubborn as fuck. The more we try to get her to do stuff, the less likely she is to stick it out or take it seriously. She doesn't think she's got a problem, at least she doesn't seem to. So why would she put a load of effort behind trying to get clean and sober?

How do we know when *we* should panic, anyway? I've always been proud of being a calming influence in states of emergency. I had to be when Emma struggled with all those panic attacks. But *I'm* seriously starting to panic now. If I take my usual, 'everything'll be alright' approach, what if I get it wrong? It's a fine line, isn't it? I know what she can handle, but I don't know what she's doing. After all those panic attacks the other year, she stayed off the coke. We both did. And I saw the change in her too. Back then, it was like she was spending the week holding all that angst in like a tightly coiled spring. Then she'd let herself really fucking go for it on a Friday night, like a slinky racing down the stairs, getting faster and faster until it lands in a screwed up, mangled fucking mess at the bottom. But she never seemed that tense anymore. And yet she was landing in that mangled mess on the floor far more than she ever did. And much earlier than expected too. Shit, it was like, barely 6pm that night we started the quiz with John and Ally when she nodded off. John did his usual, calmly scooping her up, ending the night early to put her to bed. Again. But you never saw it coming. I mean, we were used to it being a regular thing. But you couldn't tell when she was going to hit the deck cos one minute, she was fine, the next…

I'd see her with one or two beers, maybe, and that'd be it. Bam. Floored. It's what I *didn't* see that was obviously catapulting her there. It's not coke. I know that. It's different. Her mood's all over the shop but she kind of slows right down, drawling her words, her eyelids hanging like Droopy the cartoon dog. None of it is out in the open. I've no fucking idea what she's chucking down her neck. How could I possibly know if she's overdone it if all I'm witnessing is a couple of pints before knock out? I always felt kind of relieved when she was with John. He was a professional scooper-upperer. Through his work at the service, he knew what to look out for. The danger signs. The laboured breathing. The risks of inhaling puke. All that stuff - he knew exactly what to do. But I can't blame him for chucking her out. Living with that level of worry every day. I don't even know if she realised. I don't even know if she can comprehend why they split up.

I'm really, *really* fucking scared for her.

CHAPTER 26

Dor nudged me in through the church door.

'I thought you were coming with me?'

'Nope. No can do. I'll wait round the front for you. This isn't an open meeting. It's only you alcoholics can go in.'

'Seriously. I'm not…'

'You realise that you passed out with the door ajar, don't you? Any Tom, Dick or Harry could have come in and raped you.'

'Raped! Jesus Dor. Catastrophise why don't you.'

'You were alone, in the middle of the park, unconscious. Don't fucking minimise it. Go on. In you go. You're not coming back to mine until you give it a try.'

I walked in reluctantly after Dor stuck a couple of pounds in my hand. Apparently, I needed change. Perhaps we needed to buy orange squash? The one thing I did need to buy with it however I knew was unlikely to be on sale. She point blank refused to buy me anything bigger than a miniature on the way here. Fair play, I guess.

As soon as I walked through the door and could see people milling around, I had no idea what to do or what to expect. Like what happened now? Did I just take a seat in a circle and spill my guts out? God, I needed a drink more than ever right now.

'Hello there. Have you been to this meeting before?' An older lady in a cardie and a long skirt started fussing around me. Her voice was soft. She was the exact opposite of Dor.

'No. I mean, I've not been to any meeting before. Not sure why I'm here to be honest.' I was starting to come to terms with my surroundings, my reality. The fuzziness was easing up and that was the last thing I needed to happen.

Sharp edges were closing in.

'Of course, love. I'm Glenda.'

'Emma.' I held out my hand and instead of shaking it she squeezed it with both palms and a big smile.

'Welcome, Emma. Cup of tea?'

She led me over to this tiny little make-shift kitchen that was tucked away at the back of the church. We had to wind our way through some of the pews, with bibles carefully spaced out on each seat. The floor was wonky underneath my feet and the air damp. It was cold and, paradoxically, warming.

The kitchen was kind of old and tatty, with flat, white, 70s style cupboard doors and old carpet tiles on the floor. I could see a load of mix 'n' match mugs set out on the side, with tea, coffee and sugar clearly labelled in biro on scraps of paper sellotaped onto plastic tubs. Glenda dropped a teabag into a mug, pulling the boiling water down from the hot water dispenser attached to the wall.

'Here you go love. Grab yerself a biscuit and come take a seat. I'm chairing today.' I reached out to grab the mug, my hands shaking. I was sure she noticed it too.

Chairing? What was that about? It all sounded very formal against a backdrop of dark, dingy old church vibes. How the hell was this going to cheer me up? I walked over to the biscuit selection. Bourbons, rich tea, and sports biscuits. I grabbed one of each, to show willing - I guess I was starting to get a bit hungry now anyway. I still wasn't sure I could stomach anything though.

I sat down in an empty plastic grey seat. They were set out in a circle, and it all felt very…cliched. But I had to give it a go. I needed to report back to Dor, or I'd be sleeping in that bloody hut again tonight.

Glenda nipped over towards me. 'Here you go love, here's your new starter pack. See this sheet?' She pulled a blank form out of it. 'Pass this sheet around and all the ladies will pop their number on it for you.'

'Thanks.' I said, taking the pack, wondering why on earth I could possibly want all these people's numbers. I found the relevant paper and passed it onto the person next to me, feeling really uncomfortable about it all. But they were mostly all smiling. Why the fuck would you be this happy to be a useless addict? Not that they looked like useless addicts. Glenda could've been our Geography teacher. They passed my form on three times until it reached a woman who then scrabbled around in her bag for a pen and added her name and number. She smiled over at me.

'You don't need to look so worried. We're a friendly bunch. If we had more time, I'd have chatted to you more before.' Glenda said. 'But maybe we can catch up at the end of the meeting?'

'Right. Thanks.'

Soon, all the empty chairs were full, and the few latecomers were having to round up more seats from around the edges of the church. One even took a cushion from a church pew and sat on the floor.

'Hi there. Have we met before? Is this your first meeting?'

'Yeah. Hi. I'm Emma.'

'Steve. Nice to meet you.' He was wearing a suit, must've been in his late forties, early fifties maybe. I couldn't understand it. If this was a room full of alcoholics what was the problem? They were all as straight up as you could imagine. I was half expecting Cliff Richard to walk in.

I let my eyes make their way around the room and noticed a couple of people more in my age group. In fact, one looked much younger, she could have only been late teens, perhaps. The other, maybe my age or just a little older, looked like she'd come straight from work. High heels, smart trouser suit. All I could think about was having to say that line. To stand up and say, 'I'm Emma and I'm….' What even was I? What was I even doing here? This was crazy.

Glenda was conferring with a bloke sat to the side of her. He was a big fella with a friendly face, arms covered top to bottom in tattoos. I could see one crawling up his neck, too. They looked a funny couple, Glenda in her cardie with her bourbons and big menacing tattoo man.

'Right then.' Glenda cleared her throat and commanded the room's attention. For a sweet older lady, she wasn't especially shy! 'Welcome to the Friday 11.30 meeting at St Nick's.'

I was struggling to concentrate on what was being said as I was so distracted about how this was going to play out. Then somebody was asked to read from a book. So, I just sat trying to concentrate on it. Which was impossible. I felt sick and desperate.

They better not be testing us on what we heard, I thought.

There was all this talk of God and stuff. I guess that was to be expected in a church. Then Glenda announced that there would be a 'share.' With that, one of the young women I spotted at the start, the one in heels, started speaking. She opened with that line - my name's Sophie, *and I'm an alcoholic.*

God, it felt surreal. Like I was in some kind of American TV show or something. I guess it didn't help that my blood sugar levels had seriously plummeted and I could feel my heart fluttering. And given how quiet the room was as Sophie continued speaking, I felt convinced that everyone else could hear the clumsy dance taking place in my chest.

I listened attentively as Sophie talked about her mixed feelings as she approached her second 'birthday'. I guessed that was a clean and sober birthday. She talked about ditching some of her friends who weren't a good influence. How it helped her stay on track but how she missed her clubbing days. I let out a giggle when she said she could no longer dance to Josh Wink. How could anyone dance to Josh Wink? I'm not sure I was meant to say or laugh or respond or anything because I felt all eyes on me and immediately felt terrible for making light, but she looked over at me and smiled.

'You can't do Josh Wink unless you're in a higher state of consciousness am I right?'

I nodded. I realised that perhaps the others in the room hadn't spent a Friday night off their face trying to dance to Josh Wink's Higher State of Consciousness - the squeaking and shrieking synth sound that was a dance floor hit du jour for the wasted and wired.

She talked about how she was spending the weeks leading up to her 'birthday' arguing with herself. She was only 27, her friends had been in worse states than she had. *They* were all fine. Why shouldn't she go clubbing? Why shouldn't she have the odd pill and vodka chaser? Why the hell not?

She was so close, she said, and yet the tiniest little decision could change everything.

I wondered if she was maybe overreacting. Not being able to dance as well to the likes of Josh Wink or Underworld surely wasn't the be all and end all. She could go to a gig, instead maybe. Then she said something that made me realise I was way out of my depth with my naive early judgments…

'I don't want to end up back there. I can't. Next time, it'll kill me. I was lucky before. Three detoxes and a fit before I hit 25. I need to keep remembering.'

This was way beyond my league. Way beyond anything I'd ever experienced. We've all passed out, over done it, said, and done things we regret. But this….no, this wasn't for me.

But as she talked more about everyday life, something was trying to needle its way inside me. Like a little tot of familiarity. She continued: 'Those mornings you wake up and you don't know. You've no idea how you got there or what you'd been doing. You've no idea if you've really gone and pushed someone to the edge this time. And you bring it up. *Good night last night then, eh?* When what you really want to say is - *please tell me I didn't piss you all off again.*'

I suddenly felt I could relate to someone. Well, not *totally*, I mean, she'd obviously been in a worse place than I ever had. I'd never overdosed on anything or had to be detoxed. I could stop just like that if I wanted. In fact, I would prove it. So, we weren't the same, but I could understand the feelings she was describing. But we were both so young. I certainly wasn't ready to spend every night in with Dor, Trev, and an Ovaltine. Fuck's sake, even Dor wouldn't stand for that. What was the aim of coming to this place? Moderate? Or quit? None of my lot would contemplate a life beyond The Angel. No matter how much I pissed them off, they'd always respond by having a beer to chill the fuck out.

The young woman who shared came over to chat to me during the break.

'Hi, I'm Soph. First meeting?'

'Yes.' I said, wondering at this point if I had a huge sticker on my head that said I was a 12-step virgin. 'I'm Emma.'

'Nice to meet you. I added my name to your contact list, I think it's still doing the rounds.' She looked around us. 'Anyway, if you fancy a coffee sometime?'

'Yeah, sure.' I said, not believing for a second, I'd call up someone I barely knew to go for a coffee. I never 'went for a coffee'. Never mind with a stranger. She seemed pretty cool though.

'So, what's next?' I asked. 'I've been worried about having to say something.'

'Ah I know it's all a bit weird when you first come isn't it. Don't worry though - nobody expects a first timer to share. Just listen, that's all you need to do.'

'Phew.'

'Oh, and the God stuff. Are you religious?' She asked.

'I…' I didn't know what the right answer was, but she jumped in to save me from embarrassment.

'I'm not,' she said. 'These steps and all the chapters, they were written years ago. Sounds all very old school doesn't it. But I'm telling you, at least 70% of the room isn't religious. Just think of God as…. well, Josh Wink if you like.'

We both burst out laughing.

'Kurt Cobain?' I offered.

'Sure, if that's what floats your boat. Too grungy for me that one. Personally, I just hope he's getting a hair cut in heaven.'

'Oh God no.'

We both laughed. While we were the same kind of age, we were obviously of different tribal heritage - in a fashion and music sense. But regardless, we seemed to have a lot in common. Aside from the detox and fits of course.

'So, you must've been real sick then? I feel bad being here…. I've never…'

'Ah but you see, that's the point. You never think you're there 'til you've landed on the floor and crashed through to the basement. Mind you, you've decided to come here, so that's a good step. Maybe you'll never get there.'

I nodded, although I wasn't sure where or what 'there' really was.

Then the meeting was being called back and we all took our seats. More people spoke. People in their twenties to people in their seventies. Primly dressed schoolteachers, hard nuts with shaven heads covered in tats, softly spoken old fellas in cardigans, suits and ties and high heels. Every shape and size was here. And we all had one thing in common, too much of the bad stuff.

But still, I wasn't as far gone as these guys were.

CHAPTER 27

We pulled up to the car park by the beach. My favourite place. As my dad turned the engine off, I opened the door, Trev leaping out full of excitement, and swung my feet out onto the gravelly surface, breathing in the sea air.

'Ah, this was just what I needed today.'

'Yup.' He said, his face not reflecting the positivity I was hoping to inspire.

It was funny how things had changed. It wasn't that long ago me and my dad were here, finally talking about my mum after years of silence. Finally, being able to be honest with each other. For so long he'd not spoken about it, trying to protect me but, I guess, trying also to protect himself. In fact, I think he thought that if he could keep himself together that it'd help me too. I mean, I was just a kid when she had the affair. But in reality, it just sent him further down a big deep void of depression. Like a nothingness.

Meanwhile, I spent my late teens and early twenties living alongside some kind of high-octane anxiety disorder. That's what my therapist described it as anyway. I didn't even know they existed, I thought I was likely deficient in vitamins or something. I was determined to try eating more greens and topping up my iron levels before spilling my guts out to some counsellor.

Which just delayed the inevitable, really. I had to wonder if there was more to unpack, though.

As we walked along the beach, intermittently chucking a ball into the sea for Trev to show off his maximum speed and love of water, I noticed Dad was even quieter than normal. I mean, since the Barbara Carpenter whirlwind romance, he'd definitely perked up a bit - even though he remained a man of few words.

He'd started getting out more - and not just to the pub. He was always keen to take Trev out for walks and never turned down an invite for a backyard barbie. He'd found work again and his political discourse had become more passionate. Time was a great healer; a great way to get his mojo back. I just wish it hadn't taken him this long.

It took me a long time to warm to the idea of Barbara Carpenter being a part of his life. She was always…well, how shall I put it, kind of out there. You heard her coming before you saw her thanks to the loud jangle of jewellery and her booming 30-Regal-a-day laugh. Still, she seemed to make him happy, and she definitely had a heart of gold. But today, it was like he was lapsing into one of his depressive episodes or something.

'You OK, Dad?'

'Yup.'

'No come on, that's pretty much the only word you've said to me since we came out. What's up?'

I used to get worried when my dad was this quiet. Worried if his depression was coming back. Worried if he'd lost his job or something. And since he got together with Barbara, I became ridiculously over-protective of him. He couldn't face being cheated on again. It'd be the death of him.

My hackles flared - she better not have been…but just as my brain came up with fictional narratives of Barbara's indiscretions, I discovered that she wasn't the one sending him down this particular dark and gloomy rabbit hole.

'I've been worried about you Emma.'

'Me?'

'Yes.'

My heart sank. I thought I'd kept all the worry away from my dad. The drinking, the anxiety lapses…. but we were going to have to talk about it. There was no way out of it. He carried on walking, Trev returning the soggy ball and my dad scooping it up, chucking it back out to sea and wiping the sand and dog spit on his jeans. He looked ahead.

'Is it because I've been drinking too much?' I asked. 'Dor and Dave have been on my case too. But it's OK, you know. Because I've been to one of those meetings. I haven't had a drink since. Three days and nothing.'

'Three days? God, Emma. I knew you were drinking a lot, but I didn't realise it was every bleedin' day.' He looked me square in the eyes at this point and I could see the fear building up inside him, he was desperate for me to tell him it wasn't so. That this was all just a big over-reaction.

'Well. Not *every* day.' I lied, trying to get the conversation back on track and reassure him a little. And besides, I thought, I've just managed three days, I've just proved to myself that I don't have a problem. No fits, no delirium. Well, I did have to spend a good day and a half in bed, like, but…I guess that's the same as having a hangover. Without a hair of the dog. Thank fuck for zopiclone.

Dad turned his head forward and carried on walking. Everything I said seemed to be making things ten times worse judging by the furrows in his brow. 'And this thing with John, and work…' he said.

'I know. I know.' My heart plummeted, and I felt choked up momentarily. I was feeling confident about the not drinking thing, happy even. But losing John…it still made my chest ache for him every time I thought about it.

'It's a lot to lose in one go' he said.

'Rub it in why don't you.'

'This new job. The ice cream van.'

'Hut.'

'Is it helping?'

'Yeah, honestly Dad, I'm loving it. Who wouldn't enjoy serving ice cream to happy faces?'

He nodded.

'Anyway. These meetings, I've been to a couple now. They're not really for people like me, they're more for people who've got in real trouble, you know, liver problems and all that. But I think it's helping a bit anyway. And I guess it's good to get in there now, while everything really is OK. I just get a bit over-excited, I think. But I honestly don't fancy a drink and I'm feeling really confident about it. I can *totally* do it. I'm going to stop for a good time, months, maybe even a year, and reassess things then.'

'OK,' he said, sounding unsure.

'Honestly. You don't need to worry about me. I went through a bad patch. That's all. I'm coming out the other side now.'

'If you say so.'

We continued walking, momentarily in silence.

'I…um'. He stuttered. 'I saw John.'

My heart sped up. 'What? When? How is he? Is he OK?' The questions tumbled out of my mouth like curious vomit. I felt a strange mix of excitement and fear. Was he doing better now? Was he happier? Was he with another woman? I was desperate for my dad's response.

'Yeah, seemed OK.'

'Come on Dad, is that seriously all you're giving me?' I could feel my breath getting caught in my throat. I swallowed hard. 'Where did you see him? Who was he with?'

'Nobody. Just bumped into him in the newsagents. Had a chat.'

'What about?' I desperately wanted to ask if he had mentioned me, if he had missed me, but couldn't quite bring myself to.

'Just this and that. He was on his way to watch the footie. Had his sister staying with him.'

All I could think about was John and Jayney sat laughing, having fun. Joking about how he'd had a lucky escape.

Talking about the mess I'd made of the kitchen when I'd tried to bake him a cake. How I couldn't handle my drink. Oh God why did he have to tell me. My heart was in my mouth.

'Did he…did he sound OK?'

'Yeah.'

For fuck's sake. Why don't men know that when women ask that question, they don't want *that* answer. Why couldn't he just tell me he was unable to stop blubbing. That he'd made the worst mistake of his life letting me go. That he wanted me back. That life wasn't as much fun.

Why, why, why?

But I knew that was a leap too far. John wasn't thinking any of those things. He probably *was* better off. And if that's what he and Jayney had been talking about then, yeah, that made perfect sense. He wanted to settle down. I wanted to settle down. But I always wanted to settle down with a glass of wine or a vodka tonic. Or seven. Why wasn't he enough? I desperately *wanted* him to be enough.

'Anyway, it's all OK,' I said, feeling ridiculous and naive for even dreaming that John would want to rekindle something with Hull's answer to George bloody Best. Without the talent. Or the money. 'I'm totally cool about this whole not drinking thing. Some of the people at the meeting, they'd had fits and detoxes and stuff. I've just stopped. No need for any of that hospital stuff. I guess I realised before things got too bad.'

'That's good,' he said, but I could see doubt in his eyes as they drilled into me, searching for the truth.

'Honestly, Dad. I'm fine. You don't need to worry. I just needed a kick up the bum that's all. Business as usual from now on. Well, with a coke instead of a beer for a while…' I didn't tell him I was still taking zopiclone. I'm not sure he ever even knew. I kept most of my anxiety therapy and treatment from him, couldn't bear for him to even consider that he had some role to play as a single dad. The only thing he ever did was focus all his time and what little energy he had onto me, his only daughter. He was dying inside, but he kept me alive and kicking all on his own. He's a diamond is our Tel.

We carried on walking a bit further until we got to the usual landmark - a particularly spiky looking sand dune, and did our usual about turn, hollering for Trev who had seemingly found interest in a mangled-up concoction of seaweed and discarded plastic. I decided at that point to change the subject. 'Hull City doing well then?'

Finally, his eyes lit up.

CHAPTER 28

'But you and Dor told me to get back in the saddle, Dave.'

'Yeah, but not with Hula Hoop Paul.' Dave tapped his lap twice in quick succession to invite Trev up for a snuggle.

I'd taken Trev round to Dave's with me. We were having a brew - and I was telling him about my date. Of course, Hula Hoop Paul didn't call me like he said he was going to when I saw him at the job centre. He could never have called me - I've never given him my number. But when I bumped into him in the Angel car park the other night, I felt kind of sorry for him.

He was telling me about his new job. Except he didn't call it farmhand. He called it 'Rural Estates Management.' He seemed incredibly proud about it; said he had a lot of responsibility. I felt uncomfortable knowing his truth.

Dave, of course, was *not* impressed when I told him. John was practically the only bloke I ever dated that Dave actually liked. They drank pints together - even without me sometimes. We all went to gigs together. Liked similar bands. John could hold his own with my dad and Dave and their political banter. But then Dave met Ally and things kind of...well...settled, I guess. Less pub nights, less gigs, less banter.

Sure, Hula Hoop Paul wasn't perfect. He certainly wasn't boyfriend material. But I needed a distraction. And it had been like, six weeks since John broke it off with me. He wasn't going to come back.

I knew I was flirting with the idea of drinking again. Or taking something. It was like a big thrill - I was testing myself. There was jeopardy. Going out with someone like

Hula Hoop Paul would prove that I could either stay sober, or I'd end up having such a laugh anyway it would be worth it, and I wouldn't care. And he was bound to be more wasted than me.

Besides, at the end of the day, I'd done over a week sober by now.

I knew what the risk was. I knew I could wake up feeling like death after a big night. But I wanted to know whether it was my destiny to get shit-faced in company that would praise me for it rather than reprimand me? I'd know, wouldn't I? Whether this sobriety malarkey was really for me.

I argued my case. 'It's not as if I'm looking for a partner for life. I'm just trying to…have a bit of fun. Cheer myself up. I'm in my danger zone when I'm not happy. So, I'm trying to lighten things up a bit.'

'But you've been doing really well. He's the last person you want to be hanging out with. You'd never have even considered going out with him before – even when you were fucking pissed. I don't get it, you're sober.'

'He's not that bad,' I said, knowing exactly what he meant. There was a part of me that was enjoying the idea of going out with someone a bit 'dangerous.' Hula Hoop Paul wasn't exactly straight edge. He was known to knock out whatever chemical was proving popular on the dancefloors. And his idea of a good night out mostly involved some MC shouting '*come on come on come on*'. But we weren't teenagers. Our musical tribes didn't have to define us. Not anymore. I couldn't head into my thirties thinking I needed to find someone who wore the same trainers as me and liked the same gigs. Opposites attract, after all.

'Emma. I'm serious about this.'

I shot him a look. No way was Dave, all smug and loved up, telling me who I should and shouldn't go on a date with. He was in a privileged position. I, on the other hand, had been callously dumped.

'If you must go just…plan it carefully, OK?'

'What do you mean?'

'Well, you don't want to be ending up in some dodgy East Hull club OK.'

'Don't be daft. We're off out for a pub meal. 2 for a fiver. Might even get dessert.'

He didn't look convinced. The problem with Dave was that he knew me better than anyone. Better than me dad, better than John, better than Dor. He was my closest and dearest mate. And I think that was why he was a bit short tempered over the drinking thing. Me and Dave didn't dance around each other, we never sugar-coated stuff. But it was how we showed each other we cared. It was the easy route to just agree and not challenge or question. He got the third degree from me when he told me Ally was moving in part time. Well, it kind of turned into full time in the end, even though she kept her own flat. But he knew I wasn't keen. But it wasn't because she wasn't nice. It was because she was *too* nice. And kind of straight. And given where my head was at, I knew it would throw a spanner in the works with my drinking buddy.

'Look,' he said. 'I'm just worried. You did all that work - all that counselling and shit. I'm just worried about you going…I don't know…'

'Going what? Going on a date?'

'Going off the rails.'

'Seriously. You don't need to worry. I learnt a lot in those counselling sessions. Got all my mum-stuff out. I'm in a much better place today than I've ever been.'

'But that's my point. Don't throw it down the toilet.'

'As if,' I said. 'Besides, if the anxiety comes back, I've got the zopiclone. Doctor's orders. So, it's all good, all in hand.'

It wasn't enough to placate Dave. 'OK well look. Why don't I pick you up? Around ten. Then you'll know for sure that you can have a laugh, but that everything will be, OK?'

'Dave, no, you don't have to do that.'

'But I'd rather do that. Will help me sleep at night.'

'You're not me bloody dad.'

'Just trying to help.'

'Do you really think that making it absolutely clear that you don't trust me one jot to take care of myself is helping?' I spat. No way did I want him to pick me up. That would throw my fun little game of Russian Roulette out the window. That would be no fun. I'd be going out knowing for a fact that nothing was going to happen. What would that prove?

'Anyway,' I said, trying to lighten the mood. 'Let's play top fives,' he smiled. We hadn't played this for a while. It was nice being able to hang out with my best mate. Without his other half. Without him having to drag me home from the pub or out of the ice cream hut after a still very blurry day at work.

'OK. Top five…. British bands.'

'Easy,' I said. 'Well, Senseless Things are still my number one.'

'Even with Oasis on the scene?'

'You're not turning your back on our favourites, are you? Fucking traitor.'

'All right, well, so far so predictable. Give us the next four.'

'OK. Pulp has to be in there.'

'Ooh controversial.'

'Why?'

'Bit poppy for you wouldn't you say? The woman who still fancies herself as Courtney Love when she's had a bevvie too many.'

I laughed. 'Maybe. But I couldn't put Hole in here. They're American. Anyway, stop butting in. Three, Blur. Four, Happy Mondays. Five, Neds Atomic Dustbin.'

'Solid list.'

'Thanks. Yours?'

'Oasis.'

'So far so predictable' I said and gave him a wink, while Trev harrumphed on his lap trying to get a kip.

God it was nice, just hanging out, drinking cups of tea, munching on Malted Milks. Vinyl spread all over the floor. Me dropping biscuit crumbs on records, Dave telling me to be careful.

I'd missed this. And I wasn't sure if it was relationships or the fact I spent most of my time boozed up that was stopping us, but today was just perfect.

The thing was, I knew that today wasn't forever. Dave was moving on in life, his career, his girlfriend, his trips to B&Q rather than Hula Hoop Paul's place for a bit of hash of a weekend. Things were changing. And I had no idea how to move with the times.

I wasn't sure I wanted to.

CHAPTER 29

Dave

It was Geography O Level class. Emma was sat with Tammy Walters on the left, and I was in the back right hand corner with Keith Milton, open packets of pickled onion Monster Munch hidden in our laps from tuck shop. We were stuffing our faces instead of learning about arable farming or some shit.

I feel sorry for that Geography teacher, looking back. Fuck, we gave her some gyp! Hands clawed by arthritis, hair like Thatcher's and her crippling nervy presence gave us plenty of material. Kids can be such bastards can't they?

Zelda (as we so lovingly called the poor cow, after that evil character in the new Terrahawks TV show), yanked the squeaky revolving blackboard round. And there it was…

'Emma Barclay sucks cock!'

The whole class roared with laughter. I glanced up from my Monster Munch and looked over at Emma, who was already red as beetroot. Tammy was up out of her seat, heavy fringe hanging over her eyes, demanding to know *which knobhead wrote that shit*, while Emma was looking back over her shoulder, face like thunder, staring directly at the middle back row of desks inhabited by the likes of Hula Hoop Paul, Fraggle and Parky. '*The three pigs*' the girls used to call them.

'Like you'd know.' Emma hissed. 'Wouldn't go near you in a million years. Fucking prick.'

Zelda was furiously trying to scrub out the offensive chalk, dropping the blackboard rubber in blind panic, while Hula Hoop Paul started yelling something at Emma about deep throating and how she '*takes after her mam*.'

That was it. I was on top of him before he knew it. I had Hula Hoop Paul's face planted firmly down on the desk, while Zelda was frantically running to the door trying to flag down someone, anyone - another teacher, the cleaner, a sixth former, anyone - to come help her out of this teenage-hormone-fuelled hell.

'Take it back,' I ordered, ramming his head back onto the desk, harder this time, the side of his face pushed tight against the surface, spit drooling from his squashed-up gob as he continued gobbing off.

Emma could look after herself, but slag jokes about her mother? No fucking way was I having that.

'Fuck off, David,' he said, mockingly. I tightened my grip, pushed his head hard into the desk again. The whole class was cheering us on.

'David! Now, look Paul. Please. Stop!' Zelda was beside herself. The rest of the class meanwhile looked as though they'd just taken front row seats at a Big Daddy wrestling match. The energy levels were through the roof. Emma was out of her seat with Tammy at her side. 'You fucking tosser Paul' one, or both of them, were yelling, I couldn't tell in the mayhem.

Then there was that unmistakable, booming sound.

'David Chapman. Paul Townsend. My office. NOW!'

Fuck. It was Billingham. The Head. He was a right evil cunt.

I let go of Hula Hoop Paul's scrawny head and sank my trainers back onto the floor, crunching the Monster Munch that had somehow ended up down there.

We were marched immediately to Billingham's office.

That was a shit day. It wasn't particularly special getting into a scrap, it was school after all. And we were teenagers. Most days there was a fight. But my week-long after school detention paled into insignificance when I saw how upset Emma was later on.

She hadn't had her mum at home since she was eight years old. She'd got with some fella. Some prick from East Hull. And it might have been years back, but Emma never got over it. Neither did Tel, not for a long time.

So yeah, 'Emma Barclay sucks cock'. She could handle that. Everyone got some sort of flack in fifth year. But talking about her mum? Not fucking on.

Hula Hoop Paul never apologised. And Emma never forgave him. Not in all these years.

So, this date she says she's going on with him. Well, it's really fucking baffling if I'm honest.

CHAPTER 30

I was behind the counter, stocking up the Chupa Chups when I saw them. The two mummies and their pushchairs from the other week. I was mortified. I had no idea what had happened after that. Had they seen me collapse? Had anyone else? Had I said anything else? I could barely remember what I'd said to them, I just knew there was something to be ashamed of. And probably to apologise for.

But I couldn't bring myself to do it. What if there was a chance it was all in my head?

They didn't come over. I was obviously now some sort of mummy repellent. But they we definitely staring across at me. I might be stone cold sober today, but there was probably more of this shit in my closet of drunken doom that was due to catch up with me. Is this what life was going to be like now? Facing every bit of pain and every drunken mistake without a comfort blanket?

'Morning Emma.' Les' voice jolted me out of my pathetic self-pity.

'Morning Les. So good to see a happy face,' I said.

'Been getting grief off someone?'

'Those bloody snooty mums with their pushchairs.' I nodded over to where they were standing, their kids eating chocolate bars because they obviously knew they weren't going to buy ice cream from the drunk girl in the hut today.

'Ah.'

'Let me get your ice cream.' I said and began filling a cone solidly with Mr Whippy. 'Here you go.' I handed it to him and got myself one. I decided to have the same today, rather than only filling the top of mine. I was craving a sugar boost.

'So, what you up to today?' I asked him.

'Oh, just enjoying the sunshine for a bit. Then I'm off food shopping.'

I smiled at him. I wondered if he was *really* going food shopping or if he was having to scour the supermarket skips. He was looking particularly wobbly today as he stood with me. It was always strange, he wobbled like a drunk, but he didn't talk like one. I couldn't work it out.

'What about you? What have you been up to?' He asked. I wondered whether to tell him. There was something about Les that made him so easy to talk to. So, I just came out with it.

'I've been to one of those meetings, Les. I'm having a go at being a teetotaller.'

'Oh. Why's that then?' He didn't ask what I meant by meeting, weirdly. But thankfully that meant I didn't have to explain too much.

'Dor, my landlady, and Dave, my best mate. They're convinced I drink too much.'

'And what do you think?'

'Maybe…a bit. A bit of a break won't hurt, anyway,' I said. 'It's good for us all to have a detox sometimes I guess.' I said, furiously consuming the sugar laden ice-cream I'd made myself. If there was one thing for sure since I'd stopped drinking, I'd been helping myself to more and more sweets and ice creams in the hut.

I was desperate to ask him about whether he drank but I wasn't sure if I should. He didn't seem uncomfortable talking about the topic though.

'So, this meeting,' he said. 'Any good?'

Ah, perhaps he was considering getting along to one. Maybe with my newfound experience under my belt I could actually be of help, rather than being a constant drain on everyone. A hindrance. I knew people were fast losing patience with me.

'Yeah, I guess. I've been to a couple now. Well, three to be exact. They reckon I should go every day, but I really don't think I need to go that much! So, I'm just trying it out, seeing how it helps. I'm not as far gone as most of the guys there.' I said, feeling pleased with myself for not being as bad as them after all. 'They've all had detoxes and fits and hospitalisation and all sorts. One even landed in prison from drink driving. Although I'm not supposed to mention anything we talk about so best stop before I go too far.' I said remembering the code of conduct, so-called yellow card, and anonymity stuff.

'But it's helping?'

'Yeah. I mean, I've quit drinking. Wasn't too difficult to be honest. I think lots of them have all these physical dependency problems. Like, with me, I just *wanted* to drink, I didn't *need* to, so…'

'Hmm….' He said, looking at his ice cream carefully. I couldn't decide whether his 'hmm' was in response to what I was saying or how I'd made his ice cream.

'Anyway, I've got a date tonight.'

'Tonight? Well, that's good going. Hope he's worthy of you. You deserve a good 'un.

I bit my lip, knowing full well what I was doing tonight. I knew I was skirting on the edge of danger. I knew that my date would more than likely celebrate it if I did fall foul of the vodka. If I puked on his shoes, he'd probably applaud me for getting so off it.

Shit. What the fuck was I thinking? Hula Hoop flamin' Paul!

There was something in what Les said that made me ponder. Was my date worthy of me? It was a question I couldn't really answer. Months ago, I'd have said no way! Of course not. He was like a caricature. Like some low-level dodgy drug dealer off some silly TV show that we'd poke fun at. But now…well, there was no way I was going to hang onto someone normal. Someone lovely. Maybe I thought he'd feel lucky being with me? I don't know. It made me feel guilty, in a way, using him like this.

But, given who I'd become, perhaps Hula Hoop Paul *was* worthy of me. Perhaps I needed to just accept that inflicting my antics on nice blokes like John was just selfish. I was finding my level.

Les was becoming more and more like a granddad figure. He reminded me a bit of my actual granddad, in fact, but he seemed a bit more worldly wise. And cultured. It made me wonder what he used to do before he ended up living on the park.

'Anyway, while it's quiet,' I said. 'You must have some tales? What has life thrown at you? What did you used to do? I bet you've got some stories.'

'Well, in another life I was a teacher.'

'What? Really?'

'Yep. For my sins. Taught at Sir Henry Cooper School for most of my career.'

'Ouch. Tough school. Did you get grief?'

'Ah a little. But all schools are the same. I loved the kids there, though. It had a terrible reputation. Lots of poverty round there on the estate. But the kids, they were just kids. They just needed a chance. Some did really well you know.'

'Going to uni and stuff?'

'Yes, but we also produced a couple of superstars! I taught a couple of lads who went on to form the Housemartins band. Lovely lads they were.'

'No way! Oh my God, but that's what I was telling you about the other day. They're in the Beautiful South now. They're huge.'

'Oh really? That's good to hear. I wasn't sure if they'd split up.'

'No, definitely not. They're even bigger than the Housemartins. I'll bring one of their CDs into work. I've got one at home. Really good.'

'Oh, that'd be nice Emma.'

I nodded. 'Ooh, Les. I've been using that little book.' I picked his book of birds up and started looking for the page with the folded corner. 'Look, see here?' I said.

He craned his neck to see. 'The Long-tailed tit?'

'Yes, I definitely saw one. I think there were a few. Over there.' I pointed towards the trees and hedging that lined the path that cut through to the main road. 'They're like little pink pom-poms with long tails!'

'They are indeed. Little fluff balls, aren't they?' He chuckled.

'Yeah. Honestly, I was dead proud of myself. Although, I think given the length of the tail, and the name, it wasn't going to be difficult to identify them.'

'But you had to spot them first, that's the best bit. Shows you've got your eyes open, eh?'

'Yeah.'

'You should keep your eyes peeled for their nest. They make lovely little nests. Line them with feathers.'

'Sounds plush!'

'Indeed. Takes them around three weeks to build but I reckon they probably have the cosiest nests of all the birds.'

'Three weeks? To build a nest?'

'Yeah. Takes a lot of work, you know.'

'Do they pluck their own feathers out?'

'No. That wouldn't do. They'd not be strong enough to look after the chicks if they compromised themselves too much. No, they'll find the odd feather here and there, collect them off dead birds.'

'Sounds grim,' I said.

Les laughed. 'Nature is harsh. But you really weren't expecting birds to carry out funeral services now were you.'

'You're funny,' I laughed. 'Oh God.' As I looked beyond Les I felt a palpitation shooting up to my throat like a fairground strength tester. There he was. I hadn't seen him since that awful day. It knocked me sideways.

'What is it, Emma?'

I felt my throat tighten up as though I could be sick at any moment.

'It's John. My ex. Oh God.'

'It's OK. I'll leave you to it.'

'No, don't. I mean. Yes. I don't know. I can't think.'

'Why don't I just sit over there and chat to the ducks. I can catch up later if you need to talk.'

'OK.' I said, barely taking in a word he said, my eyes flicking between my compulsion to stare at John and my self-awareness of looking anywhere but, trying to prove that his gorgeous, beautiful, cosy appearance hadn't really got to me.

I'd well and truly fucked *our* little love nest up, hadn't I?

As John was getting closer and closer, my heart was racing faster and faster. All of a sudden, I felt like I might pee my pants, too. Why was my body threatening to expel all manner of gross liquids just as I was about to see the love of my life for the first time in two months?

I wiped my brow, which was starting to feel sticky, but not just from the sunshine that was streaming in from behind the trees. I had nervous sweat pouring out all over my body. Ugh.

I was trying hard to make myself look busy, but I found it difficult to know what to do, as if I'd forgotten all the things that needed doing in the hut. He was walking straight towards me. He was obviously coming to see me. What could he want? Does he want me back? Does he want to tell me that he's got a new girlfriend? To never call him again.

Oh God oh God oh God.

I shifted things about uncomfortably, re-organising lollies and chocolate bars that didn't need re-organising. When he was close enough that I could no longer ignore it, I looked up at him and smiled.

He smiled back. His dark brown eyes squinting slightly in the sun, furrowing his brow which made him look even hotter. God, I fancied him

'Hi Emma.'

'Hi.'

I had no idea why he was here or how he even knew.

'Your dad said you had a job here.'

Aha. 'Yeah, he said he saw you.'

'He seemed good. Not taking porn out on your video card any more then?'

'Ha-ha.' I laughed a little too much. Nervous giggles forcing their way out. 'No, he's still with Barbara so no need for any of that. Couple of the century apparently.'

What made everything even more weird and sentimental about seeing him here was the fact that we first met right here on this park. Almost two and a half years ago. The spot where we met was in sight. All those happy memories from when my whippet and his Afghan Hound became embroiled in coital lock after a sniff of the bums went too far. It was love at first sight for them. And for us too.

I tried not to picture us both there. I was sure I'd end up sobbing.

'How's Trev?' He asked.

'Yeah, he's good. Missing you and Dixie.' I said, instantly regretting it.

There was an awkward silence that seemed to last forever. I looked over towards the ducks, as if they'd give me some kind of wisdom. Tell me what to say. But all they were doing, of course, was quacking.

John broke the silence first. 'So, I just wanted to say hi. See how you were doing?'

Then I remembered something about Dor calling him the other night when I didn't come home. Oh God why did she have to do that. Shit, does he know I passed out in the hut?

'Yeah, I'm good.' I said, wishing he'd just tell me it was all a big mistake. He'd walk into the ice cream hut, grab me, and the You and Me Song would play, and we'd kiss and then snog and then there would be birds and wedding bells and…

'Dor said you were missing the other night. I was worried.'

'Well, you don't need to be,' I said, instantly regretting

my impatient tone. He just looked at me, directly into my eyes with his. The sadness I saw in them made me ache so so much. I swallowed hard. 'I didn't mean…'

'I know,' he said. 'You look well, though.'

'Thanks,' I said. 'Want an ice cream?'

'Sure.'

Then I realised I had no idea what his favourite was. We must've eaten ice creams together. We were together for over two years. That's two summers. Did we never come to this ice cream hut together?

'What'll it be? On the house.'

'Um…let me think…'

I felt a familiar warmth wash over me. Like the Ready Brek aura radiating around me. I remembered now. I remembered that the reason I couldn't recall his favourite ice cream was because he didn't have one. He always spent ages choosing a chocolate bar or ice cream. He loved the variety. He sometimes asked me to get him a surprise.

He studied the menu carefully.

'A feast.'

'Coming up.'

'No, sorry. A strawberry Cornetto.'

'You sure?' I smiled as he was still studying the menu carefully.

'Yes,' he said. 'Erm…no, yes. A strawberry cornetto. Thanks' He finally took his eyes off the menu and caught mine instead. I felt myself flush as his brown eyes pierced my facade, so I dived into the freezer to grab his ice cream and throw him off the scent of me pining.

'You enjoying it here?' He asked.

'Yeah. I do like it actually. I was…well, Shaw's…they…' I started to tell him about getting the sack but felt so ashamed. Then I realised that, to be fair, I'd always been getting into bother in that job. I was always late. Had always been the same since before I met John. He couldn't be shocked at my getting sacked.

'Your dad said.'

My bloody dad was good at telling boyfriends - sorry, exes - too much information. Ironic given the fact he was a man of few words. First time he met John, he told him about me 'hurting my fairy falling off the climbing frame.' Fuck's sake.

'Oh. Yeah, well, I…'

'Must be good for people watching?' He looked around the park and I noticed how lovely his neck looked, all tanned and gorgeous. In comparison to me, he was the epitome of health. He turned back to face me.

'Yeah. You get the uppity mummies, cosy student couples, the teens on energy drinks - and the whiff of hash floating through the air like Bisto bloody gravy,' I laughed. 'I honestly don't know how they think nobody'll notice. They point their bikes into a circle and the smoke comes up into the air in the middle. Looks like Vesuvius is going to blow.'

He smiled hard, drawing lines in the outer edges of his sparkling eyes and then, almost as abruptly, his smile relaxed away into a straight line.

'Anyway. I've gotta go.' He said, backing away. 'I just wanted to know you were OK.'

My heart sank. I wanted to stop him. To say something. To ask him, was he sure? Did he have no regrets? Could we not try again? But I couldn't say a word. I just felt dumb struck.

''K,' I said, struggling to keep the lump from my throat pushing my tears out into the fresh air.

He continued looking at me for what felt like an eternity but was probably about 1.5 seconds. He smiled, nodded slightly, and then he was gone.

I stood glued to the spot. My eyes pooling with water. My breath turning to a forced, random, shiver.

'Two Fanta's please!'

I took a deep breath, sniffed, and tried to shake off the overwhelming feeling that a drink might be nice right now.

CHAPTER 31

Dor slammed the cupboard shut and stared hard at me. 'You're going out with who?'

'I know, I know. But he's a nice guy, really. Good-hearted. I mean, I'm not looking to get married or anything. It's just a date.'

'A two for a fiver pub meal. You deserve better than that. Don't tell Dave he'll be fuming.'

'I've already told him.'

'And.'

'He was.... OK about it,' I lied.

'Hmm.'

I was getting ready for the pub. I'd been to a meeting, as I had promised Dave, to prep myself for being in the pub for the first time since I stopped drinking. The thing was, though, I was going for scampi and chips not a whiskey and a line of coke from some mucky toilet cistern. Those days were well and truly behind me.

We were meeting at the pub up the road that did the two for a fiver meal deal. I walked along, past the garage and the little takeaway then through the hedged pub car park. Feeling a familiar light go on inside me I walked in through the swing doors at the front of the pub. I was wearing jeans, a vest top...not my best, and a pair of Vans. Maybe I was holding back a bit. It was that contradictory voice that was racing around in my head. Go...but don't dress up for him. Go...but don't get drunk.

Go...and you might find that you don't have a drink problem at all, and you can just have a laugh because that's what under 30s are meant to be doing before everything gets serious. Christ, even Hula Hoop Paul would probably be working in an office in a shirt and tie when he hit thirty. We were meant to have fun. Life got too serious too quickly. I was behind, I knew I was behind, but everyone else was just too bloody eager to settle down and become National Trust members.

In all honesty, my heart wasn't really in this date. Not the date part, anyway. I just felt that it was something I *should* do. To move on. To get closure on the past. Perhaps it would help? Like that boyfriend bonfire thing.

'Hi Emma.'

'Hi Paul.'

He was clad in another Burberry top, different to the one he was wearing in the job centre but it still kind of felt like this must be his 'uniform'.

There was a brief moment of awkwardness. I'd known him for years, but now we were on a date the dynamic was completely different. He kissed me on the cheek, his aftershave even stronger than it was before, and he seemed to blush a little. It was weird seeing these glimpses of vulnerability in a bloke who's infamous for criminal activity. I felt oddly empowered.

'I'll get them in. Pint, is it?'

'No, I'll have a coke, please.'

'Sure?'

'Yeah.' He started to walk away with a look of disappointment on his face. 'Actually, no...' The words came out before I could even think about what I was saying. 'I'll have a pint. Thanks.' I smiled. And I thought, why not? Even kids can have an alcoholic drink with a meal. It would be like having a shandy.

'Want to grab a seat and I'll bring them over?'

'Sure.'

I found a seat by the window. It was in the smoking area. At least I could nab some of his ciggies if I felt awkward. Give me something to do.

I was wondering if I'd fucked up by getting a drink. But

it was a beer, not a vodka. And I decided that I couldn't entertain that thought anyway - it was too late now. He'd already spent the money. And if I didn't drink it, well, that would look ungrateful. So, I'd just have the one. And I'd order a huge tea - to make up for it.

He brought the drinks over.

'Cheers.'

'Cheers.' I took a sip and immediately felt quenched. Fuck, I'd missed this. Fuck, this was good. My thirst had vanished in a split second, and the anticipation of more energised me. I didn't feel bad in the slightest. There was really no problem here.

Part of me felt relieved that he didn't know about those bloody meetings and Dave and Dor's lectures. Tonight, I could just be me. I could do what I wanted. I was free. I picked the pint glass up for a second mouthful almost as soon as I'd placed it back on the beer mat. It was like a refreshing, fizzy, honey hitting my throat and awakening my brain cells which seemed to go off like fireworks. I couldn't get enough of it. Half a pint vanished almost as soon as I put it to my mouth.

'Did I tell you 'bout that time me and the lads were high on Billy? Speedin' our tits off we were, down the Marina…'

Oh, God, I thought. *I hope nobody can hear. This is gonna be well embarrassing…*

'…and this pig, like, comes up to us, and, honest to God, he said, *got any narbis*? And we're like, what the fuck? And he goes, *got any narbis*? And we're like, what the fuck is narbis, and he's like, cannabis, lads, you got cannabis on you. And we're just pissin' ourselves at this young copper fresh outta nappies tryin' proper 'ard to talk to us like he's on our level, you know, and then he goes all red, and like, gets angry cos we're all laughing, so he ses, *'ere, you're all gonna get searched*' and we're like, whatever. All the while, I'm tryin' to get Stevo to take the hint to somehow - discreetly like - throw the bag of whizz in the water, stupid bastard hasn't a clue what I'm on about so just stands there. So, this copper, well he goes to search us all. An' he finds a bag of whizz on Stevo. Fuck's sake. I'm like, this is bad, man. An' then, he searches me, but finds nowt, cos I'm not stupid like Emma, I've got mine in me kegs, an' he's not goin' in there, so then he moves onto Duckie an' he only goes n finds a fifty in his pocket. An' he's like, *what's all this then*, ha-ha, an' Duckie, he's quick on his feet is Duckie, an so he goes, 'nowt, mate. Done a car boot sale with me missus. An' he's nearly off the hook, and then he checks his other pocket just to be safe…'

Oh God…. has he finished yet? I need another drink…

'An' d'ya know what he finds? Seriously Emma. It's fucking gold, it is. A fucking signed fucking note, sayin' 'ere's fifty for the gear, Duckie. Fuuuuuck me. It was fuckin' signed. Honest to God I was like….'

I tuned out. It went on and on. I giggled occasionally when I thought he expected it. But then realised the only way to survive this excruciating ordeal was to get another round in. Besides, it was only fair. I really wasn't sure being on a date with Hula Hoop Paul was my cup of tea. I couldn't lead him on. It would be wrong of me. So, it'd only be right to get him a drink. It was just one night. Normal people drink one, two, three nights a week. Sometimes more. One night in one week, it was nothing. It was normal.

CHAPTER 32

'Jeez, Trev. Get off me legs. Trev! Trevor!'

Fuck.

Shit, shit, shit…. what the…

I woke up squashed in bed but not, apparently, by Trevor.

By Hula Hoop Paul.

Hula Hoop fucking Paul!

I tentatively looked under the covers, feeling sick because I knew what I was going to find. Yep. Stark bollock naked. The both of us. Oh fuck. What had I done?

My head was banging. My mouth tasted like a dead pigeon was rotting in it. And I could tell what had happened. Between my legs, it was sticky, rank and sore.

I leant over, careful not to stir him, and noticed a couple of condoms scattered on the floor. At least there was some sense of sensible left in me. Or in one of us. I had no idea; I couldn't remember anything about it. But between my legs… maybe we weren't that flamin' sensible after all. Jesus.

I was shit. Lower than low. A smudgy stain that I just couldn't remove from everyone else's life.

I couldn't face anything right now. In the desperate hope that unconsciousness would come, I closed my eyes, and hoped he might keep his closed too. Or at least leave quietly so I could wake up and imagine none of this had happened.

I could hear his heavy breathing verging on the edge of a boozy snore kicking into action as I tried to piece the awful flashbacks of last night together into an unwelcome jigsaw.

We definitely ordered food. There was definitely food. Did I eat it though?

Laughing outside the cash point at the petrol station. Saying I was going to pee myself. What was so funny? Why did I swear at that man filling his car up?

Ugh God what *was* that music? Bangin' techno shite. I could still feel the bass pulsating through me and the MC screaming. Ah fuck. Shit. We went to that God awful club, didn't we? The toilets - the coke. Fuck, Emma.

Then we.... Dor! Oh God, she was up. What had I done? I hope I wasn't a cow to her. She knew though. She had to.

There were pictures, awful, shameful, repulsive images, flashing through my mind. Things making their way into my consciousness that I didn't want in there.

Him biting my nipples. His arse pounding away. The sweat. *Fuck*, the sweat. The dirty, intoxicated, repulsive sweat.

Just looking at one of his discarded socks made me feel sick. His sock should not be on my bedroom floor. His dick should never have been inside me. Everything felt sore and slimy and rank. Everything inside me was toxic. Powder, vodka, spunk - all mixing with my blood, poisoning me. This was low. I'd gone really, really low. I didn't like him; I didn't even fancy him. I was…really fucking cheap.

There was no way a Cranberries CD and a mint tea would cut through the shame and darkness this time.

An empty three-litre bottle of White Lightning lay scrunched up on the floor, a tiny dreg of cider, no doubt mixed with spit, still floating in it. My jeans were crumpled, muddy...

I became restless. Sleep was not going to come and save me. My legs would not stay still. I got up - oh fuck - oh fuck.

Spunk leaking out of me, running down the inside of my thigh.

I pulled on my knickers, knowing I'd need to change them again imminently, and threw on my dirty jeans which revealed another discarded, totally fucking useless, johnny. As I did up my jeans, I noticed the angry red bruising around my nipple. The thought of his saliva all over me. In me. I was disgusting.

He was not John.

I'd done this. I'd invited this.

But I'd gone a whole week. I said I could do it. Why couldn't I do it. I wasn't like them. I'd got past seeing John without a drink. I'd got past…

I almost stubbed my toe pushing the redundant rubber johnny under the bed while simultaneously pulling on my t-shirt. It was enough to bring him round.

'You've got to go,' I panted.

'What, now?' He yawned as he spoke, and I could smell the stale booze leeching out of him. His arms stretched out to his side making his skinny chest all the bonier and pastier in the bright morning light. I wanted to retch.

'Shh. It's Dor's place. You shouldn't be here.'

'Jesus, Emma. It was your idea.'

He'd confirmed my worst suspicions. It was me. This was down to me.

'It was fun though.' He winked at me. Hot acid shot up my throat.

'Yeah. Sure.' I muttered calmly, a needling of sympathy for him shooting through me. 'Just. You need to go. Sorry.'

He got out of bed, still half asleep, still yawning. I guessed this was just a normal night for him. I ushered him downstairs as quickly as I could and out the front door, closing it as carefully as possible as he was still speaking to me.

'Bye then Emma.'

'Yeah. Bye.'

I let the Yale lock click into place and just stood there, my hand slipping off it like a heavy, defeated weight. I could shut the door, I could shower, I could gut my bedroom and leave no evidence of any of this…but I couldn't stop this from being real. Last night was physically running riot through my veins. And the risk of any other physical consequences just didn't bear thinking about. I couldn't compute the risks, not yet.

I walked back to the scene of the crime and my heart started to race. I wanted to kick and scream my way out of this…I needed to get through today.

I just needed to get through today.

CHAPTER 33

I'd tried everything to avoid talking to Dor since the Hula Hoop Paul incident. I think she must've known how sick and ashamed I felt. I'd kept a low profile since and took it steady as far as booze was concerned. Functioning levels only, I told myself.

But when she emerged from the garden a couple of days later, the garden I had previously promised to help her with, she shook her head at me.

'What?' I said, as if I could blag my way out of it.

'We haven't talked about Saturday night yet.'

'Ah Dor, come on.'

'You need to. Stop pretending it didn't happen. After everything else that's happened recently.'

'I'm clearly not pretending it didn't happen. I feel sick about it,' I said.

'Good. You must've got completely hammered that night, Emma.'

'He's not that bad.'

'Sure, deep down, he's a heart of gold, bronze, perhaps. But Jesus Christ. You have to get beneath the layers of bravado and low-level criminal activity to get there'

'I know, I know. But, anyway, you can talk.'

'Knocking a bit of baccy out is not the same as…'

'All right. I hear you.'

I felt awful. I was living on borrowed time at Dor's place. She'd been real good to me and what'd I do? Bring the local drug dealer back with me.

I spent a couple of days sat in the house, not leaving the front door once. I don't know why; it wasn't as if I was likely to bump into Hula Hoop Paul. All I had to do was avoid the pub and I'd be safe from any embarrassing 'fancy doing it again?' propositions. But I couldn't risk it. Instead, I spent two full days on the sofa. Isabella's friend was running the hut on the Monday and, well, on the Tuesday, I just had to call in sick. Said it was a stomach bug. It wasn't too far from the truth after all. I felt well and truly sick.

The sunshine was the most unwelcome visitor I had for those two days. It reminded me of the cavernous gulf between me - and what life should be. I kept the curtains drawn and mainly just slept. A lot. Those evenings, I just sat, curled up on the sofa with Trev, to watch whatever mid-week telly had to offer. Dor would often come in, tut, and pull the curtains open again in a huff. She wasn't going to let me indulge in my self-pity. She was having none of it.

The panic attacks had been plaguing me again too. After therapy I never really got rid of them completely. That was never actually the aim - so my therapist said. I needed to learn how to live *with* them, in harmony. In harmony my arse. Who can live in harmony with something that tells you you're going to die every time it shows up? Still, they *had* been a *bit* more manageable over the last year or so. But now…palpitations and sweat and a mouth that tasted like sick were a part of my everyday existence. I hadn't even brushed my teeth for, like, three days or something. Straight after the Hula Hoop Paul disaster, I'd showered thoroughly, angrily, put on fresh underwear. But then, I just stayed as I was. No more showers, no more changes of clothes. The dinner medals on my t-shirt were probably from days ago too. I say dinner medals...I hadn't been eating proper meals. The odd bowl of cereal or packet of crisps and all the chocolate I could get my hands on.

I had been running out of zopiclone fast, so I made an appointment with the doc on the Wednesday morning early doors. And there was also that other little matter of unprotected sex that needed addressing.

I really did want to stay off the booze. *I really* did. But I simply couldn't live harmoniously with the dreaded anxiety. With the shame of who I was. I needed something to help me out. To get me through each day. Now I'd committed to no booze, there was no way I could make an excuse for it. I was starting to think they - Dor and Dave - would never let me drink normally again.

I know they cared but my God, asking me about the meetings every two days was a bit much. If anything, they were driving me further into secrecy.

Yes, I'm going. No, I haven't. Yes, I feel fine.

The doctor's trip wasn't as productive as I'd hoped…

I decided to get the embarrassing bit out the way first. I never thought I'd be speaking to my GP about the morning after pill at my age. I hadn't done this since I was 17 or something. I felt like such a dickhead.

'How can I help you today?'

'I, um, could I get the morning after pill please.'

'Unprotected sex?'

Fuck's sake. Obviously!

'Er. Yes.'

'Boyfriend?'

What was this, the Spanish Inquisition?

'Erm, not really…'

'OK, so we'll probably need to rule out STI's as well. Pop yourself up on the bed, draw the curtain and tell me when you're ready.'

For fuck's sake. Could I feel any more disgusting and stupid?

'Do you want a chaperone?'

'No, I'm fine.'

I drew the curtain and rolled my eyes at no one, pulling off my jeans and letting them land in a pile on the floor. A stark reminder of what I'd done. I jumped up onto the bed, looked up at the artificially bright ceiling and took a deep breath…

'Ready,' I called, lying there naked with nothing on my lower body except an extraordinarily large piece of paper towel.

'Flop your legs out.'

'Ouch.'

'Just relax Emma.'

I wish he wasn't saying my name. I didn't want to be reminded of who I was and that I, Emma Barclay, was lying here half naked being poked and prodded. And that I was only here because I decided to lie on my back *completely* naked shagging the local drug dealer who I had zero sexual interest in. If these tests came back with a positive for the clap, I was going to fucking scream. I was going to drown myself in nothingness. I was going to make myself disappear.

'OK, just one more. Breathe in and out slowly.'

I exhaled with relief as the cold metal speculum was released from me and the ordeal was finally over.

Except it wasn't. I still needed to beg him for more zopiclone…

'But you shouldn't have run out, Emma. I can't prescribe you anymore.'

'But they've not been working. I've had to take extra.'

'If you're doubling up on the dose, you're already on you could find yourself in serious trouble. I'm going to have to stop the prescription altogether if that's the case.'

'No,' I practically screamed at him. He just stared at me with one of those looks. Like, see? It reminded me of my mum when I was teeny.

'I mean. No, I haven't. I…must've lost some.'

No more pleading was going to do the trick. In fact, it was only going to make things worse. Why would he believe someone like me? Why would he do *me* any favours? Turning up to the doctors for a clap test, morning after pill and desperate for more sleeping pills. I was hardly the model patient.

I left with only the one prescription.

There was no other way out of this. I had to swallow my pride, my shame and my God-awful flashbacks from the other night.

I had to appeal to Hula Hoop Paul.

I found him in the Angel after work later that day. Luckily, Dave and Dad weren't around. Dor neither. I made sure of that by going on a night when *Dallas* was on the telly.

He looked over at me and gave me a thumbs up. What was that supposed to mean? I cringed. But I walked over to him anyway.

'Hi,' I said, and sat at his table completely uninvited.

He was rolling a ciggie. 'Good night the other night, eh?'

'Yeah.' I smiled to ease my guilt a bit. 'Look. Can I ask a favour?'

'If you want a bit more Hula action then anytime…' He winked.

Fuck's sake. I tried with all my might to keep my smile from fading and to stop vomit hurling upwards into my mouth.

'No. I mean. Yeah, it was lovely an' all. But we're mates, aren't we? It should never have happened.'

He looked down at his pint and started wiping the condensation from the glass with his thumb. How was I going to ask him for drugs now? I'd upset him.

'I mean. I just think you mean a lot more to me as a mate, yeah?'

'S'pose.'

'Anyway. Listen. My doc's gone an' stopped my zopiclone. Can you get me anything similar?'

'Wobbly eggs?'

'Yeah. Great. How many can you get me?'

'How many do you want?'

'Um. I don't know. What can you get?'

'Wait here, I'll make a call.'

He headed to the pay phone tucked away near the darts board and I felt a rush of relief pour through me. If I had temazepam, I wouldn't need to drink. And they were pretty much the same as zopiclone. Kind of. So *really*, I was only doing what I was *supposed* to be doing. If I didn't have that stupid bloody doctor. What was I thinking telling him I was double dropping on a night? Telling him I'd had a few in the daytimes would have probably been better.

But there was no way I was waking up like I had been and going to work. I couldn't. The fear, even now, that was racing through me was high on the Richter scale. I was ready to blow. I could feel it. I just wanted to get through the day without anything weird or crappy happening. Without falling out with anyone or losing my job. I couldn't ensure that if I was on the edge of panic and ready to take a drink every hour. I might not be allowed booze, but these were prescription drugs. I was just getting my prescription from Hula Hoop Paul instead of the doctor.

Same thing really at the end of the day.

He came back over.

'Sorted. I'll go pick them up now. Meet you back here in an hour. £40, OK?'

'Jesus!'

'You've got mate's rates there.'

'Fine. Yep.'

He stood up. He looked hurt.

'Thanks.' I added, realising that this was a whole new low. I was *this* close to making the local drug dealer cry.

CHAPTER 34

Dave was clearly making an effort to spend more time with me. He was such a good mate. And he'd been through a lot himself. After he had the surgery, to remove one of his balls because of the cancer, he seemed to bounce right back. We saw Oasis not long after that op. At the Adelphi with John. And now look at them. Global bloody superstars! We were lucky. And Dave lived through the cancer and the subsequent check-ups and scans.

He was going to live forever he said. And if not, I was to remember his last wish.

Ask Noel Gallagher to smoke his ashes in a roll up. Or was it Liam? It didn't really matter anymore, thankfully, because here he was. Alive, well, and still bugging the shit out of me.

In a good way.

One thing we weren't doing at the moment, however, was going down the Angel. Our haunt. Our stomping ground. Our second home.

Today, he was trying really hard to come up with things to do that didn't involve booze. 'Remember when you had that idea to go to the roller disco? Well, what about ice skating?'

'Remember when we went to the roller disco, and I ended up sitting at the table drinking tea instead of skating cos my legs were shaking so badly with nerves?'

He shrugged. 'True.'

'It's funny how you get less confident of doing these things when you're an adult.' I mused. 'I would've been bloody flyin' round Blisters' roller disco as a kid. Not so much now when, really, we should be *more* confident not less. We've got more experience.'

Dave continued flicking through the local paper for inspiration.

'In fact.' I continued, blabbering on as if I was some kind of philosophy scholar 'that's probably why we're *less* confident. Because we've suffered the falls and we know, better than the kids, the likelihood of a sore arse.'

'Yeah,' he said, now picking up the Yellow Pages for more choice of places to go.

We were bored. We always had *something* to say, we never stopped yapping on to each other. But when you're *trying* to think of something to do and you can't, it kind of cripples your conversational flow. It took me back to the days as kids when we were stuck in the house over the summer holidays because it was raining. Again. And there were only so many times you could play battleships or Simon Says. In fact, I seem to remember Dave being so bored one day he somehow managed to stretch Stretch Armstrong beyond repair.

'Mind,' he said, clumsily trying to shoehorn a deep observation into our light-hearted conversation about falling over. 'It hasn't stopped you, you know, with the booze and that.'

'Cheeky fuck. I'm two weeks sober,' I lied. He didn't need to know about last week's slip up. Besides, that's all it was, a little lapse. Part of the recovery journey they say at the meetings. Really, I knew I was supposed to re-set the clock, start counting my sober days again. Would it *really* make a difference though? Surely it would just make me feel worse - and feeling ashamed and useless was a risk, apparently. I'd been learning all this.

I was more confident now I had the temazepam to help me out. People took that for anxiety. It wasn't a sleeping pill, not like the zopiclone. Wobbly eggs are exactly the same thing as anti-anxiety prescription meds. Because that's what they are. I just happened to have a grumpy doctor and a very hospitable drug dealer.

It kept me calm, without the high. I was calm now, calm but chatty. Which is pretty perfect.

Dave shut the Yellow Pages defeated. 'You not feeling too good?'

'Me? I'm grand, why?'

'Nothing…just.'

'Just what?'

'I don't know. I mean, I know you're not drinking. I get that. But…you're acting like my cousin.'

'Like your cousin? Which one?'

'Remember, Kevin. Used to nod off at the most inappropriate moments.'

'Oh god yeah. I remember. He fell asleep at the zoo, didn't he?'

'His head…. his head…fell…' It always cracked Dave up when we brought that one up. He couldn't speak for laughing. 'His head…in the monkey poo.'

'I know! State of him. Poor lad. He had a crush on that girl too, didn't he?'

'Oh yeah. Don't think she went near him after that.'

'What's cousin Kevin's trip to the zoo got to do with me anyway?'

'You nearly nodded off eating a malted milk earlier.'

'No, I didn't.'

'Yes, you did. I swear. You were holding it in your hand, but you looked like you were falling asleep mid-way through. It was really fucking weird.'

'Boring biscuits, Dave. You should've got the chocolate coated ones in.'

'Whatever,' he said. Dave was hardly wet behind the ears. Perhaps he knew, really. And perhaps he was just trying, gently, to coax it out - you know, trying to make me say it out loud. But I wasn't going to. The ambiguity, the lack of confirmation, it served me well. It meant I could just keep doing what I was doing. I wasn't drinking so it was fine. And I was relieved Dor hadn't told Dave about the other night. Or had she? Maybe he was testing my loyalty. Trying to see if I'd lie to him. I don't know. I changed the subject to be safe.

'OK, so what we doing? Cinema or ice skating?'

'Dumb and Dumber's on?'

'That's that then. I'll have to get my skates on.' I laughed, just as Ally headed in through the back door.

'Oh, hi Emma,' she said. 'I didn't know you were coming round today.'

'Just keeping myself out of trouble.' I tried to make light of things. I hadn't seen Ally since Dave and Dor found me on the floor of the hut. God knows what she thought.

'Yeah. You lead Dave into trouble, and he leads you out of it. Sweet really,' she said, her tone flat. I felt a wooziness come over me. 'You tired?' She asked.

'Me? No.' I knew they could tell. But if I didn't admit it, perhaps it would be forgotten? After all I'd been though, I would be tired, anyway, wouldn't I?

'Anyway. See you later then,' I said. 'Come on Trev' I called, bending over, and clapping my hands together to get his attention. He whined before standing up.

'Why don't you let him stay here tonight, Em?' Dave said.

'Why the hell would I do that?' I asked.

They both looked at each other.

'You just seem tired, Emma.' Ally said.

'What?'

'I just fancy babysitting,' Dave said. 'Miss this little fella sometimes.' Trev was standing next to Dave as Dave rubbed his face between his hands 'You're missing Uncle Dave aren't you boy? Yes, you are. Yes, you are.'

'Whatever' I said. 'If you like.'

CHAPTER 35

The park came to life like flowers blooming on a time lapse. The sunshine seemed to have energised the whole city. Hull on speed with a bucket hat and an ice-cream.

Ellesse shell suit bottoms and Nike trainers pedalling fast on bikes creating a blur of teenage colour and sass. Pushchairs meeting up here, there, and everywhere, like some kind of Tetris game operated by mums and dads - cool hip parents, huge groups with buggies and beers, sitting around in circles on the floor. Students with their music blasting out, trying to drown out the townies with *their* music blasting out. The Lightning Seeds fighting that fucking awful Rhubarb and Custard rave remix. Couples snogging and arguing and sharing ice creams a la *Lady and the Tramp*. Girls sitting in groups giggling while the boys egged each other on to make their move. Ball games and frisbee. Ducks quacking, birds singing. A perfect cocktail of sunshine and happiness all rolled into one.

And I was taking it all in. Every last drop of this beautiful microcosm of Hull.

There was so much colour and energy everywhere, but as much as it popped brightly right in front of my eyes, I felt chilled. Calm, even. The vibes were happy. It was a good balance. Just like me. I'd finally found my happy, my level, a way to keep all bad feelings in check without getting too drunk.

I peered out of the hut, scanning everyone coming towards me as I chucked coins in the till, asked who was next, filled up sugar cones and wafer cones and added chocolate and sprinkles and monkey's blood to ice-creams.

I was starting to love this job - if it wasn't for the envy

of everyone out there doing their own thing and soaking up the rays. Being in the midst of all that, it was really nice regardless.

I took a couple more tablets with a swig from my bottle to keep up with the atmosphere. When I'm feeling good, like this, in a good mood, it's all OK, see. It's only when I'm down that there's a problem, a catastrophe. I'm just chilled and happy. Safe in my hut.

I was just finishing serving a child who was obviously buying his first ice-cream independently as mum and dad looked on all proud, spurring him on. '*Go on then*' I could see them mouthing at him, hands impatiently gesturing for him to approach. As I gave him his change and he skipped away happily, I noticed something out the corner of my eye. A few blokes had circled the bench by the duck pond. I could just make out Les' tatty shoes and the bottom of his legs amongst them.

No time to explain, I dropped the hatch on the customers and legged it out towards the bench. I could see Les, his hands in the air, like he was trying to cover his face, trying to get away.

'The fuck's going on?' I yelled, my ears hearing nothing but a whoosh of confusing sounds as I ran over.

'Who are you?' One said.

'Lay off him,' I replied. I was fuming. They were laughing. I grabbed one of the blokes' arms, pushing it - and him - away from Les.

More laughter.

'It's alright, Emma.' Les was trying to play it down, but I knew he was in trouble. I knew it. I glanced at Les but felt another presence getting closer.

Then the presence appeared, staring me straight in the eyes. 'What you gonna do about it, love?'

Suddenly, I'd lunged at him.

And missed.

My trainer hit something slippy. I was arse over tit.

The laughter got louder again.

Nothing looked or felt real. Like I'd landed in the middle of a TV set, sounds coming from all directions, but not really here. Not really real.

Then the laughter stopped. I think. I couldn't hear it anymore. Had they gone?

I slowly picked up my palms and stared at them, all cracked from the gravelly path. Pieces of tiny stone wedged into my skin. Lots of them. It looked like lots of them. Shining sharply in my flesh. I surfed my finger over my bumpy skin. I couldn't feel it. Somebody grabbed my elbow. My leg slipped sideways in the slimy duck shit, but the grip on my arm was too strong to let me fall.

'You, OK?' Les asked, his arm tight around me. I had no idea if I was or not. I wasn't sure what had just happened.

'I'm fine.' I replied brushing myself down, wiping the duck shit from my jeans into the palm of my cracked hands. I didn't know what had happened. But I needed to not be here.

'I'll just go to the loo.' I said, making a beeline for the public toilets.

As I walked inside a woman was helping her little boy dry his hands. She looked at me, her face contorted, then quickly shooed the little lad out. I stood in front of the mirror. What had happened? I couldn't remember why I was there. I looked down; I was filthy. I tried to clean myself up with water, but it just made my jeans cling to my cold damp skin. I needed to get back into the hut. The safety of the hut. I could hide away. I could keep the shutters up. I could carry on doing what I needed to do.

Suddenly I was back there. And I was fine. As though I'd inhaled the sun's rays again.

Warm and fuzzy.

CHAPTER 36

I opened my eyes. It took me a moment to focus. My heart was racing even though I was just waking up. Everything felt and sounded blurry. A mush of beige and white and little blue patterns on curtains started to come into view. Like little cartoon boats on fabric, blurring in and out of focus like they were on a wavy sea.

Where was I?

I looked to my right. Les was sitting by my bed.

'What the…' I lurched upright, not knowing if I needed to run, fight, or cower. Then I felt my body slouch forwards. I was weak. I looked around. It definitely wasn't my bed. I didn't think it was anyway. I tried to think hard - what did my bed look like. I couldn't wake up properly. There was bleeping and rattling and crashing and voices everywhere. The bed felt scratchy and cool. Not the welcoming bed I have at home. Which home? Which bed? Everything was mixed up in my head. I tried to remember where I was living. With Dor?

Les leaned forward. 'You lost consciousness.'

I stared at him, confused. 'When?'

I couldn't understand it. 'I have to get out of here'. I pulled off the covers so manically I got them wrapped around me. After a struggle, I finally jumped to my feet. I had to get out. I had to get something, anything, to stop the worst from happening. If I didn't get something inside me soon. If I didn't stop these feelings…

'I need to go,' I said, desperation pouring out of me.

'What's the last thing you remember, Emma?' Les asked me, placing his hand on my shoulder. I didn't answer. All I could think about was how to get the hell out of this place.

'Emma.' He continued. 'I know you've been struggling.'

I looked in Les' eyes. It felt like the tables had turned. Here was this old homeless bloke I'd been looking after every day. Now I felt like the vulnerable one. I felt needy. I hated feeling like this. But I wasn't needy for Les - or anyone else for that matter.

'What do you mean? I fixed my eyes on his. How could he possibly know I was struggling? *What* could he possibly know? 'I don't know what you're on about Les.' I tried to deliver it with a giggle, but it hurt my head and my voice must've sounded breathless, the urgent need for peace kicking and straining inside me.

'About the pills and the booze, Emma.'

He said it so matter-of-factly. So calmly.

'I…I fell,' I said, remembering the palms of my hands. I could feel them now. Smarting. And I could feel a knot twisting inside my gut. A desperate feeling of unravelling. A great big dirty lie eager to break out from inside me. From the place where it had lived alone for so long. I couldn't let it. I couldn't. If he knew, if *they* knew, they'd put a stop to it. They'd ruin it all. It'd all be out in the open and they'd watch me like a hawk. I'd have nothing left to help me when I needed it most. It would be a living hell.

'You were trying to help me.' Les said. 'But I'm not sure why.'

'What? Help you?'

'Yeah, you seemed to think I was in trouble. With some of the young lads. They often chat. Take the mick a bit. But they're OK.'

An image started to form in my head.

'Oh…' I said, not sure if I wanted to know what had happened. I wasn't sure I could deal with it right now.

'Is there someone I should call?' Les asked.

'No. No! Please don't call anyone.'

'Well, I'm loathe to leave you alone, Emma. You're not in a good way right now. They had to monitor your heart; it wasn't beating strongly enough.'

'Well, I'm OK now. And I'm not alone. You're here.'

'I know, but close family. Friends?'

'Please. Don't., I said. And I knew it was making its way out into the open air. My secret was about to turn rotten from the oxygen my unwanted hospital visit was giving it. Keeping it inside, feeding it, it was happy that way. Letting it out, I knew, would cause chaos. Cause harm. For Dor and Dave. And my dad. Oh God and if John found out. And I wouldn't be able to carry on. I wouldn't be able to work. I couldn't feed or walk Trev. I wasn't doing a great job at it anyway. But without the help, without the numbing relief, I would be completely incapacitated. I'd be stuck. Scared. With nothing to make things right.

You should've known better, Emma. We've all told you Emma. It's bad for you Emma.

Every voice in my head was taking me a step away from what I needed. I couldn't risk that.

'Please, *please* don't call anyone,' I begged.

'OK. I won't do that. But maybe we can chat?' Les suggested.

I felt myself squirm. I had nowhere to go and every reason to run. Nothing to provide comfort or relief. Just these bright hospital lights, stripping me of any kind of cover.

'What do you want to chat about?' I asked, using one last ditch attempt to get out of it by not speaking it.

'I'm eight years sober, Emma.'

I was stunned. 'I thought you.... I thought you drank.'

He held his shaky hands up in front of us both. 'Cos of these? I'm stuck with the shakes and the wobbles,' he said. 'Nerve damage. Too many years of poisoning myself.'

I didn't know what to say. Is this why he knew? Because he had been there?

'Addiction, it doesn't want you to talk about it. It wants you to stay unwell.'

'I'm not an addict,' I snapped, disgusted at the idea.

'No, you're Emma,' he said, and smiled. But I couldn't get past it. The label, the name. Me? An *addict*? I knew at this point I had to give him something.

'OK. Fine,' I said. 'I've been struggling with panic attacks again. And I've been using beer and the occasional pill to help me feel calmer. It's the same as if you went to the doctor. It's just, it's just what I use that's different. My doctor hasn't been helping me in all honesty. I've had no support.' I could feel my legs starting to writhe uncomfortably. Angry in their surroundings of strained muscle and screaming skin.

'Hmm,' he said, a thoughtful look on his wrinkly face. A face that had transformed from vulnerable to wizened in seconds.

'I just do it to get by.'

'Emma…' Les held out his shaky hand and, instinctively, I took it and gripped it tight. But the answer wasn't in his grip. I was in the grip of something else entirely and I was just desperate to get out. My head suddenly shifted a gear, and my tone became uncontrollably snappy. 'It doesn't matter, Les. I need to leave. Now. Are you going to help me or what?'

'I've been here before Emma.'

'What? Where?'

'Where you are. This overwhelming need, this powerless, overwhelming need.'

I looked at him. 'I'm not powerless. Not if I can have my fucking independence and make my own fucking decisions.' I was scrabbling around for my belongings. 'I have to go,' I said, getting my shoes on, standing up, no idea how to get home. No idea if I even had any money on me. I patted my pockets, looked in my bag. Thank fuck. My wallet was in there. Les must've got everything together for me. I felt a pang of guilt. But it was overridden by my need for a drink. For anything.

I was being backed into a corner by my true self and she was the last person I wanted to see.

'You really should stay here, Emma. It could be dangerous.'

'If you've been here before, Les,' I said, with a tone he didn't deserve. 'Then you'll know just how dangerous it is not to have what I need.'

'Well, that's a state of mind. Physically, mentally, in the long term, you're safer here. Mark my words.'

'Sorry, can't do it.'

I ran out of the hospital, leaving him sitting there, a vigil around an empty bed. The woman who couldn't survive alone in the world. It wasn't people I needed though. It wasn't hospitals or doctors or bleeping machines or hospital food. It was a drink. A pill. Anything to get me out of this horrendous feeling. To get me a moment of calm, to think. To make a fucking decision myself. Not to be forced into hell by people who thought they knew what was best.

There was no other option.

CHAPTER 37

Dave

I just had this feeling about Emma. Something felt wrong. I hadn't seen her. Dor hadn't seen her.

I left Trev with Ally and began my walk to the hut. Mr big brother protectiveness kicking in. And beginning to terrify me if I'm being brutally honest.

All the way there I was telling myself I was being stupid. I'm not bastard psychic. It was just a feeling. Just a niggle. I was bound to be worried after everything that had happened. It was only natural, of course it was. It wasn't some kind of spiritual message.

It was dark, everything looked shut up. Empty. Quiet; I could hear the sound of a takeaway carton skimming along the path in the breeze. Maybe it was Emma's? Maybe she'd eaten. Got a bit drunk, grabbed some cheesy chips. That was a good sign. Food was a good sign. She never ate when she was bad.

Fuck's sake. I'd turned into an armchair detective. Constantly on the lookout for clues for her state of mind. It was exhausting.

But it wasn't enough to reassure me. It was a long shot. I knew that. My gut knew that. This wasn't going to be OK.

Just seeing the hut, wondering what was inside. Images flashing in my head of Emma, gone. Stone cold on the hard floor. Alone…her last moments alone.

I felt sick. I jogged the last few metres and reached the door. It was locked up. I strained to look through a small gap in the shutter, trying to see inside, to see if she was there. Maybe it was empty. Maybe she had gone home.

I tried to wipe the crack of window to get a clearer view, but it was all steamed up from the inside.

Then a wave of ice-cold prickled over me. I saw her. On the floor in the dark. Her head was facing the other way, so I couldn't tell if she was awake, and her green work apron looked twisted around her. My heart was fucking booming. I tried rattling and banging on the window. *Emma! Emma fuck's sake.* Nothing. Not a peep. Nowt. I could see her legs were lying beneath a fallen box of crisps, spewing packets out onto the floor all around her. Then I noticed her Converse sticking out. Clumsy. Duck-footed.

Fuck. They were lifeless.

CHAPTER 38

My name's Emma… and I'm an alcoholic

Shit just saying it…

Sorry. I get choked up saying it…I'm here because… because I'm terrified is the truth. I've no idea what…I just know that I was so close. I've felt it before but this time. It felt different. Like I could have really…And I don't know what else to do.

I've been here before. To the meetings. But I never wanted to come. I don't want to be here now. I just don't think there's another way is there?

I woke up in hospital three days ago. I don't know how I got there. But Les - my friend - he told me how it happened. And it really fucking scared me. Sorry. I mean. It's just. I have absolutely no memory of it whatsoever. Like nothing. This huge major thing happened and there's no memory of it.

He said I was barely breathing. Lying there, making strange noises but not breathing normally. I was lying on the floor of the ice-cream hut, where I work. Or worked. But I was on the floor. Apparently covered in duck shit because I'd already fallen over by the pond trying to start a fight with some teenagers. I thought they were having a go at Les. But I think I misjudged it.

Anyway, he said I'd had a go at some teenagers who were just talking to him. And that I'd fallen in duck shit…

They said that mixing vodka and Temazepam was dangerous. That I was lucky Les was there because otherwise…. I dread to think.

But then…you talk about rock bottom, don't you? You'd think that landing myself in hospital, covering myself in shit, you'd think that would be about as low as I could get.

But it wasn't. And that terrified me.

I woke up in hospital. I had someone there looking out for me. And I legged it. My body was just screaming for me to get out, for a drink. I just ran out…

I think I got vodka, just vodka. That's what was found next to me on the floor. An empty vodka bottle. And I was cold and wet. Jesus. I'd pissed myself. Like some kind of…

It was Dave who found me, my best mate. He found me all fucked up and pissy and…I've never felt so, *so* completely out of control.

I white knuckled it since then. I don't know how, but I did it.

No, I do know how. I couldn't have done it without him. The big stupid love of my life. He's like a big brother. Always been there. And he sat there with me, for two days, watching me, bringing me water, giving me measured amounts of temazepam to help deal with it. He was terrified though. It was dangerous, he knew it was dangerous. But he was scared I'd run away from hospital again. He thought maybe it was the only way.

The pain was screaming inside me. Like ants marching under my skin, trying to burrow their way out.

I just needed a drink. I just needed to get it all to stop. But something felt different…

At first, maybe it was because I had no money. No way of getting it, anyway. At least at Dave's, I was getting something. Some relief with the pills. If I ran out, I risked having nothing. But after a day passed, I didn't want it. Well, not that I didn't *want* it. I still felt like I needed it. But I hated it, too. I hated the hold it had.

I took that drink, after leaving hospital, because I had to. There was no choice. It was as if I had no control over my body. Or my mind. But I thought it might, I don't know, just get me through, just make me feel normal. Then I wake up covered in piss on the floor of the ice cream hut. Sat in piss and dirt, my jeans still stained with duck shit. I knew then. I had no control over it.

I never really believed in these meetings. Thought they were pointless. A bit weird, maybe. I didn't think I needed to be here. I was just trying to keep everyone happy. But I'd lost my boyfriend, my job. Perhaps even a second job after this. And then I go to hospital, and they reckon I could've lost my life. I'd depressed my heart rate so much. Scares me just thinking about it.

It's just all kind of come to a head. I've not been honest. I guess it *is* alright to go out and get wasted if you're doing it for fun. But I'm not sure I was doing it for fun. At least not for the last few years anyway. And, Dave, he, well, I kept calling him a boring cunt. Sorry. But I was calling him boring because he has this girlfriend and he'd stopped coming out with me as much. But maybe it wasn't because of his girlfriend. Maybe it was because of me? Maybe he'd had my puke on his trainers too many times or maybe he thought he needed to be on call and sober in case I needed rescuing.

I'm not even sure why I drink. There's just this awful thing, this feeling, inside me that I need to rid myself of. I don't even know who I am. Not really. And the panic attacks…

My mum left us when I was eight. She'd been having an affair. She was meant to pick me up from dance class, but instead…I never saw her again. And I was so, *so*, angry with her. Which is really fucking confusing. I've hated my mum and I've hated myself for hating her.

But I talked about it. I got counselling. Saw my doctor, chatted to my friends, to my dad. I was given pills to sleep and warned off the caffeine. It was all going great; the anxiety was getting better. But there was this one thing I couldn't get over. I don't even know what it was but something that nagged away at me and taunted me and shamed me. I was the girl whose mum had chosen to ditch her in favour of this fella. I was the girl who hated her own mother. That's what kept on going round and round.

And when I drank, that all vanished. But it didn't just vanish. It was replaced with something else. A nice, warm feeling...

And now I feel like a gullible twat because it's taken this long to figure out that it was all just bullshit. It's taken me collapsing in piss and shit to figure it out. That all those promises and all that confidence was just bullshit.

So now I'm back here and I feel dead embarrassed, but I don't think I've got any other choice. There's no nicer path to take. I don't want to stop drinking. I've said it. But I have to. And I've no idea what life will be like. I can't see a life. But I know now, that if I carry on, there's definitely no life at all.

This time it's not because I want my friends or my family to think I'm giving this sobriety lark a go. But because if I don't, like, seriously give it a go, there might not be anything left. I might really go and do it next time. I didn't mean to, but in some ways, it's like a slow suicide, isn't it? I don't want to die but I'm compelling myself to…like I just don't care cos I'd rather have nothing than not have a drink.

I don't know. I just…. I haven't got the answers. I don't even know if I'll make it. I don't know how to live without a pint or a pill. I never have. Not for years, anyway. But I know if I don't come here now…it's just not worth the risk, doing nothing.

And when Les told me he was in recovery, there was something just as comforting in those words as there was in a pint. But scary too. Like I couldn't pretend anymore. He'd been there, where I was. And he'd survived. But, he said, if he hadn't owned it, if he hadn't admitted he couldn't drink, he'd be dead, so…

I can't imagine a life without it. But now I know there isn't a life *with* it either. I'm in limbo, like fucking purgatory, Jesus.

And I'm really, *really* fucking scared.

CHAPTER 39

'Brew?'

'Thanks Dave.'

I was feeling grouchy. And completely lost. It was as though everything had been stripped out of my life and all I was left with was…me.

And tea.

Dave said he and Ally would put me and Trev up for a week or two, he wanted to look after me, he said, and Trev. He'd even taken time off work. Didn't want to leave me alone in case I had a fit or passed out or something. And Ally was falling head over heels for Trev, taking him out for walks. I think she was even taking him to that new coffee shop. But I loved that he was getting the attention. He hadn't had much from me recently. No wonder they wanted him to stay here the other night.

Part of me knew that Dave wanted to keep an eye on me in case I picked up again, but I couldn't get angry about it. I finally realised I needed help. I couldn't do this on my own. And I couldn't get over their generosity after all I'd done. The shite he'd put up with from me lately. Both, really. My bones shook with shame and regret.

Dave handed me a cuppa.

'Thanks Dave.' I took the steaming cup from him, and he sat down while I continued to sit on the floor, pouring through his records. 'What do you fancy? Cranberries? Nirvana? Hole?'

'What about something more poppy, light-hearted. Look for some Senseless Things or some, I don't know…'

'Kylie?' I laughed, finding a random Kylie album in Dave's otherwise respectable collection.

'It's Ally's.'

'Yeah, likely story,' I laughed, looking at the beautifully shot front cover before studying the tracks listed on the back. 'Stick it on,' I ordered.

'Don't be daft.'

'No come on. You want light-hearted. Stick it on.'

Dave pulled the vinyl from its sleeve and shoved it on the turntable. It crackled a little…

'Sounds well worn. You sure you're not a closet Kylie fan?'

'Get away.' He said, hitting me on the head with the album sleeve.

Confide in Me came on…Kylie's latest - and her biggest statement of being a grown-up sex symbol yet. It was slow. And moody.

'Ah, this is Kylie at her *least* light-hearted,' I laughed.

'Yeah. Sexy, mind.'

'I blame Michael Hutchence, personally,' I said.

'Ha-ha you would. You know, don't speak of it outside this room, but this isn't bad actually.'

'True,' I conceded. 'It's got a bit of an…edge. Can't believe I've just described Kylie as edgy.'

'I guess we all grow up at some point.'

'True.'

The next song started up and we realised that *Confide in Me* was probably a standout. 'Find something else.' Dave said, taking a slurp of his tea as he sat in his favourite chair, his sports socks making his feet look all cute and cosy.

I pulled out a Senseless Things record and stuck it on, ready for some glorious pop punk to make us feel young and free again, the backing vocals adding an even more sunshiny vibe to the lead singer's voice - like boy-next-door-with-an-edge - and the drums pacing it all together in a rhythm so fast you certainly couldn't feel low.

As it played, memories of our gigs and adventures came

flooding back. It was always me and Dave. No matter who was in our life, no matter who shared our bed, we were always there for each other. Like everything could change around us but it didn't matter. We were always here in the middle of it all.

'Dave.' I said, without really knowing what was coming next. He looked over at me, his hazel eyes studying me expectantly. He was a gentle soul was Dave. He had the size to create just enough nervousness without encouraging a square-up. But inside, he was just…squidgy and yet, weirdly, solid, and dependable, and, well, everything a girl could need in a best mate. 'You saved me; you know that.'

'Bollocks. You saved yourself.'

'No but. I mean…if you hadn't found me. If you hadn't got me through.' My eyes were pricking with tears. 'Seeing how much you wanted me to get better, it made me *want* to get better. Does that make sense?'

'Come here, you daft twat,' he said. And I wandered to his chair, flopped into his big bear hug, and sobbed. Big snotty tears. His hug was my home.

'I love you David you know that.'

'I love you too Emma Barclay. I mean, why else would I put up with you?'

I laughed and let out a little more snot, wiping my nose with the back of my hand like a child.

'You dirty bastard. Piss not enough,' he joked, grabbing me a tissue, giggling to himself. I had to join in.

'What the fuck are you doing with a proper box of tissues in your living room anyway?'

'Ally.'

'Of course.' I laughed, wiping my nose, grateful of her tissues and most of all, grateful for her support. 'Are you sure she doesn't mind me being here?'

'Course not. I mean, she'd be unimpressed if you decided to stay 'til Christmas. But otherwise, all good.'

'I always thought she hated me.'

'Don't be daft.'

'But you stopped coming out. We stopped hanging out, having fun.'

'That wasn't Ally, Emma.'

I looked at his sad eyes and realised what he meant. 'Thanks for sticking around,' I said. 'I know I'm not easy.'

'No bother.' His voice remained soft. 'Anyway, I brought this round from my nanna's. Fancy it?'

Dave pulled a plastic Iceland bag out from behind the side of his chair to reveal a jigsaw. With some kind of Victorian street scene on it.

'I might be a hopeless alcoholic Dave, but I haven't had a personality transplant. A fucking jigsaw?'

'Well, what do you want to do, get loaded down the…'

'A jigsaw would be great.' I interrupted. 'So long as we've got more biscuits.'

'Em.' He said, suddenly serious. 'That time you were here, when we were chatting about that stupid roller disco and ice skating and stuff…?'

I thought hard but couldn't remember what he was talking about. 'What time?'

'When you said you'd quit but you obviously hadn't.'

'Maybe that's why I can't remember it.'

'I just wondered what you'd taken then?'

'I can't remember it,' I said. 'Sorry, there's just a lot of stuff that's a blur you know?'

'You were nodding. You just looked half asleep…falling into your own cup of tea. It'd happened a few times. Benzos?'

'I guess so.'

'Wobbly eggs?'

'Probably. Thought that's what'd help stop me drinking. Not so much when you're a stupid booze-head who decides to combine the two.'

'The doc give you them?'

'Hula Hoop Paul.'

'Fuck's sake Emma.'

'I know, I know,' I said, realising I needed to tell him the whole story. 'Dave. Now you've seen me piss my pants, I'm thinking I probably shouldn't hide the other thing from you.'

'What?'

'Hula Hoop Paul.'

'Dor told me.'

'Shit Dave. Why didn't you say something?' I hit his arm playfully with my fist, just enough to make him wince.

'There was no point. You've been on one for weeks. What good would it have done. I mean - saying I told you so? Well, that would've gone down like a lead balloon. Can you imagine you, under the influence, taking that from me?'

'I guess….'

'I knew it would happen anyway. There could only be one reason why you wanted to go out with that idiot. And given that you were on a so-called date…. well…'

'I guess. Made some diabolical choices recently, haven't I?'

'Yup.'

'Yeah.' My mind was replaying that awful night. 'I haven't told anyone this, but I had to go and take the morning after pill like some teenager.'

'Emma…'

'And have the clap test.'

'And?'

'All good. Thankfully.'

'Thank fuck.'

'I know. Stupid move. Desperate times and all that. But now it's OK. I've got you, a cup of tea, and a jigsaw. I'll be grand. Now get that record turned over and I'll clear the table. Edges first, OK?'

'I'll get the biscuits.'

I never imagined that, before I turned 30, I'd be drinking tea, eating biscuits, and sorting the edges of a jigsaw puzzle from the centre pieces while singing along to Senseless Things and Blur and, to satisfy Dave's overbearing obsession, Oasis. But it didn't matter that we were doing a jigsaw rather than dancing at a sweaty gig, it mattered that he was here. It mattered that he cared.

It mattered that I was sober.

'Emma' Dave said, looking over at me. I had a gob full of biscuit crumbs. 'Hmm?' I managed.

'That wasn't the first time I've seen you piss your pants.'

CHAPTER 40

Les had been playing on my mind. Since I ran out of hospital, leaving him sitting there alone, I hadn't spoken to him. I hadn't told him I was OK.

I headed to the park to try to find him. The ice cream hut was all shut up, which made me feel guilty. I had finally plucked up the courage to confess all to Isabella, who was still dealing with her own problems, recovering from her new hip from the comfort of her sofa. After an initial angry reaction, she softened, saying she'd try and get her friend to cover while I 'convalesced'. I guess she didn't have much luck with availability today, though.

I told her that I wouldn't blame her if she sacked me, but she told me I wasn't getting off that easily. I think, in all likelihood, she probably didn't have the energy right now to train anyone else up. Not while she herself was getting close to recovery. And she thanked me for my honesty, which felt a little odd - given what I'd just told her about my irresponsible drinking and drug taking while on the job!

It didn't take me long to find Les, but he wasn't where I thought I might see him, hanging around a bench or at the duck pond. He was locking the door to one of the grand Victorian houses as I walked past.

'Les?'

He turned with a start, his eyes lighting up. 'Emma! So good to see you,' he said, as he walked unsteadily down the short path to the park edge. 'I was worried about you.'

'What are you…is this…?' I gestured to the house.

'Welcome to my abode,' he said, a modest chuckle jiggling his old bones before releasing another hacky cough.

'What? I thought…' I stopped, realising how rude it would be to tell him I had visions of him sleeping under a bench at night. What the fuck had I been thinking? Suddenly, he looked different to me. He'd told me about not drinking, sure, but now, it was like *all* my assumptions were shattered. All the stories I'd hung on the back of Les were wholly fictional and entirely unrealistic. Looking at him now, through new eyes, with new information, he didn't look like a rough sleeper at all. Not in the slightest.

Where on earth had I got the idea from?

'This is your house?' I asked, in awe of the imposing, beautiful building that stood in front of us.

'Good lord no. I rent a flat in it. It's sectioned off. Two flats downstairs, and a big spacious one upstairs that some young yuppie type has to herself. But I like it. It suits me.'

He unlocked the front door and beckoned me into the hallway. It was airy with a bike up against the wall, no carpet and a load of unopened mail sitting on a knackered old console table. He opened the inner door to the left and we walked into a big open living room. He'd clearly lived here some time. There were books, and pictures and all sorts adorning the walls. It had high ceilings decorated with raised patterns circling the lighting fixtures, an open fireplace that didn't look used, with a cast iron surround and a big bay window overlooking the park.

I felt ashamed of making the homeless drunk assumption. Was it because he was old? Or because of the shaking? Or because he was sitting on a park bench when I met him?

Ironically, *I* was the one living around the edges of my assumption. Ironically, I was the one more at risk of losing my home. I *had* lost my home, really. But also, I often hid all of my problems well. Until I no longer could, of course. But I was young, working. I had friends and family. Although I had to admit they were all being pushed to their limits. And, given I was currently sleeping in either Dave or Dor's spare room, I could quite easily have ended up roughing it before long. I'd had at least two nights' kip in the hut, after all.

'I just wanted to find you, to apologise,' I said, as Les listened intently, seemingly making no effort to interrupt me. 'I'm sorry for running out on you, at the hospital.'

'I take it you went to drink?'

'Yeah.' I looked down at my feet. 'Well, I don't really remember all that much. I remember running out, stopping somewhere to buy vodka. I vaguely remember waking up, soaked in my own piss. Dave found me. I don't know what I'd have done if he hadn't…'

'This is the thing with booze. It's a relentless killer.'

I wondered why he wasn't being more reassuring.

I nodded.

He beckoned me towards a chair. 'Sit, please.'

I parked my bum on the old leather chair, the cushion exhaling a surprise gust of air as my weight hit it.

Les sat down more slowly on the sofa opposite me, nipping his trousers away from his knees as he bent his tired legs and settled. 'You look well, though.' He said.

'You mean, well…*considering*…'

'Well, yes,' he said.

'To be fair, I'm just glad of the honesty. And to not have to hide it anymore. But…it's just…I don't know. It's a relief to get it out, but now everyone knows, I can't hide from the shame, you know?'

'It's not meant to be easy.'

'I know.'

'There'll be bumps. There might even be some crashes. But take it a day at a time. And you've got some great friends supporting you, haven't you?'

I smiled, thinking back to the last few days. 'I have, yep. Not that I deserve them.'

'You'd do the same for them, I'm sure. You're a diamond, Emma. Once you start to realise that you'll find it easier to stay sober.'

'I guess,' I said, not really sure what he meant.

'Have you spoken to your doctor? Did they give you any help with withdrawal?'

'Yeah. She was pretty good to be fair. Dave came with me. He was worried about me white knuckling it. He was giving me the odd temazepam but said it frightened him. Like he was responsible. The doctor chatted to me about the meetings, counselling, and stuff. Gave me a short course of…Librium.'

'Ah yes,' he said, looking towards the ceiling as he nodded affirmatively.

'Then Dave and his girlfriend put me up for a bit. And I've been back to the meetings too. Properly this time. I honestly didn't think they were for me. And then look what happens…'

'As is often the way. Cruel, cruel illness, addiction.'

'It still smarts when you say that word.'

'The more you say it, the least affected you'll be by it.' He had a point.

'I just, I really want you to know how much help you've been. I really thought you were lonely, coming to me, that I was helping *you*. But you knew all along, didn't you?'

'When you've been there, you can sometimes spot the struggles after a quick conversation.'

I nodded.

'Listen,' he said, looking out of the window. 'Do you fancy a brew? Looks like it's going to heave down out there.'

'Thanks,' I said, and he wandered down a small corridor off the living room, presumably towards his kitchen.

'Nice view you've got here,' I hollered, while Les had the kettle boiling and cupboard doors clattering.

'Yeah. It's a nice place. I was lucky it came up. Never want to leave now.'

'I bet,' I yelled back, while taking in his living room. His furnishings were modest, but probably made to look more so because of the size of the room dwarfing them. He had a well-worn brown leather sofa, a glass coffee table with a copy of the Mirror strewn across the top of it, bits of opened and unopened post, and an ash tray swelling with endless roll-up dumps.

Les came back through carrying two mis-matched mugs full of steaming tea. I took a sip. 'Perfect brew. I was preparing myself for a bitter milky one.'

'Do I look like a poor tea-maker?' He winked.

A clock ticked in the background, forcing me to listen, and the whole place had a feeling of calm about it.

'So, do you want to talk about it?'

'I think so,' I said. 'It seems to have been helping. Like, the more I talk about it, expecting people to get riled up at me for how stupid I've been, the less it seems to happen.'

'Well, you've not done it on purpose, that's why. I warn you, however, not everyone outside of the recovery community will see things in the same way.'

'I guess…'

'But your truth is your truth. If you're keeping yourself well by opening up in the right way—in the way you feel comfortable—and to the people you trust. You know, you don't need to take out an ad in the Hull Daily Mail.'

I laughed and slurped more of my strong sugary tea.

'Besides,' he continued. 'As a sober person, you'll find you don't need to explain yourself half as much as you used to. No more sickies from work, no more imaginary relatives popping their clogs each week so you can go to their imaginary funerals.'

A wave of familiarity and guilt ran through me. 'I've told that one before,' I said. 'Problem was, said relative wasn't imaginary, it was only their death that was.'

'You get caught out?'

'Yeah, well, it wasn't very sensible telling the boss my own bloody dad had died really. I'm a terrible actor at the best of times. But drunk? Jesus. And the guy from sales bumped into us both in Jackson's so…'

'Those lies always bite us on the arse don't they.'

'Tell me about it.' All of a sudden, we found ourselves roaring with laughter over our drinking days. 'Is it OK, you know, that we're laughing about this stuff,' I asked.

'Of course. We can laugh at ourselves whenever we want. A bit of shared black humour, it's good for the soul, Emma. And my God, after all these years of battering ourselves, we need a bit of nourishment. You can't beat laughter for that.'

'True.' I smiled, holding the warm mug between my hands. For once, not feeling like there was anywhere else I needed to be.

'You know,' Les continued. 'I once turned up drunk to work, well, once is a lie. I should've said, I once got caught drunk at work. By one of the kids in class. He was one of the mouthier lads. Deep down, he was a good kid, but by heck, he had a gob on him.' Les smiled as he looked upwards as if to draw the imagery from the depths of his shaky memories. 'He found my pop bottle and took a swig of it, then announced his findings to the rest of the class.'

'Oof,' I said. 'That can't have ended well.'

'Well, yes and no. It was one of the incidents that led to my rock bottom. If I hadn't got suspended that day, I might still be drinking. I might be dead.'

'Certainly, a sobering thought!'

'It is when you're some way towards sober. When you're drunk, the booze stops those thoughts making their way inside your head.'

Les went on to explain how he'd always drank heavily. Part of the culture in his family, he said. 'I don't think there was ever a reason to it. I just always did it, and then I didn't know how to be without it. But because people couldn't bear to be around me, I retreated. Ended up drinking alone in the house. And gradually, it took over everything in my life. All my relationships, work, everything. I landed on a few perceived 'rock bottoms' before I finally found the absolute floor.'

'What was that?' I asked.

'I was arrested and put in the cells. It was a brawl in town. Middle of the day. Me, a 60-something bloke. My daughter picked me up from the station and agreed to fund a rehab placement. I carried on drinking until we got in, I had the DTs and it got dangerous. I was fitting and pissing on her carpet. See, you're not the only one. Piss is par for the course in our game.'

I laughed. 'It's a dirty problem to have this addiction malarkey.'

'Certainly is. Anyway, one of my grandkids saw me in that state. I'll never forget that. She looked…frightened. Blind drunk, but that image, her eyes. I'll never forget it. They're engraved in my memory.'

'Shit,' I said. 'But you made it to rehab?'

'Yeah, eventually. Put me on a detox for a couple of weeks. But I was so ill, my bloods were really bad, and they ended up admitting me to hospital briefly. Then I finally went into the rehab stage. It was tough, but I did it. It was a long rocky road, but I did it.'

'Was that the first time you'd tried?'

'God no. There are many failed attempts in my past. But what happened that last time, that really shook me.'

'The arrest?'

'No. I'd been arrested before for drunk and disorderly. My rock bottom was my granddaughter seeing me covered in piss and my daughter spending all her savings to get me well.'

'Do you still see her?'

'Yeah, but not often, really. The relationship was rocky before the incident. I guess she felt she didn't have much choice though. I'm eternally grateful to her, but I've got a lot of making up to do. Her childhood wasn't exactly a fairy tale. But that's another story, eh?'

I smiled at him. For some reason, I felt like fessing up, about the homeless thing. It just felt really, honest. Everything about Les felt genuine.

'I thought you were homeless,' I blurted out.

'Really?' He laughed. 'Why?'

'I don't know now. I can't understand how I came to believe it. Something about the park…'

'Ah, the old 'drunk on a park bench' adage?'

'Maybe,' I said, feeling embarrassed. 'Also, you said you lived…'

'On the park? Yep, but these houses circle the entire park.'

I laughed. 'Sorry. It was a poor assumption. And I thought, your clothes…' Immediately I realised I was taking this honesty thing too far.

'You young 'uns are allowed to dress down in your Dr Marten boots and ripped jeans, but I'm not?'

'I didn't realise it was a fashion statement.'

'Tssk. You're out of touch missy. I'll have you know I'm the height of fashion. You'll never find these threads in Top Man. Far too classy.

I laughed.

'Seriously though, I don't have much money. My pension pot was small. So yeah, I'm not decked out in posh clobber, but I'm comfortable. I've a lot to be grateful for.'

'True,' I said. 'I think…maybe it all just feels raw and, well, I feel a bit lost if I'm honest. I mean, what do I do now?'

'You learn to live again.'

'Yeah, I've already been wracking my brain for fun sober nights out.'

'Well, there is that. But it goes a bit deeper than that,' he explained. 'That's the easiest bit if I'm honest. No matter how it seems now. You need to learn to live with what's in here.' He hammered his fingers into his chest as he spoke. 'You need to learn to love yourself. And Emma, let me tell you, once you've cracked that, you'll never look back. You'll be like, what did I ever see in that ugly bottle of vodka?''

'I hope so.'

'You will, mark my words. But I won't pretend it'll be easy. You might slip. You might pick up, lapse. You might not. But one thing I can promise you, if you always remember the dynamic of your relationship with booze, it'll struggle to take hold again.'

'How do you mean?'

'You have no control over it. One drink leads to another then another. Stay away from it, don't trust it. Because that one drink will try to fool you all over again.'

'That's what I'm scared of. The never. The idea that I can never drink.'

'One day at a time, Emma.'

'I guess,' I said.

'You've known for a long time that things weren't right, haven't you?' He said.

'Yeah. I tried hard to bury it, to deny it. It was like, I knew, but I always had an excuse, you know? I could drink because I'd had a difficult therapy session or been dumped. Or it was OK because I was drinking beer not vodka. But I was ending up in nightclubs on my own, that felt really, well, pathetic, I guess.'

'Ahh yes. I've been there. Outwardly the life and soul, dying inside.'

'Yeah.'

'You end up spending more time with strangers than you do close friends.'

'Exactly,' I said, grateful that someone understood what I was saying. 'Sometimes, I think I preferred it, because all the other stuff was unspoken. Like, it didn't matter how wasted I got, or they got, because, well, we wouldn't have to see each other again after chucking out time.'

'Sorry state of affairs that.'

'Quite,' I said, sipping the last of my sugary tea. 'Les?' I said…

'Yes?'

'There's something else. I don't know how to put it into words. But something I sort of feel I need to get out.'

'You can tell me. I mean, really, you need a sponsor, Emma. And I can't be your sponsor.'

'Why not?' I asked.

'Having a sponsor of the opposite sex is frowned upon. It's not good, really. But we can be friends. You can chat to me about things. But you do need to find someone who understands you, a woman, more your age, probably, who really gets you.'

'I will.'

'But tell me. What's playing on your mind?'

I took a deep breath and put my mug down on the floor. 'Did you ever, you know, feel like you might want to die, Les?'

'Is that how you feel?'

'I don't know. It's not like I ever…' My voice trailed off. Les walked over to me, crouched down, and put his hand on my arm. The tears started as soon as I felt his touch. He didn't rush me. He gave me time to just sit there. The clock was still ticking. The children were still playing innocently on the grass outside. The dogs still running around yapping without a care in the world. The opposite to this darkness.

Then it just poured out. My stomach jumping with involuntary jolts as I struggled to stabilise my breath. Every breath, every tear, every wailing exhale came in fits until my whole body gave in and I sobbed. Hard, regular, spasmodic, ugly sobbing. Les stood up and removed a packet of tissues from his pocket.

'Thanks,' I said, taking one, wiping my eyes. My breathing began to slow, my crying was more controlled. I took a deep breath.

'I never wanted to kill myself,' I said, tears still leaking. 'It was never that. It was…it was like I didn't care, you know? Like, the cost of getting to oblivion didn't matter. As long as I got there. As long as I could shut it all out. If it was permanent, then, I didn't mind. I didn't want to live or die. I just didn't want…to feel, I guess.'

I sniffled hard, wiping my nose with my now soggy tissue.

'I totally get that, Emma,' he said kindly. 'It's rarely about the drink, you know. We call it alcoholism, addiction, but it isn't about wanting something, it's about not wanting something. Not wanting to hurt.'

I nodded.

'It's very rare you come across anyone in the rooms who enjoys it. The enjoyment always stopped long ago. It becomes a means to an end. It's not about booze, Emma. Really. Giving up the drink, it's just the start.'

CHAPTER 41

I was relieved that Isabella was giving me a second chance. I'd had so many second chances. I got a good talking to, but she was generally pretty good with me. I wasn't sure if I deserved it, but at least I could stay on track for everyone else.

It felt like something was helping me put my life back together. I don't know if it was inside me or if it was talking to Les or just from burning myself out so badly with booze and pills that I was physically and mentally sick of it all. But something kept me going.

There was something both comforting and terrifying about being back in the hut. As I scanned the crisp boxes and the wafer cones, the snacks that always brought smiles to customer's faces, they felt tainted by my drunken memories.

It was in here, in this place, that I sought darkness. It had been my safe place, but it was the place that took me to my edge. But, as Sophie from the meeting had said, it wasn't really *my* safe place. It was *addiction's* safe place. It was where it could thrive. A place I could block out everyone and everything else. It had my undivided attention.

I needed to re-imagine the scene. I needed to get the shutters open and let the sunshine back in. I had to let people in. I flung the door open and propped it with a concrete stone. The breeze drifted through, cooling my sticky skin, and carrying the birdsong with it. I wasn't alone in here. Not if I didn't want to be.

As I finished opening up, I noticed a letter had been put through the little gap between the hatch.

'*FAO The Owner. Isabella's.*'

I assumed it must've been from a supplier or something. And I didn't want to bother Isabella with boring shit like that. Not when she was giving me one last chance. I opened it.

It wasn't a letter from a supplier. It was a sheet of paper covered in names and signatures. On closer inspection, I could see it was a petition.

A petition to get rid of me.

I couldn't believe it. It must be that bloody mummy brigade. The note read:

> 'We, the undersigned, hereby request that staffing of Isabella's is reviewed with immediate effect.
>
> 'Drugs are a serious threat to society and, as parents of young children, we do not feel comfortable bringing our kids to Isabella's whilst it is being run by a drug addict.
>
> 'We are all regular users of the park, and our only other option is to boycott the ice cream hut.
>
> 'Please advise us of your proposed action as soon as possible.'

I felt like I'd been winded. The light dimmed once more. I was a public menace. Someone unsafe to be around. Someone children shouldn't be around. I had a flashback to the woman in the public toilets, ushering her little lad out as quickly as she could. What must I have looked like? Shame enveloped me.

Then, just as I felt my mood sliding further down than it had in days, I heard his comforting tones.

'You all right Emma?'

'Not really Les,' I said. I was learning to be honest. And I could tell Les about this. As much as it sickened me to say it out loud. I shoved the letter under his nose.

'Ah. Right. I see.' He put the letter down then walked behind the hut, coming in through the back door. 'Sit yourself down. It's my turn to make you an ice cream.'

I sat and smiled as Les attempted to operate the Mr Whippy machine, creating a cornet that looked like it had a white dog poop on the top. He was humming something as he topped it with sprinkles.

'What's that you're singing?' I asked.

'Oh he-he. I didn't realise I was. It was that song that's always on the radio. You know. Der der der, de de de der der der.'

'Pulp,' I shouted with glee. 'I love that song. Der der der de de de der der der!' Then another wave hit me and my voice flatlined. 'I *used* to love that song. That's the song I was singing when I made John a cake.'

'Well that sounds nice. Memories of past relationships don't have to be bad you know.'

'It was the day he dumped me.'

'Ignore every fucking word I say,' he said, handing me the finished ice-cream, all wonky and dribbling down the cone, complete with wonky flake.

'Want to talk about it? You know, what happened with John?'

'I was drunk. I was trying to make him a birthday cake but ended up inadvertently trashing the kitchen. I honestly thought he'd be delighted. I mis-judged it.'

He nodded.

'I just remember the look on his face. Honestly, Les, he wasn't even angry. It wasn't that. He looked...broken. I was still pissed, and I'd obviously passed out. The place was a wreck.'

'He must've loved you. I'm guessing this was going on a while before that day.'

'Yeah. I think. It's hard to know the exact moment that it became a problem really. Cos I'd always been drinking. But yeah, there are drunken work-party gate-crashing memories, and red wine all over the carpet memories, and singing in the street at 1am memories...'

'Oh dear, he said. 'Maybe you owe him an apology. Have you tried?'

'Yep.'

'And?'

'I was drunk when I said it. And of course, he knew.'

'Ah,' he said. 'Anyway, what are we going to do about this petition?'

My heart sank as I was forced to face the very sobering fact that my inebriated experiences had obviously upset people. A lot of people judging by the number of signatures. There must've been 15 to 20 on there. I couldn't bear to count them up.

'Maybe I just need to resign?' I said.

'I don't think you need to do that. Why not try talking to one of the women who signed? Any idea who they might be?'

'I've a pretty good idea, yep.'

'Then try talking to them. Be honest, open. Apologetic. You've not been well, Emma. But if you take ownership of it, if you explain, you might just get a better response. They already know you were taking something. Just explain what you've been through, how you weren't coping. You don't even need to say the 'a' word.'

'Surely there's an easier way?'

'Course there is. Just like drinking vodka was easier than facing your feelings.'

I shrugged. It was going to be hell. Facing those mums wasn't my idea of fun. But he was right. I might have been struggling. But who knows what *they* might have been dealing with on the day I scooped up a pistachio cone or served a can of coke pissed up and lairy?

'OK. I'll do it. I'll face them. At least, I'll start with Isabella.'

I glanced out towards the open expanse of the park, the sun shining so brightly I could barely see what was in front of me.

Les went on his way, he had shopping to do, he said, and a meeting to go to. He was big into all this peer support stuff and urged me to keep going, and to find a sponsor when the time was right.

'Yoo-hoo!'

It was like Piccadilly Circus today. I stood up and swung

around. 'Dor. What're you doing here?'

'Fancied a cornetto didn't I. Have you got one of them strawberry ones, you know, that has the big lump of actual strawberry on the bottom?'

'We've got strawberry cornettos. No idea about the lump of strawberry.'

She tutted. 'I'll take the mint choc chip then.'

I slid open the top of the fridge and scoured the contents for mint choc chip. 'You don't usually come for ice cream Dor?'

'Look, love. I might be an old battle axe sometimes. But I'm allowed to worry about you.'

'You were checking up on me?'

'No dear. Checking *in* on you. Two different things.'

I raised my eyebrows.

'Who was that man you were chatting to before. Is that the fella who took you to hospital?'

'Yeah. That's Les. Nice guy. He's in recover…shit.'

'What?'

'I don't think I'm meant to… Fuck. Anyway, yeah that's Les. Lovely bloke.'

'I must buy him a drink for looking after our Emma. I mean, he saved your life, really.'

'No excuse to make a move on him Dor. Do you ever take time out from your manhunt?'

'It's better than hunting foxes.'

'True,' I agreed, not that the comparison made much sense. And Dor's response to thanking him just reinforced how booze was literally the answer to everything.

'But anyway, he's my friend, you keep your dirty mitts off. He might have a girlfriend for all I know,' I said, although I knew it was unlikely. Les seemed to be living a fairly solitary life. Apart from all these meetings he was going to.

'So, I'm cooking tonight. Then Dave's taking you to see a movie.'

'Jeez, Dor. Honestly, I don't need babysitting 24/7. I'm

not about to get drunk you know. And don't think I don't know that you've hidden your whiskey.'

'Well, why were you looking?'

'I wasn't. It's lived next to the cornflakes the entire time I've lived with you. Hard to miss it.'

'Well, I just didn't want you feeling…threatened.'

'It's hardly going to pull a gun out on me Dor is it.'

'No. But it could very well end up killing you,' she said, the tone in her voice harder. She was genuinely worrying about me. But the idea of being accompanied constantly, it didn't bear thinking about. Perhaps just for tonight, just this once, I'd show gratitude. I owed them that at least.

'Seriously though Dor, I do appreciate it. You, Dave, me dad inviting me on daily walks with Trev.'

'He loves you, Emma. We all do.'

'And I love you all too,' I said, my heart feeling as though it might burst any second. I truly was blessed. I'd been an absolute arsehole to everyone. Time and time again. But here they still were, they had my back, and they were doing everything they could to help me stay well.

'I'm sorry, Dor.'

'What for sweetheart?'

'For being awful. I've been so…. difficult. Ungrateful. A bit of a cow, really.'

'Well…yeah. But you're a good 'un Emma. It wasn't you; it was the booze. Or the pills. Or whatever the hell you were poisoning yourself with.'

'Well, *I* chose to poison myself.'

'Did you though? I mean, perhaps if you think about the *why* rather than the *what* it might help you?'

As our chat was interrupted by a customer wanting a packet of cheese 'n' onion and a can of Red Bull, I tried to take on board what she might have meant.

The *why* not the *what*?

Despite the shame, my behaviour, my absolute car crash of a life lately, the *why* felt much, *much* harder than the what.

CHAPTER 42

'We haven't done this since we were like, 14 or something,' Dave said.

'We haven't done this since they tripled the prices.' I replied, scanning the illuminated menus high above the fast-food counter in the cinema. 'Jesus Christ Dave, I'll need to take out a mortgage to buy a hotdog in here.'

Dave was shifting about on his feet uncomfortably. I'd criticised the jigsaw puzzle, now I was criticising his choice of night out.

I tried to reassure him. 'It's great fun though isn't it. Living like we did in our teens.'

He smiled.

What else were we going to do though. I mean, so far, I'd tried dog walking on the beach with my dad, cups of tea and chips and egg in the garden with Dor, ice creams with Les and jigsaw puzzles and the cinema with Dave. As far as non-alcoholic activities go, they were doing the best they could. I certainly couldn't come up with anything better. And it was starting to weigh me down.

We grabbed a fortune's worth of food and pop and made our way into one of the big screen rooms.

'What we watching again?' I asked.

'Oh um. That new Tom Cruise one. Mission Impossible.'

'Nice one.'

We munched our way through the hot dogs and nachos with that God awful liquid cheese on as the trailers played. There was something comforting about doing the things we did as kids. I knew exactly where my head was going to be in two or three hour's time. I wasn't about to leap out into the traffic trying to flag a cab and I wasn't about to drunk dial John, pleading, and begging to take me back. I was going to sleep in my own bed, well, Dor's bed, with my PJs firmly on and little Trev curled up at my feet.

'Is um. Is Ally OK with us hanging out together tonight?'

'Course, Emma. She thinks you're mint.'

'But I've kind of been hogging you…?'

'Shhh!' Someone in front was obviously enjoying the trailers more than expected. I decided to make only the most acceptable of cinema noises and crunched my disgusting cheesy nachos as loudly as I could.

'You're hogging me in a good way. And at a reasonable hour. It was the phone calls at nearly midnight from worried workmates she couldn't cope with,' Dave whispered.

'Shhh!'

'Alright mate. Jeez…' Dave said, twisting his neck to see who was trying to shush us up.

The film started and I realised that I needed to sit and concentrate for the next couple of hours. Perhaps if I focused hard on whatever mission Mr Cruise was finding impossible, I might be able to stop the noisy arguments going on in my head.

That was the sad thing about sitting in the cinema next to Dave. I loved him more than anyone, and we knew each other better than anyone else. But what I'd been through lately, with the drink and everything, it kind of put a gulf between us that never previously existed. How could I possibly explain what it felt like to feel that compelled to drink. Not just 'hey it's Friday night let's get hammered'—it wasn't anything like that. That had choice woven right the way through it.

The film ended and we all filed out as the credits rolled down and the music went up to sustain the dramatic atmosphere. We stepped over paper drinks cups and hot dog wrappers and nachos crunched beneath our trainers as we made our way back into the final hour or so of daylight.

'Fancy coming back to ours for a cuppa?' Dave offered.

'You sure you're not both sick of me already?'

'Nah. We've got that bloody jigsaw to finish anyway. I'm not being beaten by an old person's pastime.'

'Stubborn git! Sure,' I said. 'I'd love to.'

'Cool. We'll order a pizza.'

'We've just had hot dogs, Dave!'

'Living on the edge, Emma. Just…don't tell Ally we've already eaten.'

'You getting grief?'

'Yeah, believe it or not, now you're like some kind of model of healthy living, she's telling me to cut back on the crap. She chucked my smoky bacon away and it hadn't even gone off. I mean, what the fuck is that about?'

'She must love you, Dave.'

'Do you think?'

'Sure.'

'And what do you think? Of me and Ally?'

'It's hardly up to me. Do you love her?'

'I think so.'

'Then it's great. Perfect. Happy days.'

'But your opinion does matter.'

'Look. I was jealous that she was taking up all your time. I know how it came across. But honestly, I was just jealous. I've always liked her, that's probably why I appeared to hate her. Cos it was fucking frustrating that I couldn't find much to complain about when it came to Ally.'

'Really?'

'Really.'

'But you had John. Sorry, but I mean. When you were still with John. You weren't exactly pleasant to her.'

'Oh Dave. I don't know. My head was a fucking shed. Seriously. I was probably the most selfish, self-obsessed fucking cow on the planet. I just needed everyone's attention on me. And then, when I got it, I needed you to all fuck off again so I could have a proper drink. My fucking head, Dave. Ignore anything that I ever said, did or thought over the last year or so.'

'Yeah. I guess you have been a bit of a tit.'

'Not denying it.'

Dave stopped in his tracks, tugging on my arm to follow suit. 'I can't stop worrying about you, Em,' he said. 'I don't know how to.'

'But I'm here. I'm sober.'

'But for how long?'

'Thanks for that Dave.'

'I just mean…I don't know how to help you. How to know if you're struggling.'

'I'll tell you.'

'Will you though?'

I thought about it. I had no idea if I would if I was honest. This was all new to me. Sobriety, talking about it all, trying to get my head around everything that had happened. Taking responsibility for everything that had happened.

'I honestly don't know. I don't know how this is supposed to play out. All I know is that today feels good.'

'But what if…'

'But what if anything,' I said. 'Who knows anything? I do know one thing, though. The one thing you can do for me.'

'Go on.'

'Just keep being you. Don't pussyfoot around me, don't try to second guess. Just be you. The same you you've always been.'

'But I'm not the same. *We're* not the same anymore. Things change…'

'We know more now, sure. But what I mean is, just…go with your gut Dave. I've got my doctor; I've got my group. I've got Les to exchange war stories with. I don't need anything new or different from you other than you just being you. I veered away from everything that mattered to me the most. You and your terrible cups of tea and your terrible jokes…'

'Watch it,' he said, smiling.

'…and your loveliness.' I finished. 'That's what I need. Our normality. Whatever that is.'

He smiled at me as we stood under the concrete streetlight on the concrete path in front of the cinema and the ice rink. Then he looked out towards the sea of cars…

'Where did I park up?'

'You fucking dope.' I laughed.

CHAPTER 43

'Give me one good reason I shouldn't fire you on the spot?'

Isabella charged over to the hut, crutch under arm, face full of wrath. She took up residency next to Les, who I was having a nice calm chat with until that point.

She was clearly on the warpath. She'd been a bloody angel when I told her, albeit with a few details missing, about my hospital trips. But the petition had really tested her patience. But I couldn't *not* tell her. I mean, there were enough names on it, so somebody was going to find out and tell her straight. Les was right, if it came from me, at least there was a degree of transparency. Something I hadn't been so good at the last few months….

'I know how it looks…' I said, ready to embrace the irony that I was about to get sacked for the second time, but this time for getting sober and telling the truth. Well, sort of…

'How it looks? The facts are there in black and white.' She hit the paper repeatedly with the back of her fingers. 'You were drinking *and* taking drugs. You've just told me as much.'

'Isabella...' Les piped up.

'What the hell has this got to do with you?' She sneered. 'You're just as bad.'

'I *was* just as bad. I was just as ill.'

'Ill? Jesus Christ. Ill?' She turned back to me. 'Tell me, who forced those bloody drinks down yer neck Emma?'

'Nobody but me. Which is why I'm apologising. Honestly, I am truly sorry. But I'm getting better.'

'Once an addict always an addict,' she tutted.

'You've just had a hip replacement,' Les said. 'You're walking with a crutch.'

'What the hell has that got to do with anything?'

'Emma was ill. She'd had a traumatic time as a kid. And she used booze to prop herself up. Same thing.'

'Don't be so bloody ridiculous.'

'Please, both of you. Stop it.' I was wilting in the corner, picking at the plastic covering of an unopened tray of Chupa Chups lollies. 'Look, I get what you're saying. You've every right to sack me. I totally understand that, and I wouldn't hold it against you. But on the other hand, given you're not exactly mobile yet, you could give me a second chance. A trial run, kind of thing.'

'You've had your trial run.'

'Not since I've been sober, though. Not really.'

She looked me up and down, then her eyes darted to Les, back to me.

'They say never trust an addict.'

'Well, you don't have to. You can take it day by day. If I fu.... if I mess up, you can fire me. Balls in your court.'

'And,' Les added. 'I think you'll see that Emma's going to be trying harder than anyone else, given that she feels as though she has to prove herself to you.'

'Huh.' Isabella mulled it over.

'Honestly, I really am in a better place. I really am. I haven't touched a drop for over a week...'

'And the smack?'

I jolted with surprise. 'Smack?'

'You're a smackhead, aren't you? That's what they've said.'

'No, God no.' I had to concentrate hard to stop myself from laughing at the naïve association

'Not that it should make a difference,' Les interrupted. Isabella shot him another death stare.

'No, it's meds that the doctor's been giving me.' I thought better than tell her about the wobbly eggs I got from Hula

Hoop Paul. 'They first prescribed them a couple of years ago. I had been having panic attacks. I was in therapy about my mum leaving…'

'Your mum?'

'Yeah, well, ages ago, but she left one day and never came back, and I hadn't really…'

'Your mum left you?'

'Yeah. I was only eight or something. I've not seen her since.'

'Well why didn't you say ever say anything,' she barked.

'Well, it's not the kind of thing…'

'But if you'd said...'

'It was years ago and…'

Isabella's eyes darted uncomfortably around the hut. There was a tense moment of silence. 'I lost my mum when I was young,' she said.

'I'm sorry to hear that,' I said.

'And you're really not taking anything anymore?' she asked.

'Not had a drink or anything in almost two weeks. Longest I've been sober in years.'

'OK. Well, if, *if*, I decide to give you another chance, how do you propose we deal with the complainants?'

I was stumped. I had no idea. How *should* we deal with the complainants?

'We tell them the truth,' Les said. 'Emma has been dealing with difficult life circumstances, she became very unwell, and now she's getting help and is on the mend. Just like you,' he said, nodding towards her crutches.

Isabella blatantly didn't like the comparison, but she was definitely defrosting, the tautness of her lips beginning to relax.

'OK. OK. I will speak to the person who filed the petition. There's a number on it isn't there?'

'I think so,' I said, nervous about how Isabella was going to explain my problems to the mummy brigade.

'So, in the meantime, to help me out, what with the lost trade and everything, can you open up an extra day, Monday?'

'Sure,' I said, desperately trying to hide any resentment. But thinking on it, what else was I going to do? It would be nice to spend another day here. To fill this hut with more positive memories. To tip the scales.

Isabella left us to it, taking the petition with her. I was relieved. Relieved that she'd, albeit begrudgingly, given me a second chance. Another one. And relieved that she'd left the hut. I felt wound up in her presence. I knew it wasn't her fault. I just felt I needed to be around people I could be wholly honest with. And regardless of what I told her, I was never going to go into *all* the guts and gore of it.

'I just don't know whether I should feel glad of a second chance, or like, well, like I don't deserve it,' I said, wiping down the counter to keep myself busy and prove to myself that I was a good worker.

Les didn't respond. I turned to him. 'Les?' I said. He still didn't respond. He seemed…vacant.

I walked over to him and gently squeezed his arm, thankfully he stirred.

'You, OK? Did you fall asleep or something?'

'I'm not sure.' He seemed confused. 'I think I'm a bit tired. I've not been sleeping well lately.'

'Maybe you should get back home for a kip?'

'I think I might just do that,' he said.

CHAPTER 44

I picked up the phone, Dave, and Dor in the background, egging me on. Weird, really, given that only weeks ago they'd have told me off for drunk dialling and everything. But now, as a stone-cold sober person with a boatload of guilt, it seemed to be the right thing to do.

They had the back door wide open and were sitting in the sunshine in the yard, Dor using two chairs so she could put her feet up, Dave plumping for the tiny bit of grass that was now almost recovered from the bonfire. Every so often he chucked a manky old tennis ball and Trev went hurtling towards the bottom of the garden in hot pursuit.

I felt a rush of something shoot through my body, my head feeling dizzied by it and my mouth feeling suddenly drier than a Jack Dee comedy sketch. John might not want to talk to me. He might cut me off. He might be angry that I dare to intrude on his new life.

He might have a girlfriend. And a new puppy. And, and, and…

'Fuck's sake Emma. Just do it,' Dave hollered through. Trev was making excitable noises by Dave's side, panting around in anticipation for the next round of go fetch.

'Thanks for the support,' I shouted back, just as the ball bounced off the fence again.

I dialled the number, the number that used to be *my* number too. It was ringing. I found myself glancing down the hallway and out into the garden at Dave and Dor who looked as pale under the sunshine as I felt. A trickle of sweat dripped down my back and I couldn't decide if I was too hot or anxious.

It rang and rang. And…nothing. No answer. My heart

sank with the weight of disappointment. But I also felt relieved. I hung up the receiver and realised I was only delaying the inevitable awful conversation.

'No answer.' I announced, heading out into the yard, unable to take a seat with Dor who now had her head in Take a Break magazine, or join Dave on the grass because I just felt…restless. On edge.

Sick to the stomach.

'Did you let it ri…'

'Course! What did you think I was doing, ringing the speaking clock?'

'Well, I wouldn't put it pa…'

'Dave!' My lip developed an involuntary tremble.

'There's no need to…'

'Fuck off Dave.'

'Fuck's sake.' He sighed, slowly stood up and walked over to me, wrapping his big arms around me for a squeeze. It only served to release more of a deluge of tears. I was so glad I still had him.

I blubbed. A snot bubble growing in my left nostril. 'You snotty cow,' Dave joked. I smiled, grateful to have someone I could snot on and not worry about it.

The phone rang.

'I'll get it.' Dor practically sang as she hopped up out of her chair and slipped her flip flops back on to head inside the house.

'You can try him again,' Dave said kindly. 'I'm sure he'll be happy to hear how you're doing.'

'I hope so.' I said, picking aimlessly at the grass I was now sitting on.

'Coo-ey Emma! It's for you-hoo!' Dor was skipping back outside.

'Who is it?'

'It's John, sweetheart,' she said, carefully placing her hand on mine before I stood up quickly then felt immediately glued to the spot.

'Run along Emma.' She ordered, flicking the back of her hand towards the kitchen door. 'This is what you wanted.'

'But how did he?'

'Must've done that 1471 thing.' Dave said.

'Maybe.'

'Well, go on then.'

The pair of them were staring at me. I walked into the house, my heart racing, and found the phone receiver sitting on top of the Hull White Pages on the shelf.

'Hello?' I said, tentatively, as if I wasn't sure who to expect.

'You called me?'

My heart felt like it had plummeted through the floorboards. His tone was flat. Flat like the day he ended things. Flat like the day he found me asleep on the living room floor, cigarette burnt to ash, and the record still turning even though it had finished playing.

'I…yeah. I wanted to apologise, John.'

'What for?' He was still abrupt. Who could blame him? I had to remind myself that he didn't owe me anything. It was entirely the other way around.

'For making such a huge mess of things.'

'And how are you doing now?'

'I'm good. Well, that's a stretch if I'm honest. I'm better than I was, put it that way. Sober, anyway.'

He sniffed. 'How long?'

'Since I landed myself in hospital.' I decided there was no longer any point trying to minimise what had been going on. We'd already broken up. I was desperately trying to be as true and honest as I could be after months of lies and manipulation. I'd been awful.

'Hospital? Is everything…'

'Yeah. It is now. No long-term damage done anyway. I was…I…'

'Fancy a coffee?'

'Yeah,' I trilled. 'Yeah, that would be, just lovely, actually.' I said, more calmly now.

'I'd like to see you. To chat. Properly. I don't mean…'

'No, no of course. I wasn't expecting…'

'I just…it would be nice to know how you're doing, to see you.'

'Yeah, me too. I mean…'

'I know.' He chuckled, starting to sound a little lighter. 'Why don't I meet you at work? We can grab an ice-cream. Maybe walk over to that place that serves mint tea on the avenues?'

'Ah that'd be great,' I said.

'Great, I'll see you tomorrow then?'

'Perfect.'

'When do you close up?'

'Bout 5.'

'See you then, Emma.'

I almost melted as he said my name.

'See you then.'

He hung up and my mind was racing but this time with party poppers and sparkles rather than doom and gloom. Would there be a chance to get back together? My heart was fluttering at the very idea. But then it crashed…he said he didn't mean…he didn't mean he wanted to get back together. He was making that clear. He just wants to know I'm OK. Oh God, we *are* in the friend zone. I've got Dave for that. I don't need John for that. Could I even see John that way? Has he already started to think of me platonically? There will be no going back from that.

'You OK lovey?' Dor had come in to find me just standing in the hallway. Staring vacantly into the patterned wallpaper…paisley style swirls beginning to merge into blobs. I jolted myself out of my daze.

'Yeah, we're meeting up. Tomorrow.'

'Well, that's progress.'

'Yeah,' I said.

'What you going to wear?'

'Och, Dor, really! It's not a date. He made that clear.'

'Still?' She shrugged, a smile spreading across her face.

'No, really. It's not. He made it clear. Don't wind me up. I'll only feel disappointed.'

'OK. Well, you can try to chill out today then. Dave's snuck out down the ten foot to grab some burgers from Iceland. We're getting the barbie out. You choose some tunes and I'll grab the sun cream and a bottle of Cream Soda.'

'Ah Dor no. You two have a beer or whatever. Honestly, it'll make me feel awful to think I'm stopping you…'

'You're not.' She lied. 'I'm having a nice cold cream soda and ice.'

'Whatever,' I said feeling deflated. This was what it was going to be like from now on. My boozy affliction casting a shadow over every barbie, football match, every trip to the park when the Rainbow Fest was on …people were always going to be nervous around me. Unable to just do their thing. And to be honest, I was nervous too.

What was *my thing* going to be now?

I chucked a mix tape on and heard the back gate clatter. Dave was obviously back.

'Look at this impressive haul of meat,' he said.

'Yes, but what have you bought, Dave.' Dor said with a wink.

I shook my head and smiled.

'Oh, Emma,' Dave said as he started unpacking the contents of the carrier bag and laying them out on the green plastic table. 'I knocked at your dad's. He's joining us for a hot dog.'

'That'll be nice,' I said. And meant it.

'Good, cos he's on his way.'

'Who fancies getting the barbie fired up then?' Dor asked.

'I'll do it.' I said, pleased to make myself useful as Dor handed me a bag of charcoal. 'What are we cooking then?'

'Burgers, hot dogs, got some prawns…. oh, and some salad as a nod to healthy living and all that.' Dave's Iceland haul also came complete with two litre bottles of Cream Soda and Tizer.

'Looks like a kid's party,' I said. 'Honestly, I really don't mind if you drink.'

I couldn't really bear the thought of them drinking around me. Not so soon after quitting. I still wasn't sure how I was going to handle sobriety. And the idea of having to do it forever, Jesus. One day at a time. That's what they say. And that whole thing about not being able to drink like 'normal' people, there was something in that. I'd already proven that to myself after my first little slip up. Well, humongous fucking car crash might be more accurate.

'We're grand having a day off. Probably be good for us.' Dave reassured.

'Have you briefed Tel, Dave?' Dor asked, unstacking paper cups and lining them up next to the pop bottles.

'Course.'

'Daft sod'll probably be panicking like mad having to socialise dry,' I said.

'Well, it'll be entertaining then at the very least,' Dave said. 'Anyway, have you managed to get anything going yet?'

'Almost.' I said, looking around for something to waft the flames with. 'Two ticks.' I ran towards the shed at the bottom of the garden and found an old tennis racket.

Dave stood gawping at me and my tennis racket. 'What do you think you're doing? There's no time to play at Steffi Graf when you've been given the most responsible job of the day.'

'I'm not,' I said, as I furiously wafted the flames with the tennis racket. 'See, it's working.'

I heard the back gate clatter again and my dad's head appeared slowly from behind it, as if checking there was no danger before entering.

'Tel. Get yersel in here.' Dor called. He looked undecided as he manoeuvred his way from behind the gate into the open space of Dor's back yard. He nodded his head at us all and Trev bounded over to him, his tail wagging furiously. He dropped the soggy tennis ball by my dad's feet. He didn't pick it up. They were a bit marmitey, my dad and Trev. I sometimes wondered if Trev gave him all the extra attention just to wind him up.

'How you are doin,' Tel?' Dave asked while elbowing me out of the way of the barbecue to start loading up the burgers.

'Grand,' he said, making his way towards the fizzy drinks table. 'Ooh,' he said, his acting as stiff as a plank of wood. 'I love a Tizer, me.' And as I looked at Dave, we both burst out laughing.

'What'd I say?' My dad looked at us, unimpressed. We were beside ourselves.

'Nothing.' Dor said. 'They're just being daft. Ere, you having burgers, hot dogs, or both?'

'Both, thanks,' Dad said, sitting quietly at the table, paper cup of Tizer in hand. He sipped it, then held it away from his face, scowling quizzically at it. I nearly started again but Dave gave me another elbow in the ribs.

'So, the divorce is done then,' My dad said. 'Not that I'm a royalist, of course. Don't see the bloody point in them personally.'

'Charles and Diana?' I asked.

'Hmm. I could see that coming from the day they wed.' He added.

'How exactly, Tel?' Dor asked.

'Ah you know.'

I smiled. He didn't really have any idea I don't think. I just think he was always on a doomed autopilot.

'She was too good for them anyway.' Dor added.

'Are you blaspheming the Royals, Dor?' I joked.

'Blaspheming. They're not bloody gods you know.'

'They are in some people's eyes.' My dad added taking another suspicious sip of his Tizer.

'Jesus Christ if this is the craic without booze, I'd rather pour vodka down my neck.' I laughed.

'Me 'n' all.' Dave chipped in. I was glad we could at least make a bit of light about it all. 'How's the job going Tel?' he asked.

'Good, good.' He was a man of few words, but he was blatantly perkier at the change in subject. Funny how my dad could get more excited about work than anything else. I guess that after years of unemployment, getting up for the 6 - 2 shift was the very thing that put a spring back in his step. Well, that and Barbara Carpenter of course. 'How's yours going at the ice cream van Emma?'

'It's a hut, Dad.'

'Sorry, love.'

'It's good, yeah. I'm enjoying it. It's a nice distraction.'

'Good sugar substitute,' he said.

'Eh?'

'All that ice cream. Now you're dry and that.'

'Bloody hell Dad.'

'Just saying, love. You like it, though?'

'I do. I've learnt my wafer from my sugar cone and know how to perfect a Mr Whippy.'

'Might pop over with Babs. Say hi.'

'Babs.' I chuckled under my breath, getting yet another elbow in the ribs from Dave.

'Think these burgers are looking ready. How many Tel?'

'Just the one please.'

'Coming up.'

'Make it two,' he said, changing his mind as the smell of the charcoal and beef clearly tantalised his tastebuds.

Dave chucked a couple of burgers into buns and handed them round.

Dad placed his little plate onto his lap, suddenly distracted by thoughts of football. 'Dave fella, did you see the results?'

'I know Tel. 2-2. Bloody Scarborough as well.'

'Flamin' joke' he said biting into his flour topped burger, ketchup dropping onto his knee. He was oblivious. 'I'm tellin' you son. We've got some graft to do.'

Dave's eyes lit up. They always did when my dad called him son. 'We'll get there Tel. One day, we'll be promoted.'

'Likely story.'

They both laughed and, with Hull City chat and burgers in full flow, I realised that it was possible. We were the same four people we were with or without a drink. The only thing that changed was how much I could appreciate it.

'Bloody dog!' My dad yelled and I swung round to find Trev happily wolfing down a half-eaten burger on the lawn.

CHAPTER 45

I remembered going for that first date with John. Meeting up down the pub, him ordering in a pint. Me taking a seat, feeling nervous and panicking over whether I'd done up my fly or whether my tampon was going to leak. I had been waiting for weeks for that date. We'd seen each other at the park, at the vets…then finally, he asked me out. I'd been bursting with excitement. I knew, straight away, that he wasn't going to be a waster like most of the others. There was something genuine about him. Like, his trainers weren't the best, and he had the worst taste in furniture - his flat was like someone had just chucked together a load of random 80s pieces from a charity shop. But that's why I knew he'd be good for me. Cos he wasn't obsessed with how things *looked.*

And our first trip away, he only went and took me to a bloody caravan park in Withernsea. Jesus. That was my birthday gift. I know how ungrateful it sounds, but I worked in a bloody caravan factory. I was spending day in, day out, ordering the bloody bathrooms and kitchens for those bloody static holiday homes. He just wasn't out to impress me, he just wanted to spend time with me. And that mini break, well, it was probably the best holiday I've ever had.

Can you believe it, the best holiday I've ever had was a few miles down the road in Withernsea?

I think that's why I was so nervous about today. Because he didn't do anything for show. And there was so much expectation attached to today. Well, more, the wonder of potential. It could go either way. But at least I knew he wanted to see me. At least I knew he didn't hate me. Or he wouldn't bother, surely?

It was difficult not to let that glimmer of hope get inside my head and chuck an imaginary 'back together again' party. And a wedding. The idea that one day soon we might be moving back in together and picking it all back up again. Beach walks with the dogs, eating crisps in bed, drinking…

Why was it fucking everywhere? Was there nothing in life that was safe from the association of merry times on booze?

Hope was something I'd always been told I needed more of, but I knew how devastating it could be when it was dashed too. I needed to keep my fantasies in check.

I kept checking the time. He was coming to meet me at closing, so there were still a few hours to kill.

I breathed in the fresh air and glanced across the park.

I noticed the ice cream dribbles that a toddler had left behind on the little path, and the sound of a bird singing the same two notes over and over and over, interspersed occasionally with the sound of a heavy, rackety lorry going past on the main road behind the leafy hedges.

I strained to listen to the bird song, just as Les had taught me. Was it a Chiff Chaff? No, definitely not a Chiff Chaff, but it had a similar melody…was it telling the other birds to fuck off, trying to attract a mate or just singing happily. I was hoping it was the latter.

Les appeared in the distance so I prepared him a cone.

'Afternoon, Emma.'

I handed him the ice cream and turned to make myself one. 'How're you Les?'

'Ah you know. Bit off colour, to be honest,' he said. 'Off to see the doctor day after tomorrow.'

'You got this thing that's going around?'

'No, I don't think so. It's, I don't know, probably just a hangover from years of drinking. I keep having little blackouts. At least, I think I am. Must've killed off a few too many brain cells, eh?'

I let out a brief chuckle and studied his face. He seemed

perturbed by it. Les usually took everything in his stride, or at least that's how it came across.

His talk of blackouts worried me. What if he really *had* done some long-term damage? What if *I* had? Maybe it wouldn't be fair to be with John anyway given how much I'd fucked my body over with a cocktail of poison.

'Well, at least you're seeing the doc. They'll sort you right out.' I said, as confidently as I could muster.

'We'll see,' he said, eyeing his ice cream, seemingly trying to decide whether to go for another bite of the flake or dollop of the Whippy first.

He perked up. 'Anyway, what's going on with you?'

'I called John. You know, my ex. We're meeting after work tonight.'

'And how do you feel about that?'

'Apprehensive, I guess. I mean, I keep trying not to get my hopes up, but it's hard, isn't it?'

'It is.'

'Did you have a wife, a partner?' I asked, realising that we'd never discussed it before. I knew he had a daughter who he was all but estranged from. But we never talked about anyone else.

'I did, yeah. Kind of fucked that up.' He laughed, adding a dramatic tut and roll of the eyes.

'What happened?' I asked, suddenly feeling intrusive. 'I mean if you want to talk about it.' I added.

'Sure. Since finding recovery, I've done little else. You soon find that talking about things becomes therapeutic. It's like shaking an old rug out into the street.'

I nodded attentively.

'Joan, she was called. Well, is called. I'm assuming she's still doing OK, anyway. It just got too much for her, really. I'm not sure there's any other way of describing it. She was living under such stress, day in day out. Not knowing what she was going to come home to. She worked part time at a local chemist. And there's something seriously wrong when you're happier at work than you are at home, isn't there?'

'I guess,' I said. 'Although to be fair, this place has, weirdly, done me the world of good. I mean, it holds some scary memories, even though I've not been here long. I've managed to rack up a few dramas in this little hut, haven't I?'

'You certainly have. But look at you. You keep coming back. No matter what this place reminds you of, you're here, facing it. That's a real strength, you know.'

'Well, to be fair, I haven't got much choice. I need the job.'

There was a moment's silence that I filled by wiping down the counter with a paper towel. Les was such a calming human being. I realised how much I looked up to him. Like, if I was in trouble, I could think '*what would Les do?*'

'I'm nervous Les,' I said, honestly. 'I'm nervous about what might happen if I meet John and it's like a parting conversation. Finalising things.'

'But you're no worse off really. You're not together and you've had to get used to that.'

'I guess. It's just…that potential. I'm worried if I have my hopes dashed, I'll be back on the floor. And we know what happens then.'

'We know what has *previously* happened then. Do you feel like you want a drink?'

'No. God, no. But I'm worried I might. Like, I don't know what could tip me over the edge.'

'Thing is, you know where the edge is. You've seen it and, let's be honest, you've plummeted over it a good few times now! You're aware. You're in a totally different place.

'Well how do I make sure that I stay there? I mean, what would you do if you had something difficult, emotional, coming up?'

'Face it. And acknowledge that pain is part of life. Feel it. Look on it as an experience. You'd never be happy if you couldn't feel sad.'

'Easier said than done,' I said, feeling disappointed at Les' response.

'The best and most important things in life are never the easiest. Stick with it, Emma. You've got your group meetings, you've got your friends, Dave, and Doreen. Your dad. You've got me. You're not alone. You'll never be alone now it's all out there. As long as you keep it all out there. Don't retreat into yourself. Talking will keep you well. Secrets will keep you sick.'

'Thank you,' I said, my eyes welling up. 'Means a lot…'

'Thank *you*,' he said. 'We all help each other. It's never a one-way street. And I've already learnt so much from you.'

'What like not to mix vodka and wobbly eggs.' I laughed.

'Maybe,' he chuckled. 'But no, in all seriousness…you've taught me a lot. I called my daughter for the first time in months since you and I met. Felt like I could understand her a bit more.'

'How did *I* help with that?' I asked, genuinely perplexed by it.

'Because you felt abandoned by John, just as I felt abandoned by my daughter. But talking about it with you. If I'm honest, it reminded me that it was the other way round. *We* abandoned *them*.'

'Jeez, Les. I never thought about it like that before.'

'And as much as I've learnt over the years, we do need to keep learning, keep reminding ourselves. I had started to feel the self-pity rising. Thinking she was being cruel to me. That was nonsense so I called her and said it out loud to her. Honestly.'

'And?'

'And we're meeting up for a brew next week.'

'Aww Les that's amazing,' I beamed.

'I know,' he said. 'Anyway, I'm off to meet a pal. Good luck for later. You'll be grand whichever way it goes. I know you will.'

He waved goodbye, taking his usual de-tour around the duck pond, leaving my heart bursting with sunshine and hope.

CHAPTER 46

'99 please.'

'John!' He was early. Keen? Or keen to get it over with? 'Two ticks. I'll just cash up then I'm done…'

He looked as gorgeous as the day we met. My chest fluttered and I felt like I had a lump forming in my throat.

'No worries.' He was dressed in a brown Adidas T-shirt and his favourite well-worn jeans. I couldn't help but wonder if he'd worn them on purpose. He stood looking the other way while I finished off my jobs, kicking the back of his trainers in the dust. I watched his shoulders hunch as he thrust both his hands in his pockets nervously.

I removed my apron to reveal a still-white vest top and my own well-worn flared jeans that were frayed at the bottom thanks to many years of them dragging on the floor. I never could do heels.

I felt slightly queasy and unsure whether to have another ice cream but then realised it would probably make him suspicious if I wasn't eating.

'Monkey's blood?' I asked.

'Please.'

'Sprinkles and a flake?'

'Just the flake please.'

It was all so polite. Was he nervous too?

I made two slightly imperfect 99s, handed them to John and exited out the back of the hut, grappling with the dodgy lock and key and walking around the front to double check the shutters were properly closed. He handed me my cone.

'So…shall we stay in the park for a bit?' I asked.

'Yeah. Why not,' he said. And we walked, grateful of the

ice cream distraction to divert from the awkward silences. 'Nice day for it.' He wasn't saying much. Why would he? *I* asked to speak with him. But he was the one who had asked to meet up.

Maybe we'd lost our sparkle?

'I really am sorry,' I blurted out. It seemed like the only natural place to start.

'I know you are. But you don't have to be.'

I stared at him blankly. Why didn't I have to be sorry? Had he done worse? Had he had an affair? What did he mean?

'Well, I kind of do. I mean. It's all my fault. And that cake was the last straw.'

'It wasn't the cake, Emma.' He sounded serious, stern. I gulped hard. 'I couldn't watch you doing that to yourself anymore.'

My chest heaved.

'It was never the loud music or the disastrous baking. It was you. I couldn't bear to see *you* like that. Doing that to yourself.' He looked at me as he said it, as if waiting for me to respond. I could see tears welling up in his eyes.

I stood there dumbstruck.

'Emma, I tried, begged you to do something about it. It was heart-breaking. You just couldn't see it. You were in denial. I felt like there was nothing else I could do but watch you slowly kill yourself. I'd never had panic attacks before…'

'You were having panic attacks too?'

'Aye.'

'I had no idea.'

He looked at me, hurt. 'You weren't really here. Not for a long time. It felt as though I'd lost you completely. I couldn't trust you anymore.'

'I never cheated…' Then it hit me. Since he broke it off with me there'd been Hula Hoop Paul. Jesus, I felt sick. That would need to be said, wouldn't it? In the spirit of honesty and all that? I don't know. I didn't cheat. I wasn't even being me.

'I didn't mean that Em. I just meant…we couldn't go anywhere together without it turning into chaos. Without some blazing row.'

'I'm so, so sorry.'

'I honestly, I've never felt so angsty. Rushing home from work, hoping you'd be OK, not passed out, not slurring. The times I had to listen to you breathe while you slept. To make sure you were breathing OK. To make sure you weren't sick. It was like being on high alert 24/7. I couldn't cope anymore.'

'I never really thought. I guess…when you're as wasted as I was, you just don't realise. I was so selfish, John. So fucking obsessed with getting the next drink. It was like walking around on a mission every day and nothing else mattered. I mean, it did, of course it did. But it was like something was taking over me.'

He listened intently. 'You weren't happy. I wondered if it was me. If I was holding you back? I don't know.'

I wanted to cry at those words. 'How could you think that? You were the only thing keeping me going.'

'But I wasn't, was I? The only thing keeping you going wa…'

'I know. I know.' As much as Les said talking about it was a good thing, I still struggled to hear it sometimes. Especially from the people I loved. But I knew I had to hear it, to feel it. To understand what it was like for him. Because, at the end of the day, my own memories were sketchy to say the least.

'You weren't happy. You were just…unbelievably unhappy. I wondered if things might pick up after you left.'

'Took a bit of a nosedive to be fair.'

'Yeah, I heard. How are you now?'

'Good. Well, no. Better than I was. Sober. Clean. It's been a couple of weeks now.'

'That's great.'

'Yeah. It's my second attempt. But I don't know, the first time, I think I was just trying to prove something.'

'That you didn't need to stop?'

'Something like that'

We carried on walking and talking through the park, the breeze gently blowing on my face reminding me why it was good to feel things. Reminding me I couldn't have it all one way. Or at least, if I wanted to feel good, I'd have to feel bad. Because otherwise, there'd be nothing but blackness.

'You've got good support around you then?' He asked.

'Yeah. Dor's been a dream. And Dave's been, well, honest. I needed it, really.'

'I'm sorry I asked you to go when you were struggling. I should've thought…'

'No. It was entirely the right thing to do. I might still be drinking, we might still be in that place, both of us unhappy, if I'd stayed.'

'But anything could have happened.'

'Well, it did and I'm still here. I needed to see for myself. Nobody else was going to stop me, at the end of the day.'

'Well, you are a stubborn cow.' He laughed. And I was so relieved that the comfort in our chatter was coming back. I pushed his arm playfully.

'So, what now? Like, how are you staying on track and stuff?'

'Meetings. Meetings. More meetings. It's like I've joined a cult.' I laughed. 'I guess I need to go back to counselling though too. I think I just opened up all that stuff about my mum and everything but stopped going thinking I was fixed. And when those feelings came flooding back….and the anxiety…. I just turned the volume up on the booze.'

'Turned the volume up. You blew the bloody speakers.'

I laughed.

We looked at each other for what felt like an age, his eyes

staring into mine, moving in ever so slight flickers from side to side.

'I've really missed you,' he said.

I felt a pang of shyness. 'I don't know why,' I immediately regretted trying to joke my way out of the most important part of the conversation.

Missed me like a friend? Missed me because he was worried? Missed me because…

'I love you, Em.'

It caught my breath. I wasn't expecting it. 'I love you too.'

He moved towards me, his arm coming up as if he was going to touch me, then changing his mind and jerking it away again. He stalled, briefly. It was like we had forgotten how natural it was to touch each other. But then we just fell into it, hugging, tight. I could feel him breathing in and out beneath my grip. It was fast, but it felt like relief, too. My own breath caught in my throat again. And I felt like I could stay here forever.

I didn't know what this meant. I didn't want to assume anything. Devastate my hopes by being over ambitious in them. This was a hug. I hugged Dave. I hugged my dad for fuck's sake. But oh my God, it felt so good. It felt like home. It felt safe. But it felt exhilarating, too.

He pulled away from me, keeping his eyes locked hard into mine. 'I don't think we can just…'

'Yeah, yeah, course. I wasn't expect….'

'But maybe. Maybe we can, I don't know. See how it goes?'

'Sure. Like, as…'

'As two people who are clearly crazy stupid about each other.'

The relief poured out of me, and I felt my face burn with happiness.

'I can't go back to how it was,' he said. 'I can't watch you do that to yourself. But maybe, we can just…. I don't know. Is it too cheesy to say, date?'

'Are you asking me on a date?'

'Aye. I think so.'

My heart nearly exploded in excitement. I dropped the rest of my ice cream and flung my arms around him.

We had a real chance.

CHAPTER 47

'Pros and cons.'

'OK. Cons…'

'Why are you starting with cons?'

'Cos it's easier.'

'Glass half empty today, aren't we?'

'Bad analogy, Dave.'

Me and Dave were lying side by side on Dor's little patch of lawn, soaking up the rays, looking up to the skies with our sunnies covering our eyes and our jeans rolled up to our knees. Dave was desperately trying to talk me into trying out gigs sober.

'OK, so *cons*,' I said defiantly. 'Cons…we'll be aware of everyone else's sweat hitting us in the face in the crowd. Erm…we'll notice the dodgy vocals…we'll remember *everything*.'

'Sound like pros to me…'

'How?'

'Well, we'll steer clear of the sweat therefore avoiding any risk of zombie type contamination, we'll only go to see good bands *and* we'll remember them.'

'We do remember the gigs though. Drunk or not.'

'Do we though? I mean, think back to seeing one of your faves. What can you remember?'

'Hole playing live in Sheffield.'

'Yeah. Go on…what can you remember about it?'

'I danced.'

'And.'

'Ugh some teenagers were necking off right next to me.'

'And…?'

'I don't know.'

'What do you remember about Hole? About being in the same room as your fucking all-time favourite idol? What was Courtney Love wearing? What were you dancing to?'

'I…fucking hell, Dave. I've no idea.'

'See.'

'Can you remember any gigs?'

He paused for a moment. 'Course. But not so much the music. Although - Oasis. The Adelphi. 94. I remember that.'

'Ah yeah. That was a great night.'

'We just had a couple of beers. Cos, John. You know.'

'I was trying to make a good impression.'

'Me too. I wasn't about to scare off the only decent bloke you've ever managed to snare.'

'Ha-ha. Think we were all on best behaviour that night. What a fucking gig. You couldn't imagine it now, could you? Oasis playing the Adelphi?'

'You wouldn't have thought you'd ever see Beautiful South playing The Angel but…'

We laughed, turning our heads to look at each other.

'Think it'll work? Me and John?'

'Emma. The bloke put up with you off your face for two years. You stay sober, I reckon he could well be in it for the long haul.'

'But that's the whole point of this dating idea. That, you know, it might not work out. I might fall off the wagon. He might not like the real me. What if I become boring? Or whingey?'

'If you're anything on the booze you're boring and whingey!'

'I guess.'

'You'll be grand. He's a top fella. And I need you to do it for me, Emma. I've missed having some decent banter.'

'You cheeky fuck!'

'OK. Top five drummers…you go first.'

CHAPTER 48

The morning was cooler than it had been. And it reminded me how much I loved the contrasts life gave us.

I opened the shutter and breathed in the fresh, cool air. The council workers had been and mowed the lawn, leaving a heady scent of freshly cut grass mixed with…. eueew…. I wish people wouldn't let their dogs' doings rot in the long grass!

School had clearly started back up because there were no kids, not above toddler age, anyway. It was peaceful and calming, with the occasional quacking as ducks decided to take a run and jump up to the centre of the pond, landing with a quiet splash and shaking their feathers.

I could do much worse than working here, I thought happily.

I was going to hit 30 in a year and a bit. But I was in no rush. Rushing could upset the apple cart. Rushing could teach me to cut corners, miss out the good things, forget how I got here. I needed to take a breather. I kind of hoped Isabella might keep me on a bit longer if anything…

My first customer was approaching, so I pulled on my apron quickly and readied myself with a smile.

'Hi there, what can I get you?' It was a woman, maybe mid 30s, dressed in a skirt suit and heels - which looked great but strange choice of footwear for a park, I thought.

'Are you Emma?'

'I…I am.' I was confused. Shit, was this going to be the moment? Was she going to tell me that she was served the petition, they wanted the drunken drug addled ice-cream seller out? Was she from the council? The Hull Daily Mail?

'I'm Les' daughter.'

'Oh', I instinctively stopped wiping the scattered sprinkles and bright red drops of drizzle from the counter and looked up at her. Yes, I could see him in her grey-blue eyes, her small, rounded chin. A smile broke out across my face. ... 'Lovely to meet you, he's told me a lot about you.'

Her eyes seemed to be asking me for something. For a while she didn't blink, then she took a gasp of breath. 'He talked about you too. That's why I'm here.'

'Oh?' I felt the muscles contract in my forehead as the shock of her showing up began to sink in.

'My dad…' She stammered, her voice trailed off momentarily, before starting the sentence again with a more clear and solid tone. 'My dad died. Last night.'

The words hit me like electric shocks juddering through my body, crackling deep into my nerves. I realised I was holding my breath, and then tried to exhale the awful shock away from me.

'What? But I only saw him…'

'He suffered a major stroke.'

I couldn't speak. Everything turned grainy, unreal, I felt as if I were underwater. I staggered backwards, grabbing the chair behind me to prop myself up. Why now? Why did this happen to people I loved. It all felt so fucking unfair. An image of him raced through my mind. The time I told him about how I felt, about death. It hung there, in the air, piercing me with grief. Then I looked back on her, focusing on her. She had his face, his blood, his past, his future. Oh my God, she must be heartbroken. 'Are you, I mean, can I?'

'I'm fine.' She said, a numbness to her voice. She looked pale and washed out. Almost like she was on autopilot. I tried desperately to hold it together for her, to steady my voice, but I could feel a tear running down my left cheek. I wiped it away and sniffled.

'He, he told me about you, before he passed,' she said. 'He said he wanted you to know…'

'What happened?'

She looked up at the sky, taking a sharp intake of breath, collecting herself before looking back at me with her bloodshot eyes, pinprick bruising forming around her puffy eye lids. I wanted to hold her, but we were complete strangers thrown together in grief. Was it my place?

I bit my lip to stop if wobbling and wanted to bite down hard.

'We were out for a coffee.' She said eventually. 'He just sort of…I thought he was drunk at first. I was all ready to storm out on him. Thought he'd relapsed. Her eyes settled on mine. 'I hate myself for thinking that.'

I understood. I reached over the countertop and squeezed her arm. Everything had shifted. Everything I had come to believe in over the last few weeks.

'He just had this kind of blankness all of a sudden.' She continued. 'We rushed him to hospital and for a moment everything seemed OK. OK-ish. They said it was probably a mini stroke. He was waiting for an MRI. That's when he said about you…. then…' She looked up at the sky again, as if it might save her from the sadness clawing away at her.

'Oh my God. Oh, I'm so so sorry.' I could feel more tears wobbling out of my eyes. It felt as though I'd been punched in the gut, my chest heaving involuntarily. I wanted the ground to swallow me up. What did this mean? Why? Why did it happen? The one person who really got me, who *really* knew. What would I do now?

I tried to stuff my selfish, self-absorbed thoughts away. I didn't want to waste them now anyway; I couldn't indulge them. I needed to indulge in how horribly unfair all this was.

But for now, I knew what I needed to do.

I rushed out the back of the hut and walked urgently towards her as she stood there, drowning alone in her grief. I threw my arms around her and held her like my mum used to hold me. Tight, like I might never let her go.

I could feel the folds and creases of her suit gathering, trapped beneath my arms. It didn't matter. She released her pain in huge, breathless, belly sobs. Then so did I, my chin in her shoulder, her arms squeezing my back, like we were trying to protect each other from the pain, and worship its heavy significance all at once

How could he have gone just like that? How could this have happened?

Had this really happened?

My selfish thoughts kept bubbling to the surface. I was desperately trying to stop them, but it all felt overwhelmingly unfair. I couldn't lose him.

But I *had* lost him.

I could feel her grip loosening and I followed her lead, freeing the crumples in her suit jacket, pulling my head backwards and noticing my black make up stains on her shoulder, evidence of our shared sadness.

'Was it the drink?' I asked. 'I mean…that eventually led to…'

'No, I asked that too,' she said, pulling a tissue from her black leather handbag and offering me one too. I took one out of the little plastic packet.

I wiped my nose.

'I mean, it's what anyone's bound to think isn't it?' She said, sniffling hard as if trying to swallow the guilt she felt for making that leap. 'They said it was a familial stroke. That it likely ran in our family, given that my grandad had one too.' She started to sob again. 'I only just got him back.'

'I'm so so sorry.' I said, hugging her again as she cried into my apron.

She sniffled again and pulled her head away, looking out to the children playing in the park, carrying on regardless. 'He tried so many times. I turned him away. I was stubborn. I should never…'

'It's not easy though,' I said 'trusting someone who's spent their life glued to a bottle. It's hard. He knows that.'

'But if I had…the things we could have done. He was a granddad. I never let him…'

'It wasn't you. You mustn't think that. Honestly. You couldn't control his drinking. And who knows, if you had let him straight back in, things might have been different. He might not have been ready. You did the right thing at the right time.'

'I wish I could believe that.'

'One day, you will,' I said, desperately hoping that I wouldn't leave anybody feeling like this, confused, in pain. Regretful for the things *I'd* done.

The fluttering sound of the trees alerted us to the gap in our conversation. Two strangers. Sharing a moment. It had to end at some point.

'I guess I'd better be off…' She put her tissues back in her bag and zipped it up.

'I really appreciate you coming here. Telling me. You didn't need to.'

'It's fine. I really appreciate the friendship you gave my dad when I couldn't...' She opened the front pocket of her handbag and pulled out a business card and a pen, passing me it blank side up. 'Could I get your number? I'd like to invite you to the funeral…' She broke off again.

'Of course.' I said, scribbling Dor's number down, my arm still tense with shocks and jolts.

My head was racing with disbelief. Might she tell me this hadn't really happened. That I'd just imagined it. Was that possible? Would Les suddenly appear behind her, his lined face and his hacky laugh telling me it was all OK.

She nodded and smiled, her eyes glassy and red, and turned to walk away down the path along the pond. A slow, laboured walk in her heels and business suit. There was nothing to rush for anymore. A life that ended so abruptly needed to hang in the air for a while, it needed space to breathe, to settle. Racing through time would send it catapulting too far into the past. We couldn't forget, we weren't ready to forget.

And then she was gone, and I hadn't moved from the spot on which we sobbed and hugged.

Now what was I going to do?

CHAPTER 49

I was sitting on the floor. The bottle open and in my hand.

I wanted to indulge the pain. I wanted to qualify it. I wanted the world to know how much I hurt. I wanted to drown everything that was good in the world. It all fucking taunted me.

I wanted to disappear. Right then and right there.

I opened the bottle and breathed in the smarting fumes. I was reunited. Ready to be taken away to somewhere nicer, somewhere calmer. Somewhere where *nothing* was the order of the day.

I held it out in front of me, the sensation all too familiar and comfortable. I started to bring the bottle upwards…

But what would Les do?

Bam! It was like something hit me like a bolt of lightning. I lowered the bottle slightly. I could see Les' face. I could hear his words. I could lose him forever or cherish the friendship we had. He wasn't in the vodka. He was in my soul.

But oh my God, I really, *really* wanted a drink.

What would Les say if he saw me now? What would he say?

His words rang through my head. He'd tell me not to do it. He'd tell me I had a choice. He'd tell me that I've got the privilege of choice right up until I take a sip. Then it would be gone. And with it, everything else too.

I thought about John, Dave, Dor. I thought about my dad. About my little lad Trevor who depended on me.

But then, I thought about me. Who was I living for? Les would tell me that *I* mattered. He *did* tell me I mattered.

It was the end of the line. I'd already smashed through the floor. I needed to climb back up.

After all, if I couldn't do it for me, I couldn't do it for anyone.

CHAPTER 50

Dave

They can tell, you know. They definitely know when something's up. They retreat. Backwards. Bums to walls, or noses poking out from underneath the coffee table. Some kind of emotional intelligence, Ally says. Whatever it is, we've definitely come full circle with Trev. He's got his whippet spring back in his paws. I barely noticed the change until he had already snapped out of it. Until Emma snapped out of it.

It was like she was in some kind of thick fog for months. A Campbell's mushroom soup kind of fog. Then something happened. A trip too many, a fall too hard, fuck knows. I can't get my head around it. But *something* snapped for her. I don't even know what it was, there had been so many serious bloody incidents lately. It was like, how much of a fucking scare did she need for the kick up the arse to work?

Then again, maybe those scares were easier to deal with while she was wasted? Maybe she simply couldn't bear to face them in the cold light of day. To sober up and deal with the aftermath that was getting bigger and bigger. Fuck knows. None of it makes sense. She's like one of them impossible drawings on the front of your O Level maths book. I can never tell what the real picture is. Or whether there will always be an upside-down Emma hiding in there somewhere that might just reappear in front of us when we're least expecting it. I just know that, for now at least, for today, I've got my mate back.

And there's definitely looser shoulders all round. I can see it in Dor, Tel, Trev. Even Emma. Even me.

I was secretly blaming Al's healthy cooking for the relentless shits I'd been getting. But it's definitely more of an effort on the bog now, which has to be a good thing.

It's not completely gone though. The worry's still there, in the background.

I've no idea how long Emma'll stay dry for. But even for a day, it's like major fucking respite. Even if I wasn't with her, I was worrying about her. But just for today, I know she's safe.

Ally's invited Emma and Dor round for tea. And Trev. And she's told me I'm cooking. Which is fine if you like spaghetti carbonara. My repertoire's not exactly eclectic. But that's the things. Normally, Ally's happy cooking in the kitchen while I deal with whatever drama Emma had going on. She always said she gets off lightly, listening to some tunes in the kitchen while chucking veggies onto a sizzling frying pan and drinking a glass of Chardonnay. It's better, she says, than sitting in the living room having to deal with whatever mess Emma had gotten herself into this time. But not tonight. Ally's not reluctantly *putting up* with her. She's happily *hanging out* with her. And her confidence in my best mate is nudging my confidence in Emma higher up the barometer.

Something's changed this time. I hope it's enough.

CHAPTER 51

My name's Emma. And I'm an alcoholic.

I've been good, lately. In recovery terms, I guess. Because I've been in floods of tears more than I can ever remember. Crying because I lost a good friend, crying because I realised how much of a horrible cow I've been to my boyfriend. Crying because my dog puked up on the carpet. But I've kind of just let these things happen. I've let them hurt me.

And I realised that was normal.

There's something I really struggle to get my head around and that's this whole feel-the-pain-but-don't-pity-yourself kind of thing. Like, it's taking a while to understand how I can let the pain in without feeling sorry for myself. Without indulging it.

Then I watched little Trev, he's my pet dog. He's a whippet. I reckon having your chew stick taken off you for doing something wrong is probably like having your leg chopped off for a dog. God the bloody drama. But then it changes. When he realises, he's not getting it back, he just gives up and goes into the garden. Forgets about it. Yes, it's shit. He wanted that chew stick. But that's life.

Ridiculous example. But it kind of made me realise. Whatever happens, well, it happens. The control I have over it is not making shit happen in the first place by being a drunken twat. But also, by just taking it. Feeling winded for a bit isn't going to kill me, no matter what it feels like at the time. It passes. And when it passes, everything feels so much brighter because it's all relative isn't it?

Sometimes, I lie in bed in the morning, and I just smile and I'm just happy in that moment, content. Like feeling more comfortable and not fidgeting or wishing I wasn't awake. And it's OK.

I lost a good friend recently. It almost broke me. I had the bottle in my hand. And then I thought of him. He was called Les. He was in recovery too. Eight years under his belt. And I thought - what would Les do?

And I poured it all on the floor. Got rid of it.

It didn't make me feel better - but it didn't make me feel worse. And instead of delaying the inevitable, I just sat and cried, really hard. It's weird that, in sobriety, things gradually get better. Brighter. When I was drinking, the after effects always got worse and worse, and the initial moments of excitement and relief always became less and less.

I still cringe. And there's a lot I can't remember. Some things I've needed to know. Like how much I pissed people off. I kind of had to know that. I think it helps, doesn't it? But I guess there are some things I can do without going over. Cos I'm not sure what good it'd do.

I know I'm not, like, cured or anything. I know I'll have to keep an eye on myself forever. And fuck, it's hard. Like everything around you, it's all about booze. Every gig, every quiz night, every match. But then I started to wonder.... maybe I was bored of those things anyway? Maybe the reason we only stuck to the usual routines was because we made them more exciting than they really were with booze. Maybe it was an opportunity? To broaden my world a bit. I don't mean geographically. I'm Hull through and through! Although a trip to Spain wouldn't go amiss. But I mean, like what I choose to do.

So, I went strawberry picking. Honest to God, I'd have told you to fuck off if you asked me to go strawberry picking a few months ago. But me and my mate Dor did it and we had a right laugh. Her chat was still as dirty and outrageous as ever. In fact, probably more so, because I was hearing it sober. And she had me in stitches. She's in her bloody 70s. And we were there, straw hats on just to look the part, carrying bloody Kwik Save carrier bags because we didn't have a wicker basket. God love her.

I still think about it. Every bloody day. Will I ever drink again? Will I take drugs again? What if I hurt so bad? What if I just want to have a laugh down the pub. But those memories that hurt, they're really important, and in some ways, I appreciate them, because they keep me safe. Not dwelling on them, but just knowing they're there, as a reminder.

But the one thing that always helps, no matter what's going through my head is to think about Les. To think about everything he told me. It sometimes makes me cry. But then, he would say that's a good thing. He'd tell me that I only cried because I was lucky enough to have things or people in my life that I missed. That I was lucky to have those experiences. He would have told me to just be honest. To tell someone if I was feeling edgy. If I felt like I was in trouble, close to picking up. He'd tell me to stop and listen to the birds sing and remember my place in the world.

So, whenever I wobble. Whenever I think this time, I might just fuck it all up or this time I might be able to have a drink and everything will be OK I just think, what would Les do?

EPILOGUE

We took our seats. Jesus, it was cold in there. I even noticed a couple of people around us sitting with blankets on their laps.

'Ere Dave' I whispered. 'We'll have to nab that blanket out the back of your car next time. Seems to be the done thing.'

'Yeah, bang on trend in this place.' He laughed. 'Are you really that cold?'

I looked at him sitting there in his thin jacket and t-shirt, his arms looked taut. 'You're trying to prove a point, aren't you? Because I warned you Dave. I told you to wear your winter coat.'

'What are you my bloody mother?'

'No. I'm your responsible best mate, get used to it.'

He laughed. 'OK, OK. I'll admit it. I'm freezing my bollocks off in here.'

'Your bollock you mean.'

'Cheers Emma.'

We both smiled as we waited for the game to start. Some strange little tractor type effort was going up and down on the ice, preparing it for the players.

'Think we'll win?' I said.

'These lot blatantly do,' he said, looking around him at a quarter full but highly lively arena. 'They're bloody buzzing.'

'Yeah, well. They've probably given up on the footy.'

'You really going there?'

'Well, they've let us down far too many times, Dave. And I have to put up with yours and me dad's sulking. Thank Christ John's a Geordie.'

'You what Em?' John returned with Ally, both carrying trays full of hot dogs and chips and slush puppies.

'I said, thank fuck you're a Geordie. You don't have to deal with the constant let downs that we do.'

'Football?' He asked.

'Yes mate,' Dave said, taking a drink and trying to suss out which chips had vinegar on them.

'Scuze.' Ally said, squeezing her way in front of mine and Dave's knees to get back to her seat.

'She'll never get past you Dave, you big lump,' I laughed.

'Ah you don't need to do you love?' And he pulled her onto his knee giving her a big squeeze.

'Dave,' She screeched. 'My bloody Slush Puppie.'

I let the two love birds finish their squabble and turned to John.

'You seen the Hawks before John?'

'I've not. I'm a Hawks virgin. Or something.' He wrinkled his nose.

'Ha-ha me too.'

'You never told me that. You were talking like you knew what was going on? I thought you must've been a regular as a kid or something.'

'Don't be daft. Just studied the back pages in the Mail.'

'Ah. Like one of those cheats who reads the Trivial Pursuit questions before inviting the neighbours round for a game.'

'Yeah, I've been known to…' I slurped my bright blue slushie.

The music was blaring around the arena, with some DJ I couldn't understand a word of - his voice a mash up of echoes and MC bullshit.

'Hey look, they're here,' I said, pointing to the pitch.

'Jesus Christ. They're dressed as if they're about to get a battering,' Ally said.

'That's cos they are.' Dave added. 'This is going to be fucking immense.' He piled about five chips into his mouth at once.

As the puck was hit, the arena broke out in whoops and cheers and boos. None of us really knew what was going on but it was bloody mesmerising.

Thwack! Two players crashed into the corner near us, with Dave losing a few of his chips as he almost jumped out of his seat.

'Fucking hell. Bit rough this.'

'I thought that's what you were looking forward to, love,' Ally gently jibed him.

'Yeah, I'm just saying, that's all.'

'Adrenaline rush just watching,' John said.

'You don't have to go making up 'natural highs' for me. I'm already happy being here you know,' I joked.

'There's nowt natural about what we're drinking Emma. Jesus Christ. It's blue.'

'It's a slushie. It's bloody lovely,' I said.

The game continued with the puck seemingly heading straight between our eyes before thankfully hitting the transparent barriers between audience and rink.

'Fuck me.'

'Jesus.'

'That was close.'

'How come no bugger else is worried?' John said, looking around him nervously.

'Goooooooooal!' As the puck hit the back of the net, I was up out of my seat with the rest of the Hawks fans. John, Dave, and Ally all looking up at me with a confused smile.

'Certainly was,' John said, giggling.

I sat back down feeling embarrassed. 'Just…lost myself in the moment there.'

'You did,' he said and pulled me towards him by my jumper. As our foreheads clattered together and we both winced, I heard him whisper those words. Words I desperately wanted to hear. Words that took us beyond ice-hockey and just-for-laughs.

And this time, I heard every single one of them.

'Fancy kipping at mine and eyeing up some birds tomorrow then?'

THE END

ACKNOWLEDGEMENTS

This book has been written and produced with the support of a brilliant and talented team of people. Huge thanks must first of all go to my wonderful (and patient) agent Jo, who has been there every step of the way. Many thanks also to my editor, Sara Cox (particularly for going over and above and for caring so much about Trev), my typesetter and all-round publishing guru, Caroline Goldsmith (who also deserves praise for her spot-on political commentary), and my awesome cover designer, Kirk Teasdale (who patiently replaced perfectly acceptable ice cream pictures when my mucky mind conjured questionable metaphors).
Big thanks also to my lovely husband Chris who got to know these characters inside out when adapting the book 27 for the stage, and my step son Sam, who possibly brought the biggest crowd of cheerleaders to see it!

I also want to say a particular thank you to my friends at Recovery Connections, who not only provided invaluable feedback on my work-in-progress, but who do amazing things every single day to support people into recovery and beyond (www.recoveryconnections.org.uk).

ABOUT THE AUTHOR

Lucy is a writer, mental health campaigner and PR consultant whose work has appeared in *The Independent*, *The I Paper*, *NME*, *Red Magazine*, *Den of Geek*, *Huff Post* and many more. She is also a former columnist with Sarah Millican's *Standard Issue* magazine. She is passionate about challenging mental health stigma and particularly addiction stigma, has worked with the media in PR and marketing for over 18 years and has experienced anxiety for even longer. Lucy works closely with many mental health and recovery charities, supporting campaigns and raising awareness.

Her first book, *A Series of Unfortunate Stereotypes*, was released in 2018 and her first work of fiction, *The Twenty Seven Club* (which published in 2021) was recently adapted for the stage by her husband, Chris Connel, for Live Theatre.

Follow Lucy on:

Twitter: @lucyenichol

Instagram: lucyenichol

Facebook: Lucy Nichol Author

Sign up for Lucy's newsletter: lucynichol.substack.com

Also by Lucy Nichol

THE TWENTY SEVEN CLUB

It's 1994. The music industry is mourning Kurt Cobain, Right Said Fred have re-emerged as an 'ironic' pop act and John Major is the country's prime minister. Nothing is as it should be.

Emma is hurtling towards her 27th birthday, riddled with anxiety that her idols Joplin, Hendrix and Morrison all died aged 27, and now Kurt Cobain has gone too. Will Emma be next to join The Twenty Seven Club?

Emma, a rock music fan from Hull, with a penchant for a flaming Drambuie and a line of coke with her best mate Dave down The Angel, is troubled. Trev, her whippet, has IBS, and her job ordering bathroom supplies at the local caravan company is far from challenging. So when her dad, Tel, informs her that her music idol, Kurt Cobain has killed himself aged 27, Emma is consumed with anxiety.

Why have so many legendary musicians gone aged 27? Is there a link between the members of the so-called Twenty Seven Club? Is this why her mum had an affair and left them? And could Emma be about to join The Twenty Seven Club too?

The 27 Club is a nostalgic, often humorous, drug and booze-infused tale of friendship, discovery and anxiety as Emma tries, for once, to focus on life, rather than death.

Printed in Great Britain
by Amazon

12596111R00171